MORA'
THE MUR

C000101792

KATHERINE DALTON R

born in Hammersmith, London in 1881, the only child of a Canadian father and English mother.

The author wrote two well-received early novels, *Olive in Italy* (1909), and *The Sword of Love* (1920). However, her career in crime fiction did not begin until 1924, after which Moray Dalton published twenty-nine mysteries, the last in 1951. The majority of these feature her recurring sleuths, Scotland Yard inspector Hugh Collier and private inquiry agent Hermann Glide.

Moray Dalton married Louis Jean Renoir in 1921, and the couple had a son a year later. The author lived on the south coast of England for the majority of her life following the marriage. She died in Worthing, West Sussex, in 1963.

MORAY DALTON MYSTERIES
Available from Dean Street Press

MORAY DALTON

THE MURDER OF EVE

With an introduction by Curtis Evans

DEAN STREET PRESS

FOOLS RUSH IN

MORAY DALTON'S *THE MURDER OF EVE* (1945) AND *DEATH AT THE VILLA* (1946)

> "I am John Bull to the background, yet I do want to see
> Italy, just once. Everybody says it is marvelous. . . . ."
> Caroline Abbott, *Where Angels Fear to Tread*,
> E. M. FORSTER

FOR British novelist E. M. Forster, "Italy was to stand for passion," observed American critic Lionel Trilling in his 1943 study of the author. Forster's 1901-02 tour in Italy with his mother released the young man's smoldering creative fires, resulting in the publication three years later of his acclaimed first novel, *Where Angels Fear to Tread* (1905), the title of which draws on the famous line from Alexander Pope's *An Essay on Criticism* ("Fools rush in where angels fear to tread") in telling the story of the consequences of free-spirited widow Lilia Herriton's marriage in Italy, much to the consternation of her straight-laced British in-laws, to Gino Carella, a handsome younger man. Born in 1881, making her just two years younger than E. M. Forster, British mystery writer Moray Dalton (aka Katherine Dalton Renoir) likewise must have toured Italy at some point in her youth around the turn of the century, likely with her own mother in tow for chaperonage. Her first published novel, *Olive in Italy* (1909), which followed into print Forster's *Angels* by four years, is the story of "an unconventional. . . . clear-sighted girl who goes to Italy in a spirit of high adventure" and is similarly suffused with Italian light and color. Recalling the case of Lilia Herriton in *Angels*, Moray Dalton at Brighton in 1921, three years after the death of her father and when she herself was just shy of forty years of age, married one Louis Jean Renoir, by whom she bore a son the next year, though the couple seems soon thereafter to have separated.

The bewitching spell which Mediterranean magic cast over Dalton is readily apparent as well in the crime fiction which she published from the 1920s through the 1940s, nowhere more so than in the novels *The Murder of Eve* (1945) and *Death at the Villa* (1946), a pair of uncommonly rich mystery thrillers that she wrote in the waning months of the Second World War. Doubtlessly Dalton was a confirmed Italophile, having during the previous World War even published poetry celebrating the martial heroism of Italy, the country having been, from the British perspective, on the right side in that conflict. How difficult it must have been for the author to bear witness to the terrible actions taken by Italians during the two decades when her beloved *bel paese* fell under the sway of brutally charismatic fascist dictator Benito Mussolini. *Il Duce* finally was summarily executed for his monstrous crimes by Italian partisans on April 28, 1945, merely a couple of months after the publication of *The Murder of Eve*. On February 27 the *Liverpool Evening Express* had roundly praised Dalton's novel as "an imaginative thriller."

Excepting its epilogue, *The Murder of Eve* takes place four decades previous to its publication in the year 1905, perhaps the very year in which the author herself first visited Italy. It opens with a somewhat *Lady Chatterley*-ish shipboard romance between Roger Fordyce, an ingenuous British planter in Malaya returning home to visit his schoolgirl sister Penny and their spinster aunt, Polly Fordyce, at their home in Stratford-upon-Avon, and Nina, Lady Craven, a sophisticate who is on her way to Rome with her sickly husband, who is seeking medical treatment there. Roger and Nina meet for an assignation at the Albergo Del Castello, a once splendid but long-derelict villa located in a little town in the Apennines outside Rome that has been partially restored as a hotel by a handsome, ambitious, young Italian, Mario Laccetti, and his formidable sister Maddalena, whom we are told resembles Leonardo da Vinci's reputed Medusa. As the passionate affair—passionate on young Roger's part at least—burns itself out at the villa, Roger while wandering the grounds one morning imagines that he espies in a water tank a dead body, long black hair eerily afloat. When told of this by her lover, Nina objects to making any mention of it to local authorities, fearing exposure of their affair, and Mario later explains to Roger that the dead creature in the water tank was merely a mongrel dog. Roger and Nina part ways, with Roger returning to England, but the time which he spent at the villa ripples outward with fearsome consequences for himself and many others, both in England and Italy, including not only Penny and Aunt Polly, but disgraced *émigré* piano teacher Lily Oram (who recalls the title character in *Olive in Italy*); earnest British embassy official Ronald Guthrie; high-placed Italians Commendatore Rinaldo Marucci and Marchese Luigi de Sanctis; and British writer Francis Gale, his lovely schoolgirl daughter Anne and Francis' estranged ex-wife, the artist Eve Shandon. . . .

Reviewing the novel in March 1945, the *Plymouth Western Morning News* praised "the descriptions of life in Italy before the Great War," the in-depth characterizations ("The author is not content to outline his *[sic]* characters sketchily") and the "unexpected twist" at the end. Certainly *Eve* is an ambitious period thriller in a deadly serious vein, eschewing the stock formulae of the Edgar Wallace school of English shockers—works which seem, whatever their merits as popular entertainment, jejune by comparison. In *Eve* Dalton ironically has Roger Fordyce reflect, as he begins fumblingly in Italy to investigate what may be a case of murder (or murders), on the contrastingly comforting nature of the fictional stuff: "It was comparatively easy for the detective heroes of the thrillers he most enjoyed. They usually had the resources of New Scotland Yard at their disposal, or, if they happened to be amateurs, they had a faithful, though thick-headed, friend in attendance, or a valet who was also a boxing champion and an expert photographer."

Later in the novel the Marchese de Sanctis bracingly pronounces: "Poetic justice is so satisfying, but we live in a world of prose." *The Murder of Eve* is surprisingly modern in its refusal cheerily to tie up every loose end around a pretty, if predictable, package. Instead it looks ahead to modern crime fiction, where packages contain surprises—and by no means all of them pleasant ones. Yet the English characters in the novel remain stubbornly determined to try to do right as they deem it in Italy, whatever the dangers—and they are manifold—which may befall them. As one Italian character bemusedly reflects: "These English are a pest.

Always poking their noses where they are not wanted. . . . . How is one to deal with such people? They are without sense, when you offer to buy they will not sell, they are hard when you expect them to be soft, and soft when you think they will be hard, and somehow by accident, they have acquired an empire."

Despite the menaces which "these English" face in Italy, Polly Fordyce—surely as formidable a spinster as *A Tale of Two Cities'* Miss Pross, who braved France during the tumult of the Revolution—earnestly tells the Marchese: "I think you must know how much the English have always loved and admired Italy and the Italian people. I hope our countries will always be friends as they are now." Surely Aunt Polly was speaking as well for the author, whose John Bullish sentiments, typical of popular British authors of her day, invariably were softened by her warm Italian sympathies.

* * * * * * *

"All this blood and violence. God help us. It is like a bad dream. When shall we wake?"

Reverend Mother Superior at the Convent in the Via Due
Macelli in *Death at the Villa*

THE second of Moray Dalton's Forties Italian mystery thrillers, *Death at the Villa*, takes place during the Second World War during the summer of 1943, when an Allied landing was imminent and the Mussolini regime teetered on the very brink of collapse. On the night of July 9-10, Allied forces launched Operation Husky, a successful invasion of Sicily, resulting two weeks later in the *25 Luglio* (the 25th of July), in which Benito Mussolini was ousted from power by King Victor Emanuel III and placed under arrest. On September 3, as the Allies launched an invasion of southern mainland Italy, the neophyte Italian government signed the Armistice of Cassibile, which declared a cessation of hostilities between Italy and the Allies. The publicizing of the armistice rapidly resulted in a German commando raid freeing Mussolini;

the occupation of northern and central Italy by German forces; the establishment of the Italian Social Republic, a collaborationist puppet state nominally headed by *Il Duce*; and the beginning of the nearly twenty-month Italian Civil War, during which German forces committed numerous atrocities against the Italian populace, resulting in thousands of civilian deaths.

Turbulent and terrible times indeed, and Moray Dalton dramatically captures their early days in *Death at the Villa*. Like much of *The Murder of Eve*, *Death at the Villa* is set at an old country mansion in the Apennines, this time the Villa Gualtieri, ancestral home of the Marchese Gaultieri. While the widowed Marchese occupies himself in Rome with his accommodating mistress and other dilettante interests, his country villa is occupied by his widowed young daughter-in-law Chiara (her husband Amedeo, the Marchese's son, recently went down in his plane over the Mediterranean, six weeks after the birth of their child) and her young companion and poor relation Alda Olivieri, both of whom are under the supervision of middle-aged widow Amalia Marucci, a vague distant cousin whom the Marchese took in, along with her implicitly gay son Silvio, an ardent Fascist, after the death in Venice of her husband Ettore. (Could Ettore Marucci have been a relation of Commendatore Rinaldo Marucci from *The Murder of Eve*?)

Alda's quiet, recessive country life is disrupted when buxom local farmer's daughter Marietta Donati reveals that her family has taken in a wounded English paratrooper. With the help of a kindly local priest, Don Luigi Cappelli, Alda shelters the handsome Englishman, Richard Drew, in an abandoned Etruscan tomb, all the while attempting to evade the prying eyes of Amalia Marucci, who is eager, for purposes of her own, to discredit Alda and evict her from the villa. Soon, however, Amalia's wicked machinations bear poisonous fruit, as the war inexorably closes in on them all. Can a stalwart young Englishman come daringly to the rescue of a fair damsel in a tumultuous foreign land where he himself stands in need of rescuing?

Death at the Villa is unique in the genre in coupling private murder with public terror. (In terms of subject matter I am reminded of British crime writer Michael Gilbert's innovative 1952 novel *Death in Captivity*, a mystery, drawing on the author's own personal experiences, which is set in 1943 in an Italian prisoner-of-war camp.) It makes, to my mind, gripping reading, with the last third of the novel in particular constituting the essence of the term "page turner." A contemporary review compared *Villa* to "classical Italian opera," avowing that its "narrative of jealousy, violence, tragedy and innocence against a somber background" made for "convincing and gripping reading." More recently the late crime fiction connoisseur Jacques Barzun praised the novel's "tense situation, beautifully plotted and narrated," and its "admirably diversified characters and . . . picture of the times."

For my part I was reminded, when reading *Death at the Villa*, of the dark French television wartime drama series *Un Village Français* (2009-2017). I imagine that *Villa* would make a similarly compelling television production—as would, for that matter, *The Murder of Eve*. In both of her non-series Forties Italian crime novels Moray Dalton clearly aimed to take her crime writing in a more realistic and relevant direction, one where murder really matters. In this I believe she succeeded admirably.

Curtis Evans

Chapter I
THE BLACK DOG

1

"Roger—"

It was dark on deck, but the silver tissue of Lady Cravenach's dress gleamed as she moved a little nearer to him. Roger's heart pounded against his ribs. She was so lovely, and she had seemed so unattainable, and she would be leaving the ship in a few hours.

"My poor boy," she said softly, "you have been looking so unhappy. Do you mind so much?"

"Mind? Of course I mind. Oh, Nina—you said I might call you Nina—"

She slipped her hand into his. He gripped it so hard that she winced. "Be careful. Someone may see us. Listen, Roger. If you could leave the boat at Naples too I might be able to manage something. You know we're going to Rome to see some specialist Henry heard of. He'll probably have to go into a nursing home for a bit. We shall be staying at the Russie. I don't want you to come there—"

He laughed a little ruefully. "I couldn't afford it in any case."

"Stay wherever you like, only let me have your address, and if I am able to fix up anything I'll write you a line. Only—I shall be running a big risk. If Henry ever suspected—"

"I'd ask you to come away with me. I can't bear to think of what you have had to suffer," said Roger fervently. "But I haven't anything to offer."

"I would not leave him, Roger," she said. "He has hurt me so often, but I don't want to hurt him."

"You are too good for him."

"Hush. I must go now. Don't forget the Russie. Good night, darling."

Left alone he fumbled in his case for a cigarette. He would have to tell the purser, pack his cabin trunk, write a card to Aunt Polly to tell her not to meet the boat, as he was coming home overland. Those few words from Nina had changed all his plans, they might change his whole life. He had never been in love before. And this was so impossible. He was just an ordinary middle-class young man coming home to England on six months leave after two years as assistant manager on a plantation in Malaya. He had to help pay his young sister Penny's school fees out of his salary, but he might be able to afford a wife in a year or two. She would have to be a sensible girl, prepared to rough it; living on tinned food, with some native dishes; and making her own clothes from paper patterns in the magazines sent out from home. That was over now, of course. There would never be any woman but Nina in his life. Nina, so fragile and so exquisite. Roger, who was completely unaffected, and rather young for his age, told himself earnestly that she was like a hothouse flower.

The next morning when the passengers who were to leave the ship at Naples were collecting he saw Sir Henry Cravenach for the first time. He had not left his cabin during the voyage.

He was tall and thin and white-haired, and he leaned heavily on his stick. Nina followed, looking about eighteen in her white frock and big shady hat. Roger overheard someone saying that she was more like Sir Henry's daughter than his wife. The Japanese valet, with his mask-like face, went after them, laden with rugs and hand luggage.

Roger took a second-class ticket to Rome. The Cravenachs, he knew, would be travelling first. It was hot in the train, and the second-class carriages were crowded, but Roger noticed neither the heat nor the noise and discomfort. He was dreaming—

2

The only vehicle waiting in the station yard was an omnibus in the last stages of decay, drawn by two bony mules, whose harness had been mended with string. Roger followed a withered old woman, carrying a bag full of vegetables and a live hen, who had been the only other passenger to alight at Vallesca.

The driver, who had been asleep in the shade, scrambled to his feet, and seized Roger's suitcase.

"The signore is going to Sant Andrina? Another Inglese? A signora arrived last night. Che bellezza!" He blew a kiss into the air as a tribute.

Roger mumbled something. His cheeks burned. So she was really there, waiting for him. He had her letter in his note-case.

"I shall be staying at the Albergo del Castello, in a little hill town called Sant Andrina. A woman I know discovered it last year and raved about it. Call yourself Smith."

Call yourself Smith. If Roger had been less in love that might have struck a jarring note. As it was he tried to forget it.

Nina was being divinely kind. It would be unforgivably mean to criticise her for taking some necessary precautions. It was not her fault that they had to meet in this—this hole-and-corner way.

The omnibus had no windows. Sun and air were excluded by flapping leather curtains, cracked and green with age. Roger noticed that there were two little round holes in one of them that might have been made by bullets. The mules toiled on, up a winding road that climbed a wooded hillside and across a bare ridge where the black volcanic rock was patched with the gold of the wild broom. Roger, parting the curtains as they broke into a weary canter, saw blood running down their lean flanks and realised that the driver had been using a goad. He longed to take it from him, but it would not do to draw attention to himself by having a row with the man, so he dropped the curtain and sat back. His fellow passenger was telling her beads, but though her withered lips moved in prayer her beady black eyes were watching him. She said something, but he did not understand her dialect. He had taken some lessons in Italian at the Berlitz school years ago, and had a chance to exchange lessons with a young Maltese in Singapore, and so far he had got along fairly well.

The driver pulled in his mules presently, and turned in his seat to speak to his passengers.

"Ecco Sant Andrina—" He pointed with his whip.

Roger drew the curtain and looked across a narrow and deep ravine at the little walled town that clung to the olive-grown slopes beyond like a swallow's nest. It must be a mile away, but in that crystal-clear air every detail was visible. He saw the built-up terraces, the huddled red roofs, the cypresses of the Campo Santo, like the spears of a besieging force camped outside the gates. Beyond, on a jutting piece of rock that was like the rowel of a spur, there was a building that appeared to be in part a ruin. A winding path seemed to lead down from it to the road through vineyards and olive groves, and came out where there was a gate and a tumble-down shed.

"That looks like a short cut?"

"If you were on foot, yes," the driver said. "But the land belongs to the people at the Albergo and they don't allow anyone to use it."

"Not even people staying with them?"

"Who knows? You can ask them for their permission if you like, signore. It is no affair of mine," the man said gruffly. Roger, happening to glance at the old woman, saw that she was making the sign that averts the maleficent influence of the evil eye.

He wondered, rather uncomfortably, if she thought there was something wrong about him.

The road was winding up again now in a series of hairpin bends. They stopped under the narrow span of a massive gateway while an official of the dogana asked them if they had anything to declare, and clattered up a dark stone-paved street to a piazza where a few children were playing in the dust in the shade of the plane trees while their mothers fetched water from the fountain in big copper jars which they carried on their heads. Roger got out and took his suitcase. The driver directed him.

"Go round behind the church and follow the lane."

He lounged off, swinging a bucket, to get water for his mules.

An old blind beggar, incredibly ragged, crouched on the church steps. He stretched out a dirty claw as Roger approached and the young man felt in his pockets for soldi. It must be so awful, he thought, to be blind. The beggar turned his head sharply to listen as he pocketed the coins. Another stranger. He knew the foot-steps of everyone who passed that way. A young man, young and gay, going to meet happiness, one could tell that from the quick springing tread. Generous, too, for he had given silver.

"I shall know him again," he thought. "I will say a prayer for him. Something tells me he is in need of prayers." He fumbled in the filthy folds of his shirt for his rosary of black wooden beads.

The villa of the Duke of Sant Andrina, known to his contemporaries as the mad duke, had been built early in the eighteenth century from the stones of the grim old fortress from which his forefathers had defied the Pope on their southern borders, and the grand dukes of Tuscany to the north. The family had been impoverished, and was now extinct. The house had stood empty for years. The lawyers administering the estate were glad enough to let it to the young fellow who had come to them, saying that he meant to turn it into an hotel. His brother-in-law had been a chef on the Riviera, his sister had been a chambermaid. It was to be a family affair. His name was Mario Laccetti, and he was standing in the main entrance as Roger, after pausing for a moment to gaze at the imposing façade, with its triple row of shuttered windows, crossed the grass-grown square.

Women had been known to gasp audibly at their first sight of Mario, but Roger, excited and preoccupied, did not even notice his spectacular good looks. Mario, bowing and smiling, took his suitcase from him.

"Mr. Smith? You came by the omnibus? Madame is expecting you. Will you come this way? Madame chose rooms at the back because of the view. After the sun has set it will be cooler, and you can dine on the terrace if you wish—"

He spoke English fluently, though with a strong Italian accent. Roger followed him up a vast marble staircase and down a long passage. The walls were covered with faded frescoes. Their voices echoed. Roger hazarded the guess that only a few of the innumerable rooms were furnished. Mario said, "Madame has been resting in her room since lunch—"

He knocked at a door and stood back to allow Roger to pass in.

3

They dined alone on the terrace.

A full moon hung like a silver lamp over the wooded hills and the illimitable plain. Below the terrace broken fragments of a more ancient building showed here and there in a riot of myrtle and oleander and overgrown rose bushes. Farther down the slope there was a small one-storied building that might have been a gardener's cottage. There was an occasional croaking of frogs, but no other sound to break the silence of the summer night.

Roger hardly noticed what he was eating, but Nina enjoyed her dinner, the minestrone, the carcioffi al olio, the vitello alla Milanese, the zabaione. "The cooking is simply marvellous. The dinner last night was just as good. It really is a pity in a way that I can never bring Henry here. But he could never face those hours in a slow train, and the drive from the station. Mario tells me they are hoping to get a clientele of English and Americans who are tired of the tourist-ridden beauty spots and want to get right off the beaten track. They may succeed, but they'll have to wait some time before they get enough to make it pay. They have a few of the local people coming every night for dinner in the restaurant, the doctor and the lawyer and officers from the garrison, but when they had gone last night I was quite alone on the first floor. It was rather eerie. It's such a vast place. But I was so tired after that journey that I slept like a top. And it's worth it, don't you think so? A perfect setting. We shall always remember it, Roger. This terrace, and the moonlight and those divine cypresses. We might walk that way to-morrow. It must be a garden."

"It's the Campo Santo," he said.

"Oh. We won't go there then. There's a garden here actually. Terribly neglected, but the roses haven't quite turned into briars—"

Mario had just brought their coffee. He said, "Pardon, madame, but I would not advise you to go down there. It is a wilderness and there are many thorns. You would tear your dress. And I killed a snake there yesterday. Also there are scorpions—"

"Then we will stay here, Mario," she said pleasantly. "Thank you for warning us."

When he had gone she said, "The poor boy seemed quite worried. I suppose it would not be a very good advertisement for the hotel. I gather that he and his sister and her husband have put all their savings into this place. They are running it without any outside help. With his looks he ought to go to Hollywood. I don't wonder that—" she broke off to light her cigarette from Roger's, and she did not finish her sentence. He was gazing at her adoringly, but she could see that he was not paying very much attention to what she was saying. It was just as well, she thought. The white wine of the country which they had been drinking at dinner was stronger than she had realised and making her feel rather light-headed. She knew she would have to be careful. Roger had idealised her. He was so young, so ingenuous, but he was not a fool. It would be easy to disillusion him, and one of the ways would be to betray too much interest in an hotel waiter, just because he happened to be good-looking.

She smiled at him, and whispered, "Darling—"

Mario carried his tray into the hot lamplit kitchen where his sister Maddalena was ironing sheets and pillow cases, while his brother-in-law, having cooked the dinner, was poring over a two days old copy of the *Roman Messagero*.

Maddalena was older than her brother, bigger boned, rougher in every way. There was something formidable about her. They were the same material cast in a different mould. It was the difference between an axe and a rapier. As a servant she had been sullen but efficient, scraping, saving, hating her servitude and looking forward always to the day when she would be la padrona. That day had come, and she worked harder than ever. Beads of sweat stood on her upper lip as she bent over her ironing board.

"Bene—" she said. "How long are they staying?"

"I do not know. A few days perhaps. They are lovers, not married. She is older and more experienced," said Mario, smiling, "she amuses herself, that one. Also, she is rich, and he is poor. Perhaps she will stay on after he has left," he said thoughtfully.

His brother-in-law grunted. "We've had enough of that if you ask me. How did you learn so much in so short a time?"

"I have seen their hair brushes. His are much worn and have wooden backs. Hers are of tortoiseshell with a gold monogram that does not include the letter S. And there are other indications."

His sister, whose dark sunken eyes had been fixed on him with a strange intensity, said, "A letter came by the last post while you were still in the dining-room. It has the Orvieto post mark. I think it is from the father of Laurina. Here it is."

Mario snatched the letter from her hand.

"Yes. They could not come last week because he had an attack of gout. They are better and they will arrive tomorrow or the day after."

"Let us hope the parents will be favourably impressed," said Maddalena anxiously. "The sooner you and Laurina are married the better, as you are still mad about her. God knows what you see in the silly little puppet, but the money she will bring will be useful."

It was not until the third morning of their stay at the hotel that Roger found an opportunity to explore the foundations of the old castello. Nina never left her room until just before lunch, and the afternoons and evenings were spent lounging on the terrace in basket chairs, moving now and then to keep in the shade. Roger tried to persuade her to go for walks after sunset, but she had been into the town once, the day before he arrived, and she said it was smelly; and the paths through the vineyards and olive groves that covered the hillside were thick with grey volcanic dust and would have spoiled her high-heeled white suède shoes. Besides, even in this remote place, she was afraid of being seen and recognised, she was one of those women, mentally inert, who can sit for hours, quite happily, smoking cigarettes and polishing their nails, their vanity satisfied by an admirer in attendance who will tell them at intervals how marvellous they are looking. Roger, on the other hand, soon began to feel bored. The truth was that, apart from their mutual passion, a passion that was burning out as quickly as a fire in stubble, they had nothing in common.

Roger had not quite reached the point of facing this fact, but, as he sat down to breakfast on the terrace, he was not sorry to be alone. It was only just after eight, and the air was still cool and fresh. The coffee was delicious and so were the rolls. As he looked down on the overgrown wilderness that had once been a garden he decided that he would spend the morning in exploration, keeping a sharp look-out for the snakes. There was a stray dog, too. He had heard it every night, howling, and once he thought he had seen it moving among the bushes. There was no one about and he saw no need to ask for permission to go down to what was virtually a piece of waste ground. Some of the paths, however, had been recently used. The long grass had been trodden down and overarching briars broken or bent back. He made his way towards the one-storied building. Its windows were shuttered. It looked like a derelict summer-house, or perhaps a gardener's cottage. There was a padlock on the door. Both the padlock and the staples looked new. Roger noticed something shining in a drift of dead leaves, and stooped to pick it up. It was the screw stopper of an oil-paint tube with a smear of cobalt on it. He held it for a moment, idly, on the palm of his hand, before he threw it away. Evidently one artist at least had discovered Sant Andrina. There was a subject at hand, a moss-grown statue of Pan with one arm missing, against a background of wistaria pouring over a shapeless mass of masonry. The scent of the heavy purple clusters of flowers drifted towards him. Beauty in decay, he thought, as he went on, following a crumbling line of stones towards the tip of the spur.

As he moved on, slowly, for there was little trace of any path here and the undergrowth was very dense, he was overcome by a curious depression of his spirits. The heat was intense and he was plagued by a cloud of flies, and he began to notice a faint unpleasant smell that was certainly not that of the wistaria. He was about to turn back when he saw what seemed to be a stone tank partly sunk in the ground. Its heavy wooden lid was partly displaced as if someone had been there recently to draw water from it. Roger was one of those people who are fascinated by water. He liked to linger on bridges and quays, and to hear the clash of a bucket running down the windlass of a well.

He could not leave the stone tank without looking in. It was fuller than he had expected, coming up almost to the brim, and it had a dark glaucous surface. He thought, "It's stagnant. I hope they don't get their drinking water from here."

He moved the lid an inch or two farther back and as he did so he saw bubbles rising.

4

"You're very quiet," said Nina after lunch. There was not much shade at that hour and they had moved their chairs close up to the house wall. "I say," her voice was suddenly sharp with anxiety. "You were down in the grounds all the morning, weren't you? I saw you from the window. You haven't got a touch of the sun or anything. You can't possibly fall ill here, you know."

"I'm all right." He leaned forward, knocking the ash off his cigarette and staring down at the stone pavement. He was very pale.

"The fact is, Nina, I got a shock, and I don't want to upset you, but I think I've got to talk to you about it."

"Go on."

"I don't know how to tell you. I was poking about in the undergrowth trying to trace the lines of the old castle walls—there's very little left. I suppose it was used as building material by the Sant Andrina who put up the villa in the seventeenth century, or whenever it was. It's a marvellous position for a watch tower, guarding the pass from Tuscany into Umbria—"

"Never mind all that," she said impatiently. "What happened?"

"There was a stone tank, a reservoir for water with a heavy wooden lid. It wasn't quite shut and I shifted it a few inches. There—" He stopped to clear his throat. "Something was floating just submerged. I—I'm afraid it was a body. I could see—black hair."

"Rubbish, Roger."

"I'm sorry, Nina. I wish I could think so. I could have touched it with my hand—but I didn't. I felt pretty awful coming upon such a thing suddenly. The question is, what are we to do about it?"

She looked at him. "The answer is nothing at all. I am supposed to be spending this week with a friend who has a villa at Fiesole. I am going on there from here. I can rely on her. But if there was any kind of trouble here involving the police God knows how it might end."

"Yes," he said slowly. "Yes, I see."

After a moment she said: "Are you really quite sure?"

"Unfortunately, yes. Thinking back I realise that I felt before I got there that there was something wrong. There's something depressing, in any case, about a neglected garden, but this one has what my aunt Pollie would call a bad aura."

"You didn't see any snakes?"

"No. But it was very hot and airless, and there was a queer smell. I had to tell you."

"I suppose so," she said coolly. "It's a pity you had to spoil our last day though."

"Is it the last?"

"I think it had better be. If I leave to-morrow at about four o'clock I can get a train from Vallesca to Orvieto and join the diretto to Florence there. You'll go back to Rome, I expect, to pick up your luggage."

"Yes."

She lit another cigarette. "Poor Roger," she said more kindly. "Don't look so down in the mouth."

He said, without looking at her, "You've been sweet to me. I—don't know how to thank you—"

"Don't be absurd, it's been very amusing. I've enjoyed every minute until just now. You really have been tiresome to-day, darling. You should have taken Mario's hint, he warned us, you remember."

Roger was startled. "Good God! Nina, you don't imagine these people here know—"

She smiled at him, but it was a smile that did not reach her eyes, and he had an uncomfortable feeling that when she had described him as tiresome she had meant what she said.

"I don't imagine anything. They've made us very comfortable. Mario is most attentive, and the cooking is marvellous. That's all that matters to us, I think."

"All right."

He narrowed his eyes, looking across the plain, golden in the clear light of the summer afternoon. He was realising that the parting to which he had looked forward with such heart sinkings would not move him at all, that the woman he had worshipped, the ill-used wife, patient under indignities, yielding at last to her lover out of sheer kindness, because she could not bear him to suffer, had never had any existence outside his imagination. Three days and three nights with Nina had taught him that she was very well able to take care of herself, in spite of her apparent helplessness. Nina would always get what she wanted. She had wanted him, but not for long, perhaps she was equally disappointed in him.

That evening, before dinner, he went into the hotel dining-room to speak to Mario, who was busy laying the tables for the clients who came from the town every evening.

"We shall be leaving to-morrow. Will you let me have the bill in the morning?"

"Sicuro. I am sorry the signori are going so soon."

Their table was set, as usual, at the far end of the terrace where they could watch the moon rise over the plain. The night was very warm and so still that the candles burned without a flicker except when moths blundered into the flame to fall on the white cloth with singed wings.

"Why are insects so idiotic?" said Nina irritably.

Mario brought them a special wine. "So that one day you will come back to us," he said, smiling. Nina watched his profile as he filled their glasses. It was as perfect as that of a head on a Greek coin.

For the last course he served a zabaione, and that was special, too, fragrant and satin smooth. He smiled at them as he cleared the table. "You have eaten it all. That is good."

When he had left them Roger looked up at the great bulk of the villa with its rows of shuttered windows, dark against the starry sky, and yawned. "I don't know how it is. I can hardly keep my eyes open."

Nina got up and, coming round to the back of his chair, rested her hands on his shoulders and dropped a butterfly kiss on his head.

"Poor little sleepy boy," she whispered.

Roger roused himself to make the required response.

He came down an hour later than usual the next morning. He had slept heavily and woke with a headache.

Mario poured out his coffee. "Signore, I have a confession to make, and then a piece of news that will please you, I think."

"Really? What is it?"

"Yesterday afternoon the signori were sitting over there, near an open window. I was there, cleaning the forks and spoons, and I could not help hearing. I was greatly surprised and greatly troubled to know that the signore had found what he thought was a body in one of our old water tanks. I thought I would see for myself when I had the time. And so last night I went down the garden and I shifted the lid—"

"Well?"

"The signore was perfectly right."

"Good Heavens!" Roger set down his coffee cup. "You take it calmly. Have you called the police? I say—" he remembered Nina.

"I mustn't be brought into this—"

"Lasci fare. If you will come with me I will show you—"

"I don't want to see it," said Roger violently.

"But, signore mio, it is nothing, un affare di niente. There was a body, but it was that of a dog. I would like you to see it before I bury it. This way—"

Roger, already half ashamed of his reaction, drew a long breath of relief. "Well, that's a weight off my mind," he agreed. But as he followed Mario across the terrace and down the steps he was remembering uneasily that the conversation Mario had overheard had probably betrayed their secret. The young waiter must have guessed that Nina was not his wife. Perhaps, so long as he did not know who she was, that did not greatly matter. They were both leaving in a few hours, and it was not likely that either of them would return to Sant Andrina.

The body of the dog lay in the shade of a myrtle bush. It was a mongrel, but its mother had probably been a retriever. Runnels of water from its thick curly black coat had trickled into cracks in the sun-baked earth. Flies buzzed over it.

Roger looked down at it thoughtfully. He was fond of dogs.

"Why did you bring him all this way?"

"Ma—to show the signore."

"Very good of you. He must have been heavy to carry."

"I am strong. It was nothing."

"I wonder how he got into the tank."

"Perhaps he was thirsty, and tried to drink, and overbalanced."

"But the lid—"

"Some days ago I noticed that the lid was nearly off and I replaced it. I did not see the body. The water is not clear."

"It isn't your dog?"

"No, signore."

"Who owned him? They'll have to be told."

Mario shrugged his shoulders. "He was—how do you say—a stray. Sometimes he would come to the kitchen door for scraps, and then for days and sometimes for weeks we saw nothing of him. He could be troublesome. It is a good riddance."

"I've heard a dog howling in the night."

"Si, signore."

"But if he was several days in the tank—"

"True, signore. Then it would be another dog. There are others. I shall bury him now."

Roger nodded and turned away.

He supposed that he would have to tell Nina. No need, perhaps, to explain that Mario had overheard them. She might not like that. He had paused, on the terrace, to light a cigarette, when Mario came up with him, a little breathless with the haste he had made.

"Scusi, signore. I wished to say that I have a very good quick horse and a carrozza that I keep in a shed at the foot of the hill. I could drive you to the station. And if you and the signora could walk down the path through the vigna you would save three miles of road."

"But what about the luggage?"

"My brother-in-law, Luciano, and I can carry it down after lunch," Mario said eagerly. "I keep this conveyance for the use of our guests," he added, with a youthful pomposity that was rather engaging.

"Very well," Roger said. "We've been very comfortable. You all work so hard. You deserve to succeed. It's a pity Sant Andrino is so inaccessible."

"You will see," said the young Italian confidently. There was an almost fanatical gleam in his beautiful dark eyes when he talked of the future of his beloved hotel. "We have the means to advertise a little at last. And some day I shall buy an automobile. Then the distance to and from the station at Vallesca will not seem so great."

"Nasty smelly things I've heard," said Roger carelessly, "and apt to stick at hills, but they may improve them. Anyhow, I wish you luck."

A few hours later he and Nina were in a local train on their way to Orvieto. The express to Florence would come in first. Roger would have two hours to wait.

"You had better not see me off," Nina said. "There might be someone I know on the train. No need to run unnecessary risks. Was the bill very extortionate?"

"Not at all. Very reasonable."

"You must let me pay it."

He turned very red. "Certainly not."

"But you haven't any money, and I have heaps," she argued. "Henry has his faults, but he isn't mean."

"I'm glad to hear it," said Roger stiffly, "but—oh, Nina, can't you see how horrible that would be—"

She smiled. "Darling, aren't you straining at gnats? Never mind, if it gives you a feeling of moral superiority it's probably worth the money. And now don't let's talk. I woke with a head-ache, and I've still got it—"

"I'm sorry."

He sat looking out of the carriage window at the sun-baked vineyards and the little fields of maize. Just as well, he thought. They had nothing to say to one another. Their mutual passion had flared up and gone, and physical intimacy had not led to any real understanding. When he had come to Sant Andrina he had believed himself to be on the threshold of a great experience. He was gradually awaking to the humiliating fact that he had been merely taking part in a sordid little intrigue.

He got up to lift her dressing-case down from the rack.

"Here we are. Orvieto. Better say good-bye now, I suppose."

"Good-bye." She offered him her lips, but casually, almost absent-mindedly. "Mind that case. I do hope I shall get a porter—"

CHAPTER II
A HOME COMING

ALL the tenants in the block knew that Francis Gale had married again. There had been a good deal of unpleasant publicity about his divorce, but that was five years ago, and it was more or less forgotten. He had lived a bachelor existence ever since, casual, untidy, but not in any way scandalous. He was a freelance journalist, with a knack for writing light whimsical stuff that brought him in a steady income. He was no longer very young, but women still found him attractive, and the sweep of white hair brushed back from his forehead gave him an added touch of distinction. Only a few of his older friends knew that there had been one child of his first marriage, a girl, and that he had been given her custody. He never brought her to the flat. Leila found her photograph within half an hour of their return to the flat after their honeymoon, when she was running a comb through her yellow curls before going into the kitchenette to put the kettle on for tea. It stood, in a silver frame, on Francis' dressing-table. Francis had gone out to buy cakes for their first meal together in the flat. Written across one corner in small precise letters was the dedication: "With lots of love from Anne."

"Darned cheek," said Leila.

The telephone bell rang and she went to answer it.

"Oh, Billie, my sweet, is that you?" Billie had been in the chorus of the same musical comedy on tour, and they had shared diggings. Billie was resting at the moment, and she had been offered the use of the flat while the Gales were away on their honeymoon.

"Yes, everything's all right. I say—do you know anything about the girl whose picture Francis keeps on his dressing-table? Yes, pretty in a way, I suppose."

Billie's voice came thinly over the wires.

"My dear, I haven't an earthly. But, believe it or not, she came to the flat one evening. We'd been having a bit of a binge, and there was a ring at the door. Brian answered it, and unfortunately he was as tight as an owl. You know he's really quite harmless, but I fancy he scared her."

"How do you know it was her?"

"My dear, I heard him talking and I went to see what was happening. I saw it was the girl in the photograph. She just turned tail and fled down the stairs. We might have been Gorgons. But it's just as well, isn't it? I mean, what's past is past, and all that—"

"You've said it. Thanks, Billie."

When Gale came back with his arms full of paper bags Leila ran to meet him.

"Darling—"

"Look out. I've brought raspberries and they're coming through the paper. And cream—"

"Angel—"

"Aren't I. You'll find plates and things in the dresser."

She would have liked him to watch her admiringly as she flitted about, but he had sat down to read the letters he had found on the mat when they arrived.

"Anything exciting?"

He answered her absently. "Not particularly. Mostly bills. Old Peridew wants me to do a weekly series of essays, some facets of London life—rotten title. That ought to pay for our bust in Cornwall. I don't generally stay at the best hotels. The average pub is better fun actually."

Leila reddened. "Are you trying to tell me that you were bored?" He looked up at her, smiling. "Of course not. Come here"—he drew her to him. "You baby," he said fondly.

She was twenty-four and had been earning her living on the stage since she was seventeen, but her small figure and round childish face gave her a deceptive air of extreme youth. "Nice boy," she whispered, and rumpled his hair.

They enjoyed their tea.

"Don't bother to wash up," he said. "The woman will be here in the morning. Leave everything stacked in the sink."

"All right. Where shall we go?"

"Go?"

"I mean a play, or the flicks. We can't just sit here twiddling our thumbs," said Leila gaily.

"Well, as a matter of fact I ought to be starting on the first of these essays. I have to work, you know."

"Not in the evenings, surely."

"Peridew wants the first instalment to-morrow."

He was taking the cover off his typewriter as he spoke. Leila threw one of the sofa cushions at him. He fielded it with his left hand, but he did not return it. Leila's full red lips drooped at the corners. She did not look so pretty when she sulked.

"How dull. Well, I'll ring up Billie and ask her to come round."

"Please don't. I'm sorry, my dear, but this is a small flat, and the walls are thin. I know I should hear a most distracting chatter even if you shut yourselves up in the bedroom. I have to be quiet when I'm writing. Can't you read or something? Plenty of review copies of novels about."

"Read," she said contemptuously. "What do you take me for."

He made no reply. She watched him as he slipped a sheet of paper into his typewriter. He was too old for her, of course, and not really her sort, as Billie had warned her, but she loved him. He was so handsome. "And he's mad about me, too," she thought. And then, with a sharp prick of jealous fear, she remembered the photograph in the silver frame.

She had been silent for ten minutes, curled up on the sofa, and he had written his opening sentence. The keys of the typewriter pattered like machine-gun bullets, and ceased, and began again.

"Francis—"

He answered curtly, without turning his head. "You've got to understand that I can't work if I'm interrupted."

"You should have married a deaf mute. Francis, who is the girl whose picture you've got on your dressing-table?"

"That? That's Anne."

"Thank you for telling me," said Leila sarcastically. "I'm as wise as I was before. One of your has beens, I suppose. Well, I'm not much good at sharing, see. There's a photograph of me that'll go very well in that frame—"

Gale got up and went over to the mantelpiece to fill his pipe from the tobacco jar. "Steady on, Leila. You don't understand. Anne is my daughter."

She stared at him. "Your daughter!"

"Yes. She looks older than she really is in that picture. She's— Good Lord, I suppose she must be sixteen."

Leila whistled. "So I'm a stepmother, am I? Well, I'm damned."

He struck a match. "I ought to have told you—but I was so afraid that if I did you wouldn't marry me. I knew that girl—Billie What's-her-name—was persuading you to turn me down."

"Are there any more? You may as well make a clean breast of it while you're about it."

"No, no. Only Anne. She's at school in Brighton. She would have enjoyed Cornwall, Leila. Another time, perhaps. I don't see why you and she shouldn't hit it off. She's been with me to Normandy and last Easter we did a walking tour through the Lake district. I've felt rather guilty about putting her off this time—"

"Wasn't she thrilled to hear about me?" enquired Leila, adding, half to herself, "I don't think."

"I haven't told her yet," Gale said. He looked troubled.

"It was so near the end of the term. I hadn't the time to explain properly. She's sensitive, and at that age it's so difficult to make them understand. I didn't want her to be hurt. I just said I was called away on business, and she was to go to Cousin Agatha."

"Who is she?"

"A cousin of my father's actually, and about the only relation I have left. I used to stay with her sometimes when I was a kid. I haven't seen her for years, but I sent her a reply-paid telegram and she was quite willing to have Anne. The child will be safe with her."

Leila was not angry now. She thought she could cope with a step-daughter. But she was curious.

"Is she like her mother?"

"I hope not."

"Like that, was it? But it might have been your fault. Perhaps you hammered on that machine when she wanted to go out."

"I'd rather not talk about it if you don't mind, Leila. I divorced her five years ago. She could have seen Anne now and then if she had wanted to, but she didn't bother. I believe she writes to her and sends her presents."

"Has she married again?"

"No."

"The other man let her down?"

Gale answered shortly. "There was more than one. Anne knows nothing about it, and I hope she never will."

"Why does she suppose you parted?"

"Oh, incompatibility. That sort of thing. Leila—I know I ought to have told you all this before. It wasn't fair to you. Forgive me—" He sat down by her and drew her to him.

His lean face, sombre in repose, lit up when he smiled. Leila heaved a sigh of content as she snuggled into the hollow of his arm. Never mind Billie, with her "marry in haste—" and all the rest of it. Billie was probably envious of her happiness. As for the girl, perhaps the relative she was staying with would adopt her. If not, she would have to be found a job as soon as she left school. Not the stage. Nursing, perhaps, she looked one of the serious kind. "Mercifully," thought Leila, "there isn't room for her in this flat."

And then she remembered what Billie had said when she rang up.

She made a small involuntary movement. Gale glanced down at her.

"What's the matter? Cramp?"

"No. Nothing. At least—" Leila hesitated. She realised vaguely that the information she was tempted to withhold might have some importance. On the other hand, Francis would fuss, and they were so comfortable as they were. "Nothing," she said more firmly.

"No use trying to work now. I'm no longer in the mood." He looked at his watch. "We'll go up West and have dinner somewhere."

They went on the top of a bus in the golden glow of the summer evening, and came home in a hansom.

Leila loved hansoms, the light swaying motion and the jingling of the harness bells, the horses threading their way so cleverly through the traffic. They said a horse would never knock anyone down if it could possibly help it. "Oh dear," she thought, "I'll have to tell him." Brian had been tight, and had scared her. She thought of Brian with distaste. He was one of Billie's admirers, a pimply youth, and he could be a beast if he was not kept in order. She thought of the girl in the picture, looking so young and—somehow—defenceless.

"You're very quiet," said Gale as he followed her into the living-room. "Are you tired? A spot of whisky and soda?"

Leila threw her cloak on to the sofa and turned to the mirror over the mantelpiece before she sat down.

"Francis, there is something—while you were out getting the cakes and fruit I rang up Billie—"

"Did you tell her we had already seen the holes she and her pals burnt in the Persian rug? Why people can't use ash trays—"

"No. Listen. It wasn't Billie's fault, but somebody rang the bell one evening when she was throwing a party. One of her young men went to the door, and unfortunately he was a bit squiffy. Billie heard a girl's voice, and I suppose she sounded scared. Billie went to see, but it was too late. The girl ran off down the stairs."

Gale frowned. "Well, we shall have to try to live it down. You and I are not likely to annoy the other tenants by giving rowdy entertainments."

"It isn't that," Leila said. She finished her whisky and soda and set down the glass. "Billie said it was the girl whose photograph you keep in a silver frame on your dressing-table. She was chipping me about her. Of course, she had no idea—"

"Anne," said Gale loudly. "It couldn't have been Anne. She's with Cousin Agatha at Bognor. She wouldn't come here. She knew I was going away."

"All right. Don't get excited. I daresay Billie was mistaken. After all, she only saw her for a second, and there isn't much light on the landing."

"It wasn't Anne," he said again, trying to convince himself. "But I tell you what, Leila. I'll go down to-morrow and make sure."

"Do. You might break it to her at the same time that I exist."

"Yes. Yes, of course."

He was thinking that the whole evening had been wasted. He would have to work in the train. If he could rough out his essay on the way he could type it when he got home. Leila would have to realise that he could not give up all his time to running around with her. Eve had been just the same. Women were so exacting. How was he going to explain to Anne that he had to have Leila? Something about her—the impudent little snub nose, the curve of her upper lip, too short for beauty. That was how a man was caught, maddened, until he was like a drug addict craving for the peace that only his beloved poison would give him. Peace. But it didn't last. He couldn't say anything like that to Anne, and, if he did, she wouldn't understand. She was too young. She would think he had spoilt everything, and so he had from her point of view. A pretty and rather common stepmother, only a few years older than herself.

He squirted a little soda water into a liberal allowance of whisky and drank it down.

"Oh, hell," he said. "Let's go to bed."

CHAPTER III
THE SEARCH BEGINS

MISS Agatha Wrenn had lived as long as anybody could remember in the last house of a terrace of tall, narrow, stuccoed houses standing alone in a road that had been begun and never finished on the outskirts of Bognor. After her house the pavement ended, abruptly and beyond there was nothing but an expanse of flat fields, most of them lying fallow. In winter the prospect was inexpressibly dreary, in summer it had a certain charm, being so open to the sky, but, in any case, Miss Wrenn never noticed it. Her father had built the terrace in the seventies of the nineteenth century. All the houses were alike, with basement kitchens and a great many stairs. Agatha, ever since she came into the property, had refused to make any repairs, and the tenants had left one by one. She had the terrace all to herself now. Most of the windows were broken and grass grew on the steps leading up to the front doors. It did not matter. She had a sufficient income from other sources. Consols, she thought, and other things. She did not really spend much. The fishmonger and the milkman. Such nice men. Not that she ever saw them. She wrote on a slate, and they left what was required. And it really was a good thing she had gone, letting in so much air and refusing to take poor Beauty on her lap. As if she could help having sores. Knock. Knock. Wake Duncan by your knocking. That was in a book, wasn't it. Or a play. And now the ringing. Let them ring. But it went on and on. Miss Wrenn lost patience at last, and went down to the door. The latch was rusty with disuse. She always used the servants' basement entrance when she went out, which was seldom.

She opened the door a few inches and said in an angry voice: "What do you want?"

The man who had been knocking and ringing for the last ten minutes was tall and good-looking, with thick white hair brushed back from his forehead. A stranger: but he reminded her of someone she had known long ago. She blinked at him doubtfully.

Francis Gale moistened his lips. "Miss Wrenn—"

"I am Miss Wrenn."

"Good God! I mean—I beg your pardon. You don't remember me. It's so many years—I stayed with you more than once for my holidays when I was a boy. I am Francis Gale. My little girl is with you now."

"Oh," she said hesitatingly. "Perhaps you had better come in—"

She held the door open just enough to allow him to squeeze past her. The hall was dark and stuffy, with a peculiarly fetid fishy smell.

"Where is Anne?" He tried to control his voice.

"Oh, dear." Her eyes, pale and restless, avoided his. "It's very inconvenient just now, with poor Beauty so ill. You must come down, I suppose. I can't leave her long—"

He followed her down a steep flight of uncarpeted stairs to a black pit. She opened a door and he looked over her shoulder into a kitchen whose only light came from a closely barred window, crusted with dirt, looking into the area. It was a warm day, but a large fire was burning in the grate. The place was full of cats, sleeping on the chairs, gliding about in the shadowy corners, rustling the piles of dirty old newspapers and accumulated rubbish under the table. One, lying in a basket on the hearth, turned its head feebly as Miss Wrenn bent over it.

"I'm here, Beauty," she murmured. "Mother hasn't left you."

Gale saw that it was blind and covered with sores. He felt slightly sick.

"Anne—"

"She went away after—I forget exactly how long—was it two or three days? She couldn't adapt herself to our ways." Miss Wrenn sat down and a big black tomcat leapt on to her knees and stood there, purring, and arching his back under her hand.

"Where did she go, Cousin Agatha?"

She looked about her vaguely. "I'm afraid I don't—she left a note, but I mislaid it. Don't look like that. You mustn't be angry with her. It is Frankie, isn't it? You spent your holidays here years ago. We used to go for long cycle rides together and bathe in the sea. I haven't been able to go out for a long time because of my pussies. They don't like me to leave them."

"I understand," he said gently. He remembered now that she had been a little odd, even in the old days. He blamed himself bitterly for not having taken the trouble to come down and see her before sending Anne to her. She seemed harmless, but she was obviously mad. The child must have been terrified, afraid to stay, and not knowing where to go. He felt tolerably certain now that she had come to the flat. He had sent her two pounds for pocket-money, not much more than enough to pay her railway fare to London. After that—what? She was sixteen, shy and reserved, young for her age in some ways, inclined to be dreamy.

He said:

"Can't you remember at all where she was going? No, that's no use. She came to my place, and I wasn't there. What about her luggage?"

"She had a little wicker case, one of those light Japanese things. Her box is still upstairs in her bedroom."

"May I go up and have a look round? There may be some indication—you see, Cousin Agatha, I don't know where she is."

But the flicker of interest in something outside herself had died down. She said, "I can't come up with you because of Beauty. That girl wanted to fetch the vet. I wouldn't let her. I knew what he'd say. He's a wicked man."

Anne had occupied one of the attics at the top of the house. The window was broken, probably as the result of her efforts to open it. The room was bare, but it was tolerably clean. Anne's school trunk stood at the foot of the old-fashioned iron bedstead. He had hoped to find the note she had left for Cousin Agatha on the dressing-table, but it was not there.

He went down again to the ground floor and hesitated at the top of the stairs leading to the basement. He could hear Miss Wrenn shuffling about and talking to her cats. Would she expect him to go down and say good-bye, or had she already forgotten him? Characteristically he decided that she would not notice his going without taking any leave of her. The habit of shirking unpleasantness had become ingrained. He wanted to forget the details of his visit as soon as possible.

He drew a long breath as he closed the door after him, filling his lungs with clean air. After that dark, silent, malodorous house it was good to come into the busy main street and to find the railway station crowded with cheerful trippers, young men and girls with tennis rackets and bath towels, and children carrying buckets and spades. Gale took a ticket for Brighton. It had occurred to him that Anne might have gone back to her school.

But his heart sank as he approached the house and saw painters at work on ladders. The maid who answered the door was doubtful.

"I don't know if you can see Miss Blane, sir. She's going on a cruise, and she's busy."

"Please tell her it's urgent."

She took his card and went away. After an interval she came back and he was shown into a drawing-room where the chairs were covered with dust-sheets.

Gale waited uneasily, feeling very much as he had felt when, as a boy, he was summoned to the head's study. Miss Blane's manner to parents was invariably bland, but she allowed them to realise that from her point of view they were a regrettable necessity.

He smiled nervously as they shook hands.

"Sorry to disturb you—"

"Not at all. But I'm afraid I haven't much time. What can I do for you? I hope you are taking Anne away for the rest of the holidays. She was bitterly disappointed that you could not come for her as you always have done."

"I know. It couldn't be helped. She—she isn't here then?"

Miss Blane looked surprised. "Here? Certainly not."

"You haven't heard from her at all?"

"No. Why? Is anything wrong? Fräulein bought her ticket for Bognor and saw her into the train. There was only one change, at Barnham Junction. Quite simple even for such a daydreamer as Anne."

"She got there all right. But, unfortunately, the relation she was to stay with has become very eccentric. Anne—she seems to have left after a couple of days. There—there's some evidence that she called at my flat in London."

"Dear me. Please go on, Mr. Gale."

"The people there had no idea who she was. There was a party going on. Rather a rowdy affair apparently, and I'm afraid she was frightened."

Miss Blane looked at him gravely. She had never quite approved of Anne Gale's father. It was not his fault, she knew, that he had no home to take the child to, but he was too casual, too easygoing to be a good influence. He was selfish, of course. All men were. But she did not doubt his affection for Anne.

"When was this, Mr. Gale?"

"Yesterday week."

"Has she no other relations to whom she might go?"

"None. I thought she might have come back here."

"I wish she had. But would she have the money for railway journeys?"

"I sent her two pounds for pocket-money while she was at Bognor. The fare up to London from there would come out of that. Could she have gone to one of her girl friends? She was always talking about a child called Brenda at one time—"

"Brenda Sims. But she left last term and she's gone to Australia with her people. Wait a minute. Penelope Fordyce and Anne were in the same dormitory. Penelope is one of those slow, heavy and thoroughly reliable girls who are apt to devote themselves to someone of an entirely different type. Yes, she and Anne—I think it might be worth trying, Mr. Gale."

"Thank you. Can you give me her address?"

"Certainly." She opened a drawer of her bureau and took out a notebook. "She lives with an aunt, Miss Fordyce, at Stratford-on-Avon. It's rather an odd address. The Poor Player, Sheep Street."

"Is she on the telephone?"

"I'll go there at once."

"You—forgive me, Mr. Gale—you'll be discreet. You'll understand that with a school like mine one can't be too careful. Any unpleasantness, the least breath of scandal, and some of the parents would be taking their children away at once. I—you will remember I stretched a point when I agreed to have Anne five years ago. I have never regretted it, she is a dear child, but I can't afford to take any risks."

"Do you mean that you don't want her back next term?" he asked bluntly.

"That depends, Mr. Gale. I am being quite frank with you. Girls of her age are difficult. We watch the children who are committed to our care very carefully—but we may sometimes be mistaken in our estimate."

"Are you trying to suggest that Anne may have run off with the music master? She wouldn't see any other men here, I suppose."

"Please, Mr. Gale, don't lose your temper. I made no such suggestion. I hope you may find her staying with the Fordyces. I am going away for three weeks on a cruise to Norway. Perhaps you will get into touch with me when I return. And do believe that I am very sorry about this. I share your anxiety. It was such a pity you weren't able to come for her as you always have done. The child worships you, Mr. Gale, and I'm afraid she took it very much to heart."

She glanced at the clock. He took the hint and stood up.

It was past ten o'clock when he reached Stratford, after catching the last local train from Leamington. It was late to be making a call on strangers, but he could not bear to wait. He had had too much time during his tedious cross-country journey to reflect on what might have happened to Anne. If she was not with the Fordyces he would have to go to the police. And what could they do? He tried to remember how many hundred people disappear every year from their homes without leaving any trace. No doubt a large number of those disappearances were voluntary—but the others—

The little Warwickshire town looked very peaceful, its ancient roofs and tall church spire silvery under an August moon. A policeman directed him to Sheep Street.

"The Poor Player? Half way down, on the left. But it'll be closed."

"It's not a pub?"

"No, sir. A tea shop."

He found it easily, for it was marked by a swinging sign. The shutters were up, but a light showed through the curtains of the window of the room above.

Gale knocked on the shop door and heard someone coming down the stairs. The door was opened by a young man who said, "Hallo, you two, you're earlier than I expected"—and then—"I beg your pardon. I didn't see. I thought it was my people. They had seats for *Twelfth Night*—"

Gale said: "Does Miss Fordyce live here?"

"Yes. My aunt. She's at the theatre. She'll be back soon."

"And Penelope—"

"My sister. Do you know her?"

"She is a friend of my daughter's. My name is Gale. Is Anne here?"

"Not that I know of. But she may be. Won't you come in, Mr. Gale?"

"Thanks."

"I'm Roger Fordyce. This way—"

Gale followed him through the shop and up a steep flight of stairs to the parlour above.

"You'll have a whisky and soda," said Roger hospitably. As he tilted the shade of the lamp he had noticed that the visitor was no longer young, and that he looked pale and weary.

"Aunt Polly and Pen are ardent Shakespearians, as, of course, they ought to be, living here and making a living out of visitors to the shrine. I prefer musical comedy myself. Had to swot the old boy at school. Ah, here they are," he said. "Just a minute, sir—" He clattered down the stairs.

"Somebody called to see you," he announced. "He's upstairs, lean, distinguished-looking bloke with white hair. He says he's the father of a friend of yours, Penny."

"Goodness," said Penny. "Oh, Roger, you should have come. The Duke was sweet. Such legs."

"His legs were better than his enunciation," remarked her aunt. "Penny, a glass of milk and straight to bed, please."

"But, Auntie, oughtn't I to see this whoever it is?"

"He's up in the sitting-room," said Roger. "Fidgeting round like a cat on hot bricks."

"Most extraordinary," said his aunt. "None of Penny's school friends live within a hundred miles of us."

"Gale is the name."

Penny squealed. "Anne! Is she with him? What a thrill—"

"No one," said Roger, as he and his aunt followed her up the stairs, "no one could say Penny is light on her feet. She charges about like a baby rhino."

"She'll outgrow it," said Miss Fordyce placidly. She was a little woman with a long, humorous face and that faintly equine appearance that so often denotes brains in a woman. She had adopted her orphaned nephew and niece, and worked hard to pay for their upbringing. Lately Roger had been able to help her out of his salary. He was assistant manager on a rubber plantation in Malaya, and had just come home on his first leave.

Penelope burst into the sitting-room and stopped short in the doorway. "Oh, I thought—are you Anne's father?"

"Yes. Is she with you?"

"No. Was she coming round? Are you staying in Stratford?"

He answered heavily. "I don't know where she is. I hoped you might."

Miss Fordyce edged her way round the solid figure of her niece. "Do sit down, Mr. Gale, and tell us all about it. We'll help you if we can. I've heard a great deal about Anne from Penny."

He remembered that Miss Blane had advised discretion. He said rather carefully, "Anne has always spent her holidays with me. I try to give her a good time."

"Simply gorgeous," cried Penny. "She makes the other girls green with envy, walking tours in the Dales, and following the Roman Wall and the Italian lakes last Easter. Scrumptious."

He smiled faintly. "This year I couldn't, so I arranged for her to stay with an old cousin of mine at Bognor."

"I know." Penny was irrepressible. "She was frightfully fed up about it. You only let her know the day before we broke up, didn't you? I heard her crying in the night, and the next morning you could hardly get a word out of her. I was worried, but, of course, we were all catching our trains—"

"That will do, Penny," said her aunt. She had seen Gale wince.

He said, "I was afraid of that. But it couldn't be helped. I meant to make it up to her later. The fact is—" he flushed as he turned to Miss Fordyce. "I've married again. There wasn't much time. Leila was going to sign a contract for two years and going to South Africa with the company. I persuaded her to marry me instead. It was all a rush. I simply hadn't the time to explain it all to Anne."

"I see," said Miss Fordyce dryly. She had taken Francis Gale's measure. She glanced at her niece and saw that she was deeply shocked. Roger had faded tactfully into the background. Gale, aware that, for the moment at least, he had lost their sympathy, struggled on.

"When we came back from Cornwall I learned that Anne had come to the flat one evening last week. We had lent the place to the girl my wife had been sharing rooms with. There was a party going on, a noisy affair apparently, and Anne went away. She may have thought she had come to the wrong flat. I've never had her there. I went down to Bognor this morning and found that she had left there. My old cousin has become very cranky. I should never have sent her there if I had known. I went on to Brighton and saw Miss Blane. She thought there was just a chance that Anne had come on to you."

"I wish she had," said Penny. "I understand now—"

She broke off abruptly.

Gale looked at her. "Please," he said, "if you can help me, if you have any ideas—I must find her."

Penny shook her head. "I'm sorry."

"Are you sure?" He looked so wretched that Miss Fordyce was touched. She said, "It's very late and Penny is tired. She might think of something if you give her time. You'll be spending the night in Stratford?"

"Yes. I booked a room at the Swan on my way from the Station."

"Will you come and see us again to-morrow morning as early as you like?"

"Thank you," he said humbly. "It's good of you—"

Roger saw him out. When he came back he turned on his sister. "Look here, Penny, you know something. Why you didn't tell him at once I can't imagine."

"If you had a very great friend," said Penny, "would you betray her confidence?"

"Don't be a little idiot," said her brother crushingly.

"This may be serious—"

His aunt stopped him with a warning glance at poor Penny, who was evidently on the verge of tears. "Not another word to-night," she said briskly. "Off to bed, both of you. Roger, did you bolt the shop door?"

Penny had retreated. Roger lingered. "Do you think she really knows where this girl is?"

"No. I'm afraid not. We shall see to-morrow. Don't be too hard on the child, Roger. She adores you, and she has been counting the days. Don't bully her now you are here."

CHAPTER IV
TROUBLE FOR A STRANGER

GALE called soon after nine o'clock. "I hope I'm not too early," he said apologetically to Miss Fordyce, who was superintending the display of home-made cakes in the window.

"Not at all," she said. "I've talked to Penny, and she is going to tell you all she knows—which isn't very much, I fear."

She left the shop with her assistant, an earnest, bespectacled young woman in a green overall, in charge, and took him upstairs. Penny, red-eyed, and subdued, was waiting for him. Roger was not present.

"I'm sorry about last night," began Penny, when they were all seated, "but it was difficult. You see, Anne said don't tell anyone and underlined it twice. Even now I'm not sure I'm doing right—"

"You've heard from her?"

"I had a card from her last week. Here it is."

She drew a rather crumpled picture postcard of the Traitor's gate in the Tower of London from the pocket of her cardigan. Gale took it from her and read the few words scrawled in pencil on the small space reserved for correspondence.

> Darling Pen, I am going to my Mother. I've often wanted to, but now something has happened that has made up my mind for me. Don't tell anyone. Always your loving Anne.

"Good Heavens. She can't mean—" gasped Miss Fordyce.

Gale, glancing at her, saw that she had turned very pale. "Not that," he said hurriedly. "I'm not a widower. I—there was a divorce some years ago. I had Anne. She hasn't seen her mother since."

"Anne always hoped you would be reconciled," said Penny.

"She told you that?"

Penny nodded. "Nobody at school was supposed to know her parents were divorced, but, of course, everyone did. We all thought it very exciting. But Anne always said it was only a separation. She wouldn't believe either of you had done anything really wrong."

Gale sat turning over the card in his hands. It had been posted at 5.30, six days earlier. That would be Thursday, the day after that unlucky visit to his flat. He had no idea where Eve was, but Anne would know since she kept up a correspondence with her mother. That was all right, then, he would have to get her back, of course, but meanwhile she was safe. Eve would not let the child come to any harm: he would do her that justice.

He said, "That's a weight off my mind. Thank you very much, Penny," so charmingly that she was inclined to revise the unfavourable opinion she had formed of him.

Miss Fordyce eyed him thoughtfully. He looked tired and careworn in the strong morning light. She noticed that there was a button missing on his coat and drew the conclusion that his second wife did not know how to look after him.

"Forgive me," she said, "but has your first wife married again?"

"No."

"The court gave you the custody of the child?"

"Yes."

"You will now go and fetch Anne away? I was thinking that if you cared to bring her back here to spend the rest of her holidays with us—we have no spare room while Roger is home, but she could share Penny's."

"That would be lovely," said Penny fervently.

Gale was really touched. These people were kind. "It is most kind of you. I should be very grateful—until I can make other arrangements—" His voice died away. The longer he could put off bringing Leila and Anne together the better. He knew well enough what Anne, with the intolerance of youth, would think of her stepmother. She might even say it. "Pretty, but common, with bad manners. Oh, Daddy, how could you!"

"Where is Mrs. Gale living now?"

"That's the trouble. I don't know. I believe she has no settled home. She's a painter, quite well known under her maiden name.

Eve Shandon. She has a show in one of the Bond Street galleries now and then. She does small oil landscapes chiefly. She travels a lot. The United States, Egypt, the Levant. So, you see, she might be anywhere."

"But Anne couldn't get far, could she? I suppose she had not much money?"

"About two pounds, less the fare up from Bognor—and I suppose she spent Wednesday night somewhere. Another eight-and-six for bed and breakfast."

"I suppose you can get in touch with Mrs. Gale through her Bank," suggested Miss Fordyce.

"I might," he said doubtfully. "I must try that, of course."

Penny, who had been fidgeting on her chair, said, "She was in Italy last term. I know, because Anne had a letter from her with Italian stamps on it, and she gave them to one of the girls who collects them."

"That's a help," he said. "Did Anne tell you anything about it?"

"She said it was a place her mother had been to before, but only for a few days, and that she was staying longer this time because it was simply gorgeous and full of subjects."

"You don't remember the name of the place?"

"She didn't tell me that. But, anyhow, she couldn't possibly go all that way by herself. Why, we aren't even allowed to go to the station at Brighton without one of the mistresses to take our tickets and make sure we're in a Ladies Only." Gale was silent, looking down at the card in his hand. The Traitor's Gate. Would Anne regard his second marriage as a betrayal? These young people were so hard. Anne might have heard of his marriage from the caretaker at the flats. He would have to find out from the man if he had seen and spoken to her. He had not faced it before but, in fact, he had always known how bitterly Anne would resent what she would regard as Leila's intrusion into his life. He sighed. "I know. But I'm afraid it's not impossible. She went to Como with me only last Easter."

"About money—" Miss Fordyce reminded him.

"She has a gold watch and some bits of jewellery and an extravagant gold-mounted dressing-case Eve gave her on her last birthday that would fetch something, I expect. But I'm hoping that Eve is back in England. I must go to Town now and find out. Thank you for all your kindness."

"Bring her to us if you like—" said Miss Fordyce as they shook hands.

"Thank you. Here's my card with my address. I'll let you know how I get on."

She went downstairs with him, leaving Penny in the sitting-room.

"Will you forgive what may seem an impertinence, Mr. Gale. Are there valid reasons why Anne should not stay with her mother?"

"I think so," he said. "Eve is charming, but she's completely amoral. She dragged my name through the mire five years ago. I expect she would say that was my own fault. I had only to shut my eyes. Anne doesn't know—"

She stood in the shop door and watched him go up Sheep Street and turn to the right for the station.

She called Penny down to help in the shop, for the Poor Player usually had a good many customers round about eleven for morning coffee, before she went into the kitchen to start cake-making for the afternoon. Roger had gone over to Birmingham to lunch with friends and did not return until the evening when the shop was closed. He found his aunt sitting by the open window in the sitting-room enjoying a well-earned rest. Penny, still rather pale and subdued, was reading a novel by Charles Garvice. She did not raise her head as he entered, but Miss Fordyce gave him a questioning look.

"Well?" she said. "Did you have a good time? Were all the girls at home?"

He was unreasonably annoyed that his aunt had not forgotten that in his early youth, that now seemed to him so far away, he had admired Irene Wilkinson.

He said, "So far as I know. I didn't count."

Miss Fordyce did not resent his brusqueness. Roger had only been home two days, but it had been long enough for her to see that, for some reason, he was restless and unhappy. It was not like Roger to be short with her or to snub Penny as he had done more than once. Normally he was cheerful and had a naturally quick temper well under control. Miss Fordyce had been hoping that he would become engaged during his leave to some nice and not too exacting girl who would be willing to go back to Malaya with him. One of the Wilkinsons would have done very well. She wondered if he had had some unfortunate affair on the voyage home. She leaned out a little to watch a young man in flannels who was walking down the street towards the river. "There goes Feste, Penny. I suppose he isn't in the play to-night."

Penny ran to the window to feast her eyes on the actor's back view.

"He was sweet when he sang 'Come away, Death', but Shakespearean jokes are a bit pointless, aren't they—or am I too young to understand? I'll get the supper, shall I? There's a pork pie, Roger."

"Good," said Roger with more enthusiasm than he actually felt. He was ashamed of his bad temper. It wasn't his aunt's or Penny's fault that he had gone up like a rocket into the starry sky of romance, and come down like a stick. He said, "It's a warm evening. What about hiring a boat for an hour after supper? It will be cooler on the river. What do you say, both of you?"

Miss Fordyce looked pleased, and Penny beamed, her woes temporarily forgotten. But clouds came up, and it began to rain before they had finished supper. Penny was so disappointed that her brother, anxious to console her, remembered some native-worked embroidered silk he had brought home for her. He routed it out of his trunk and took it into her room, standing there, with his hands in his pockets, observing her collected treasures critically, as brothers will.

"George Alexander, and H.V. Esmond as Little Billie, and some of Louis Wain's cats. I should think you'd see enough actors at close quarters here wolfing teas, to put you off them." His voice changed as he said, "Who is this girl?" Penny came over to him. "Isn't she lovely?" she said enthusiastically. "Taken like that in profile. It always reminds me of Browning—we do a lot of him, our literature mistress is simply nuts on him, but he's rather good all the same, I think."

"Why Browning?"

"Oh, you know—'I would I had her little head upon a background of pure gold.'"

"Yes," he said. "Who is she?"

"Why, that's Anne Gale." Penny, who was very proud of her friend's beauty, enjoyed the impression she had made.

Roger said "Good Lord!" and replaced the photograph very carefully on the rickety shelf where it shared the best place with a china pig.

"By the way, did her father come again this morning?"

"Yes, and I told him I'd had a card from her posted in London and saying she was going to her mother."

"But I thought—"

"They were divorced," explained Penny. "Anne hadn't seen her mother for years, but she used to hear from her and get some ripping presents, Spanish lace and ivory and coral and things. She used to travel about in places like India, staying with Rajahs and all that, but this summer she's been in Italy. When she was in India she painted a racing cheetah. We had to look that up in the dictionary. It's a sort of leopard, but more doggish in its mind. She does gardens a lot. She sent Anne several tiny little sketches last term in one of her letters. Anne gave me one and I'm going to have it framed. Look."

She opened a drawer and took out a small unmounted sketch in water colours. It was a study, very firmly drawn and coloured, of a moss-grown statue of Pan, with one arm missing, against a background of purple wistaria.

Roger felt as if his heart had missed a beat. He had seen that Pan before and quite recently. Surely he could not be mistaken. And yet—there might be hundreds of such garden statues, and wistaria was common enough. A chance resemblance reminding him of something that he wanted to forget.

Penny said, "What's the matter, Roger? You do look queer."

"I'm all right. Where was this painted?"

"Somewhere in Italy. But I think it was done last year. She told Anne she'd gone back to the same place and was working hard so as to have plenty of stuff for a show at one of the Bond Street galleries next Spring."

"I see. Did you tell Gale?"

"Yes. But it wasn't much use as I didn't know the name of the place. He's going to try to find out through her Bank."

"You think Anne may have tried to go out there to her mother?"

"I don't know," said Penny doubtfully. "Anne's so quiet, and one never can be sure with quiet people. There's Auntie calling."

She replaced the sketch in the drawer and they went back to the sitting-room.

Miss Fordyce, ignoring Penny's protests, sent her up to bed at ten o'clock. She wanted to give Roger an opportunity to tell her his troubles but he did not seem disposed to take it. She was knitting, and he seemed to be reading, but she noticed that he had not turned a page. At last she could bear it no longer.

"My dear boy, is there anything wrong?"

"Nothing, Aunt Polly. At least—nothing I can talk about to you."

"Is it money? I might be able to help. I have a little put by."

"No. It isn't money. I made a fool of myself, but that's over and, I daresay it's taught me a lesson, only it leaves one feeling a bit flat for a bit."

"Very well, dear, if that's all. We all make mistakes." She finished a row before she added. "I have been wondering if I did not make one to-day."

"What was that?"

"When I told Mr. Gale we should be pleased to have his daughter here. After what he had told us I felt so sorry for the child—but she may not be a good companion for Penny."

"Why not?"

"Well, Roger, I hope I'm not narrow-minded, but there is something in heredity, I suppose—I know you often remind me of my poor brother—Mr. Gale may be well enough, though I should say he was self indulgent and inclined to be shiftless, but I gathered that the mother is not a nice woman."

"I think the girl must be all right," said Roger, "or Penny wouldn't have taken to her. I hope you asked him to let you know when she's found."

She looked at him quickly. "I fancied last night that you thought he was making an unnecessary fuss."

He said "I've had time to think it over—some of the things that might have happened to her—"

His aunt sighed. "I know. But don't worry too much. It's no business of ours. We aren't responsible."

But when Roger had gone to bed, and was lying awake until the sparrows began to twitter under the eaves he was not so sure. When, at last, he fell asleep, it was to dream that his sister Penny was being attacked by a black dog, and that he was prevented from going to her rescue by something warm and stifling wound about his neck. A woman's arms, or a rope. He woke shaking and drenched with sweat. It was only a dream, but it had served its purpose. At breakfast he announced that he had to go up to Town on business.

"I'll be back to-morrow probably."

"Just as you like, dear," his aunt said. "Penny, I shall be making a batch of lemon curd cakes. You can come into the kitchen and learn how to mix them. Penny is going into partnership with me when she leaves school, Roger."

"Glad to hear it."

Yes, Penny was safe enough; she would be happy and busy helping to run the tea shop, and his dream about her had been fantastically irrelevant. But there were others less fortunate. He remembered a plaster cast he had seen in an art school where he had gone for lessons in wood carving—a girl's face, faintly smiling—someone had told him it was a death mask taken in the Paris Morgue from a subject found drowned in the Seine. Why was she smiling? Was it because she had nothing more to fear?

He had lunch on the train, and it was still early in the afternoon when he arrived at Camperdown Mansions. He saw from the list of tenants that Gale's flat was on the fifth floor. There was no porter and the automatic lift seemed to be out of order so he walked up the stairs. Gale himself answered his ring and stared at him blankly for a moment, evidently failing to recognise him. He looked haggard and heavy-eyed, and had not troubled to shave. "My name is Fordyce. You came to see us at Stratford. I happened to be in Town so I thought I'd call—"

Gale blinked at him, and Roger realised that he had been drinking. "Very good of you," he said, "won't you come in? Nothing much to offer, I'm afraid. Finished the whisky just now."

"Thanks. I don't want anything," said Roger hastily.

Gale waved his hand. "Sit down. Anywhere," he said largely. Roger glanced about him and took the only chair that was not encumbered with books or articles of clothing. The living-room was in great disorder, and there was a good deal of crumpled tissue paper about on the floor.

"Packing," explained Gale with tipsy solemnity. "My wife is packing. After seeing me off at Victoria the day before yesterday she went on to the agents. Believe it or not, she got a shop without the leasht, I mean the least difficulty. Theatrical slang. In plain English, my boy, she's going to Australia with a touring company. Chorus, and understudying one of the principals. She was gone when I got back yesterday. Left a note. My fault perhaps. I should have told her about Anne. Part of stepmother wasn't in her contract. Well, there it is."

He sat staring at Roger for a moment, his tired face twitching, before he said very quietly, "So I've lost them both."

Roger felt sorry for him, but he also felt some youthful contempt. He said, "Do you mind if I open the window? It's stuffy in here."

He suited the action to the word, and came back to his chair. "What have you done—about finding your daughter?"

"I went to Eve's Bank. They didn't know where she was. Wouldn't tell me, anyhow. I remembered the address of a friend of hers, another painting woman. Couldn't get anything out of her either. She always hated me like poison."

"Have you been to the police?"

"Yes. Called at Scotland Yard yesterday. They took down the particulars and rang up the hospitals to find if anyone answering to her description had been brought in to the accident wards. They said they'd make enquiries and keep a look out. They asked me when she disappeared, and when I said ten days ago they said it would be difficult, all but one chap who kept on smiling until I wanted to swipe him, who said that in nine cases out of ten after the police had gone to a lot of trouble the object of their search was found to have been staying with friends."

"Then you aren't any further?"

"Yes, I am. I've talked to the porter of these flats. She spoke to him when she came downstairs after being scared away by my wife's rotten crowd of friends. He told her I'd married again and was away on my honeymoon. That put the lid on it, of course. She asked him if a jeweller would be likely to buy a gold watch. He advised her to go to a pawnbroker, and told her of one not far from here in the Vauxhall Bridge Road. Quite a well-run place. I've been there now and then myself as a matter of fact. I went to see him and told him what I was after, and he was very decent about it and allowed me to question his assistants. One of them remembered Anne. She's striking, you know, with those long plaits of silvery fair hair, and her very white skin and her blue eyes. Unusual colouring. She went there the next morning with all the jewellery she possessed and her dressing-case. They seem to have given her a very fair price. So you see it's no good thinking that she can't have gone far."

Roger hesitated, wondering if Gale's head was clear enough to follow what he was about to say, but he seemed unaffected, apart from the thickness of his utterance, by the whisky he had drunk. "Look here," he began, "I came here because I believe I know where Mrs. Gale was staying up to a short time ago, though she had left when I was there last week." Gale, who had been about to light a cigarette, paused in the act of striking a match.

"Mrs. Gale? Eve? What the hell are you getting at?"

"I'm home on leave from Malaya. I came overland from Naples and spent a few days at an hotel in a little hill town in the Apennines between Rome and Orvieto. Yesterday evening Penny showed me a sketch Mrs. Gale had made in the garden of her hotel. Anne had given it to her. There was a statue with one arm broken and part of a wall covered with wistaria. I recognised it. I remember thinking at the time that it was the sort of thing an artist would want to paint—and somebody had been painting there recently. I picked up a half finished tube of cobalt close by."

"Well, that's possible, I suppose," said Gale slowly. "But Eve wasn't there?"

"No."

"She'd be out all day, sketching, perhaps. You might not have seen her."

Roger shook his head. "We—" he broke off reddening.

"There were no other guests staying in the place. It's a new venture. A few of the natives came in the evening for dinner. The people who run the show are hoping to get artists, I fancy, but they'll have to advertise to make it known, and they haven't the money. It's a large building, a nobleman's country villa, built in the seventeenth century out of the stones of the old castle. Only a few of the rooms are furnished. It's very remote. Off the beaten track of tourists."

"Did you notice her name in the visitor's book."

"No."

Roger was remembering his own discomfort as he signed the book, "Mr. and Mrs. Smith." He said, "You can't go altogether by hotel books. As a matter of fact I was travelling incog. myself. I—I wasn't alone."

"I see. All right. You can trust me not to give you away. I suppose you don't want your aunt to know. But—my head aches so damnably I can't think straight—what do you imagine may have happened?"

"My idea is that Anne may have gone out there to join her mother only to find that she had gone, leaving no address. She would not have enough money to pay her fare back to England or her hotel bill for more than a few days. I don't say there's any cause for alarm if that is the position. Mario, the waiter, speaks English. The British consul would help her—but there isn't one nearer than Rome. In your place, sir, I'd go out there and see for myself."

"You may be right," said Gale reluctantly. "But it's all supposition. Eve had left before you arrived. Anne is just as likely to have joined her somewhere in England. I don't feel like dashing off to Italy without further evidence. I don't want to waste time or money. I'm hard up as it happens. Leila—and, thanks to this mess up I've lost a commission to do a series of weekly articles—"

His tone was fretful. Roger was inclined to think that he resented being roused from his stupor of self-pity and goaded to take some action. He had thrown away his cigarette and sat leaning his head on his hands and muttering, "Lost. Lost. I am quite alone," in an ecstasy of gloom.

Roger said sharply. "We can't leave it, sir. I'll lend you twenty pounds, if that will do. The banks will be closed now, but I can come round again in the morning. Meanwhile, why not send a cable, reply prepaid, to the hotel to ask if she's there? That ought to settle the matter."

Gale was perceptibly cheered by this suggestion. "That's the best idea yet," he approved. "I'll do that. As to a loan, I won't say no. Decent of you. I don't know why you're taking all this trouble for a stranger, young fellow."

"She isn't exactly a stranger," said Roger. "My sister Penny is very fond of her."

Gale looked at him. "You don't really think—"

Roger avoided meeting his eye. It could do no good to tell him why he disliked the notion that Anne had arrived, alone and unheralded at the Albergo del Castello, either just before or just after he and Nina had stayed there. He repeated the address and Gale wrote it down. He thanked the younger man again effusively, but it was apparent that he wanted to get rid of him, and Roger was not sorry to go.

He called again the next morning a little before half-past ten, Gale was just fastening the straps of his valise. He had had no answer to his cable.

"I was awake half the night, worrying," he said, "and I've decided to go. I'm catching the boat train at Victoria at eleven."

"Good," said Roger heartily. "I've brought the money." Gale wrung his hand. "I'll never forget this."

Roger, feeling awkward, mumbled, "Not at all. You'll write a line when you find her? My aunt and Penny will be anxious—"

"Of course. The very moment—"

They left the flat together and walked up the Vauxhall Bridge road to the station. Roger hated seeing people off, but Gale, though he had shaved and was wearing his best suit, looked much older in the morning light, and seemed so flurried and forlorn that Roger had not the heart to leave him.

He always remembered that last five minutes, standing on the platform looking up at the older man as he leaned out of the window of his compartment.

"I'm a bad traveller," he said, "and a rotten sailor. Still, in August the crossing shouldn't be too bad. And Anne's all right. She must be. Only—somehow—I have an ill divining soul—" He still leaned out to wave as the train steamed slowly out of the great dim echoing station, wistfully, as if they had known each other for years instead of hours, as if Roger was his last tie on earth.

Absurd, thought Roger, as he turned away: he dramatises everything, he should have been an actor, not a journalist. But he felt oddly depressed.

Chapter V
RESULT OF AN ACCIDENT

1

Roger returned to Stratford and to the normal life of a young Englishman home on leave. His aunt had plenty of friends, and he and Penny were asked to picnics on the river and tennis parties. He visited his tailor in Birmingham and made an appointment with his dentist.

It was while he was turning over the magazines and papers in the dentist's waiting-room that he received an unwelcome reminder of something he was trying to forget. Nina smiled up at him from a page of the *Tatler*. It was a studio portrait, very carefully posed, and she looked about eighteen. He read the caption.

Lady Cravenach, who, before her marriage, was Miss Nina Truitt, and the loveliest débutante of her year. Sir Henry and Lady Cravenach have just passed through

London on their way to their fine old place in Devonshire, which, before Sir Henry acquired it in 1898, had been for three hundred years in the same family.

There was a snapshot taken by a press photographer on the opposite page that showed the couple leaving their hotel. Sir Henry was leaning heavily on his stick. Nina walking beside him, smiling, and the Japanese valet following with a rug over his arm.

Roger studied Sir Henry's face. It was a hard face, thin lipped and narrow eyed, the face of a man who would not easily forgive an injury. Nina would certainly have to be careful.

It was a pity, he thought, that she was so much photographed. Still, it was unlikely that a copy of the *Tatler* would ever find its way to a remote hill town in Umbria, or that if it did anyone there would he reminded of an English couple who called themselves Mr. and Mrs. Smith, and had left after only four days. Unfortunate, of course, that he had had to admit as much as he did to Gale, but it could not be helped, and it did not implicate Nina.

Miss Fordyce and Penny talked a good deal about Anne. They had heard nothing from Gale, but they imagined him already on his way back to England with her. Penny took a sanguine view and quite expected that Anne would be spending the last part of the holidays with them.

"I shan't mind if you fall in love with her," she told Roger.

He laughed. "Thanks. I'm not a cradle snatcher."

"She wouldn't be too young if you waited a year or two," she argued. "She's sixteen, and you're only twenty-four."

"No, thanks. These raving beauties are a fearful responsibility. I'd rather have someone plain and solid who can cook, like you."

"Beast."

One evening Penny had gone to the theatre with some friends, leaving her aunt and Roger to spend the evening together.

After supper Miss Fordyce, who had been very quiet all day, said: "I'm glad the child isn't here. I want to talk to you about something I saw this morning in the paper."

She took it from the side table and held it out to him. "Page twelve. The obituary notices."

He looked and saw the name of Gale.

"Good God, it can't be. Francis Gale, who has died in Rome as the result of an accident, was a minor poet and a writer with a considerable talent as an essayist. Readers of more than one popular weekly will miss his regular column, written in the light and whimsical style characteristic of him. He was forty-five. He was married, but his marriage was dissolved some years ago. His one published volume of collected verse, *Moon Vapour*, is now out of print'."

"They didn't know about his second marriage, evidently. Not that it matters, I suppose. But what does it mean, Roger?"

They stared at each other, like stout Cortez, with a wild surmise.

Roger cleared his throat. "Accidents can happen to anyone. They'd be very likely to happen to him, I fancy."

"Why?"

"Well, he was a dreamy, unpractical, inefficient sort of bloke. If he was excited or worked up about things he wouldn't look where he was going. When I saw him off I felt he really needed someone to look after him. I wonder if the girl was with him at the time. I say, this is rotten for her."

"Yes," said his aunt, "I wish we knew more. I don't like it. He promised to write to us."

Roger was studying the notice. *"Moon Vapour,"* he said. "Holy snakes and ladders! Poor Gale. He was pathetic somehow. Well, a fond farewell to my twenty quid."

"You lent him money?"

"He was hard up. Spent more than he should on his damn silly honeymoon."

Miss Fordyce adjusted her pince-nez. "Roger," she said firmly. "I'll pay your expenses. It's not Quixotry. It's for my own sake. I shouldn't be able to sleep for thinking of that child who may be out there, alone, and in trouble."

"All right," he said. "She's probably quite safe, if she's there, being looked after by the English consul, or the chaplain's wife, or something. I'm to bring her back here, if they'll let her come with me unchaperoned?"

"Of course."

"When do I start? As soon as possible? I'd better do a spot of packing now then."

"I hope I am doing right, involving you in this," she said uncertainly. "Did he tell you how he found out where his first wife had been staying in Italy?"

"He got hold of it somehow," said Roger, reflecting that he would have to be careful with Aunt Polly. She was as sharp as a needle, and he knew she had been surprised to hear that he had gone to see Gale in London.

Miss Fordyce sighed. She knew that her nephew was keeping something from her and that it had something to do with his return overland from Naples. She said: "Take care of yourself over there. What sort of an accident? One can't help wondering. Of course, Roger, if the child is with her mother we can't do anything about it."

"Naturally. I just say howdy and come back without any sheaves. Don't worry, Aunt Polly. We just have to make sure that the kid is all right."

Penny saw him off at the station. She had not known of Gale's death when she came in from the theatre, and had goaded her brother into telling her the little he knew. Penny was nothing if not persistent.

"Roger! How ghastly for poor Anne. She simply adored him, that's why she was so fearfully upset when he married again. Of course, you must go and fetch her back. I'm sure her mother won't want her. Anne doesn't realise it, but I'm certain she's one of those women who grab at every man in sight, and a daughter like Anne would cramp her style."

2

The Consul was away on holiday, and the vice consul was unwell.

The English-speaking clerk was civil and sympathetic.

"You are a relative of Mr. Gale? He was a journalist, we think. There was a card from the editor of an English weekly paper in one of his pockets, but no other papers to enable us to get into touch with his family. We wrote to the gentleman in question and he replied that he knew nothing of his contributor's private life beyond the fact that he was separated from his wife. He was arranging for a suitable obituary notice in the London papers. He had to be buried within twenty-four hours. That is the law over here."

"I understand. But"—Roger was assailed by a sudden doubt. "There was no one to identify him. Was his identity established? That's important."

"Naturally. Apart from the card his linen was clearly marked F. Gale, and that was the name written in the lining of his hat. We have got his description here." The clerk turned over some papers on his desk "Here it is. Age between forty and fifty. Height, five feet, eleven inches. Slight build. Features regular. White hair. Some bridge work with three artificial teeth in the upper jaw. Apparently a heavy smoker, but organically sound."

"There was a post mortem then?"

"Oh, yes. A matter of form. The cause of death was obvious. Did you say you were a relative?"

"No. I represent the family," said Roger. "I've come to settle things up and take his daughter home. My aunt will look after her."

The young clerk's expressive face registered surprise.

"His daughter? He appeared to be alone. We have not seen or heard anything of a daughter. Surely if she had been with him—"

"One moment," said Roger. "I understand that his death was the result of an accident. What was it?"

If Anne was not with him where was she? Presumably Gale had gone to Sant Andrina and drawn a blank there. What had he been doing in Rome?

"To be sure. He fell down a lift shaft. It was in one of those new blocks of cheap flats in the San Lorenzo quarter. The lifts there are automatic. You know, if one of the gates is left unlatched the carriage remains at the bottom of the shaft. His body was found on the roof in the early morning. It is assumed that he fell from the top floor. There is no light on the stairs or the landings. It may be some comfort to his friends to know that he was killed instantly. His neck was broken."

"What was he doing there?"

"As to that, the two flats on the top floor are unoccupied, but all the tenants in the building were questioned. Not one of them admits to having had a visit from an Englishman."

"What sort of people would they be?"

The clerk shrugged his shoulders. "Poorish, struggling. What you would call the lower middle class. There might be one or two pretty ladies of the more discreet type among them. But I must remind you that he was not robbed. He had some Italian and some English money, a watch and a gold pencil case."

"No railway ticket, no hotel bill?"

"No. You would be surprised," said the clerk, "how many English people drift about the Continent with nothing about them to enable the authorities to identify them. Passports are only needed for Russia. Sometimes we feel that is rather a pity. In this case I must warn you that unless you are prepared to pay the funeral expenses his effects will have to be sold for what they will fetch."

"If you can wait a few days," Roger said. "He isn't a rich man, I know, but I think I can promise you will be paid out of the estate. Please don't sell his watch, in any case. I expect his daughter will be glad to have that."

"He was buried in the English Protestant cemetery. Where your poet Keats is," said the clerk, "that is always something, is it not? It is a quiet spot, and there are violets there in the grass, in spring."

Roger thought of *Moon Vapour*, Gale's one published volume of verse, whose sales had been negligible, and said, gently, "Yes. That would please him, I'm sure."

The clerk became business-like. "I will take your address. Are you returning to England immediately?"

"I shall stay here for a few days, I think." Roger gave the name of the quiet and rather dingy little commercial hotel near the Central railway station where he had stayed before. "I shall go and have a look round the block of flats where the accident happened," he said, "just to satisfy myself," he added vaguely.

"You can if you wish, of course," said the clerk. "The police are perfectly convinced that his death was accidental. You realise that?"

"Quite. But I don't understand how he came to be there at all."

"It is remarkable," said the clerk oracularly, "how little we really know about our nearest and dearest—or even about ourselves. We will retain his effects for the present since you accept responsibility for all necessary expenses. The address is 105 Via Romeo Poldini."

"You speak English very well," said Roger as he prepared to leave. The young man flushed, possibly with pleasure or possibly with annoyance. "I am English," he said. "At least I am an English subject. I am Maltese."

Roger lunched at a trattoria in the Via Sistina and went back to the station to get his bag from the cloakroom before booking a room for the night at the hotel. The stout padrona sitting at the desk in the hall recognised him and greeted him cordially.

"The signore was here two or three weeks since. Ben tornato. Yes, the room he had before is at his disposal. Giovanni, take the signore's bag? Will you use the lift?"

"No, thanks," he said hurriedly. "I'd rather go up the stairs."

"Ah, you heard of that affair?" she said. "A compatriot of yours. Poverino. He was in too great a hurry, or perhaps he had drunk too much of our good Roman wine."

"He wasn't staying here by any chance?"

"Here? No, signore. They could not find out where he was staying. They think he may have gone directly to that house from the station."

"But no one in the house knew anything about him—"

"So they say," said the padrona. "One does not want to be mixed up with police enquiries. That is only natural."

Roger decided against taking one of the shabby cabs drawn by bony little horses, whose drivers cracked their whips and shouted to attract his attention as he left the hotel. He had been sitting in trains for so long that he felt he needed some exercise. But the Via Romeo Poldini was in the new working-class quarter between Santa Maria Maggiore and the great cemetery of San Lorenzo and he had to enquire his way twice before he found it.

He was seeing Rome from a different angle. When he had come to it before he had gone about sight-seeing during those hectic days of waiting to hear from Nina. In these mean streets the Rome of the Caesars and the Rome of the Popes seemed equally far away. You could live here for years and never experience the shock of surprise that stills the heart as you drop the leather curtain and enter the vast nave of St. Peter's, or catch more than a glimpse of the ruined walls of the Colosseum or the cypress-crowned Palatine hill, from a passing tram.

The house he sought was built, like most Roman houses, round a courtyard. From each floor lines of drying linen were strung out, dazzling against the deep blue of the sky. A stout woman in a loose white cotton jacket screamed a greeting to a friend at a window facing her own, and held up a tiny, brown, swaddled baby for inspection.

Roger noticed that the lift appeared to be in working order, but he preferred to use the stairs. They were of cement, with an iron rail, and very dirty, littered with nut shells and cherry stones and cigarette ends. An accumulation of match ends outside all the flat doors indicated tenants coming home after nightfall had to find their keyholes. Roger was rather proud of his deductions, but they did not seem to lead to anything beyond the obvious fact that a stranger, fumbling about in the dark, might mistake the open door to the lift shaft for that of one of the flats. He trudged up to the seventh floor. The lift came up here into a kind of iron cage. The gate had been secured with a padlock. One of the flat doors had an ill-spelt notice scrawled in purple ink announcing that it was to let unfurnished.

Roger sighed. There was nothing here to show why Francis Gale should have met his end in this place more than any other. "I'm not cut out for a detective," he thought. "I'm wasting my time."

He went slowly down the stairs, slowly because he heard the lift ascending. It stopped at the sixth floor landing just as he came to it, and a young woman got out. She was carrying several paper bags and a string bag stuffed with fruit and vegetables, but she managed to shut the gate with her elbow. She was wearing a blue cotton frock, and a red belt that matched her straw hat, and was thin and dark and anxious, and might have been rather pretty if she had had time to rest and more to eat. Roger looked at her, hesitated, and passed on.

There was a metallic clang just behind him and an English voice, sharp-edged with fatigue, exclaimed, "Damn! That's my key—"

Roger turned quickly and stooped to pick it up for her. Inevitably their heads knocked together. Roger's hat fell off and he bent again to retrieve it. She smiled as she put hers straight. Her dark face, so much too thin, seemed all eyes and teeth. She had set her bags down by her door.

She said in Italian, "La ringrazia. Were you coming to see me? About lessons?"

"No. You're English, aren't you? Do you live here?"

She looked at him warily. He fancied that she was often on the defensive. She said, "I do at present. The flat has been lent to me while the tenants are away. They are pupils of mine. I give English lessons."

"A friend of mine was killed here last week. He fell down the lift shaft."

"I did not know him," she said quickly. She had turned very pale. "The police made me go to the mortuary to see if I could identify him. It was—horrible—and I missed two lessons. My pupils live so far apart. I am always running—"

"You look very tired now," he said, "and I'm keeping you standing. But this is a very worrying business. I don't know what to do next—"

She said in a warmer voice, "I can see you're all in. I daresay you feel the heat. Most people leave Rome in August, even the Romans. I couldn't afford it this year. Come in, if you like, I'm just going to have tea."

"It's very good of you. Let me carry some of these bags—"

"It isn't. I don't often get a chance to talk to a fellow countryman. Just sit down while I get it ready—"

She left him in a dusty, airless, over-furnished salotto and came in presently with a tea tray and a plate of biscuits.

She said, "I was loaded, wasn't I. The fact is, some of my pupils pay me in kind. The child I was teaching this afternoon is the daughter of the people who keep the pasticeria round the corner, so I get rice and coffee and cheese. Often those people are kinder and more considerate than the grand ones. But most of them are very decent. I have some real friends among them. It's only some of the men—I hate Italian men."

He said, "Are you quite alone?"

"Quite. I've been here six years. But don't let's talk about me. Have you come over from England? I think about it sometimes, green and damp and restful, and all the birds. They eat them here. Larks and thrushes and all."

"I know what home-sickness is," he said. "I've just come home on leave from Malaya." He sighed with content as he set down his cup. "That tea was just what I wanted."

She laughed. "Italians think that is one of the maddest things about us. I miss it dreadfully when I stay with them. They say it's like medicine."

He said, "You don't know my name. It's Roger—Roger Fordyce."

"Mine is Lily Oram."

"Are you sure you can't help me, Miss Oram?"

"You mean about your friend?" She pushed the heavy waves of dark hair back from her thin temples with a nervous gesture.

He thought, "She works too hard, and doesn't eat enough."

She said, "I believe I heard him. I was in bed, but I hadn't been asleep long. A dull heavy thud, not any cry. I looked at my watch. It was ten minutes to one. But I never dreamed—"

"He had come to Italy to fetch his daughter. She had run away to join her mother. The parents were divorced, and he had the custody of the child. The question is, had he come after her to this house?"

Lily shook her head. "I know all the tenants to speak to, or by sight. There aren't any English among them. There used to be a German woman in the flat over mine, who had lodgers, but she left last month just after I arrived. There's nobody up there now."

"Look here," he said, "I'd like to tell you the whole story. You might be able to advise me. But am I taking up too much of your time?"

"No. I've no more lessons until to-morrow morning."

She accepted a cigarette from his case and lay back in her chair, smoking with evident satisfaction. Roger was secretly rather surprised, for at that date very few women smoked in England, but he did not misunderstand Lily Oram. She was no longer on her guard, but that was because she had decided that she could trust him. Her manner was frank and friendly, without any trace of coquetry. She listened to him without interrupting, and because it is easier to make damaging admissions to a complete stranger than to friends and relations, he told her everything, or almost everything. Nina had to be kept out of it, naturally. He referred to her, vaguely, as a friend.

She said, "I suppose he went directly to the hotel at Sant Andrina. If his wife had been staying there she might have given them an address to have her letters forwarded. Would she be likely to take a room at a pensione like Frau Haussman's—that's the German who was in the flat above—a cheap, free and easy place."

"I don't know. She's a painter. I think she sells her stuff and has plenty of money to splash about."

"Then it isn't very likely. But it would explain how he came here, wouldn't it? He'd find the flat empty and think he'd go down again in the lift—" she shuddered. "You'd think he'd be more careful, in the dark, and a strange house."

"Perhaps I should follow up this Frau What-is-it," he said. "She could tell me if Mrs. Gale had been staying with her—or I should say Eve Shandon, for she used her maiden name. Will that be possible?"

"Easy. Her furniture was moved by Passerini. I saw the vans. There wasn't any secret about her destination. She had taken another larger flat in the Via della Croce, that's a street running from the Piazza di Spagna into the Corso, a much nicer part of Rome than this, so it looks as if she had turned up trumps."

He said, "Eve Shandon must have left Rome—if she ever was here—before Gale arrived."

"Why are you so sure of that?"

"There were accounts of the accident in the papers, weren't there? The padrona of my hotel referred to it as if it had made a lot of talk."

"Yes, it did. It's the dead season. Nothing much happening. Luckily for us there was a nice juicy murder in the Trastevere the next day to take off their attention. They had begun to hint that he must have come to see me, I being English too, and my denying all knowledge of him was suspicious. They don't have to be so careful about libel here as they are at home. It didn't really matter, but my pupils who lent me the flat might not like it."

"If his wife had been in Rome she must have heard about it. Surely she would have gone to the consul. I know they were divorced—but still—"

She looked at him. "If you really want to carry on I'm afraid you'll have to go back to Sant Andrina and find out how he got on there."

"I'll go to-morrow," he said, "but perhaps I ought to interview this German woman first. I'll go on there now. Will you dine with me later? What about that restaurant in the Piazza Colonna? We could sit at one of those little tables outside afterwards and listen to the band that plays in the square. I wanted to do that when I was here before, but I was alone then."

"I'd love it," she said. "If any of my pupils see me they'll be bursting with curiosity, but I shall tell them you are my cousin. Wait a minute. Why don't you leave Frau Haussman to me? I can go and ask her terms and what vacant rooms she has and get at what you want without asking any direct questions. She's rather a formidable female. Of course, if you want to do it yourself—"

"I don't," he assured her. "I'd be eternally grateful if you would cope with her. Will you meet me afterwards?"

"Yes. Nine o'clock. Mind you are there first. They won't let a woman alone in."

"I'll be there."

CHAPTER VI
MR. SMITH IS UNWELCOME

MOST of the chairs set out on the pavement outside the restaurant were occupied by music lovers who had come to enjoy a concert for the price of a cup of coffee or a vermouth, for the band of a famous regiment was to play in the piazza. Roger found a seat and ordered beer. It was still very hot and he envied some of the men who were wearing light alpaca coats. He was surrounded by family groups, Romans of the borghesia, clerks and tradesmen, with their wives and children. They were all well dressed and well fed, especially, perhaps, the latter. The southern races run early to seed, and men who were probably not over thirty tended to become paunchy, while their womenkind, exquisite at seventeen, sleek at twenty-seven, were only too apt to wobble like badly-set jellies ten years later.

Roger listened unashamedly to the conversations going on all around him and the outspoken comments on his own appearance. He knew they would assume that, being an Englishman, he would not understand. They found him simpatico: his teeth did not stick out and he had not the carroty moustache of the stage Briton, but his clothes betrayed his origin.

He finished his beer. The band was playing the overture from *Lohengrin*. Roger looked at his watch. Lily Oram was late. And then he saw her threading her way through the groups of people standing about in the piazza. She had not changed her dress and her heavy dark hair looked untidy and uncared for, pinned in a careless knot on the nape of her neck.

There was a loud chorus of criticism from the Italian women who observed her approach. "See the Englishwoman, alone at this hour." "Brutta. Secca." "How ugly she is, all skin and bone." "How ugly."

Roger was surprised at the violence of his own reaction. He could only relieve his feelings by rising very quickly and greeting her with a warmth that seemed to startle her. She released her hand. "I'm afraid I'm late. Did you think I wasn't coming?"

"No. No. Come along in. I've booked a table—"

In a sense, of course, they were right. If you wanted curves you would not get them with Lily, and she was careless about herself. The blue cotton frock was crumpled and he could see a safety-pin fastening torn gathers under the cheap red leather belt. Her arms, bare to the elbow, were painfully thin. It would have been better to cover them. Like all the other women she carried a paper fan and fanned herself between the courses.

"They give you good food here. I've heard my pupils talk about it. I haven't been before myself. I just eat when and how I can, sometimes at their houses, a meal instead of a fee for a lesson, but they keep on asking me how to spell words and so on, so I don't get a chance to eat. They're kind, but they want their money's worth. That's only natural. And one gets so tired of pasta with pomodori, though I must say it's filling at the price. And here I am talking about myself again when you want to be hearing what I've found out at the Pensione Haussman. There isn't much, or I'd have told you at once."

"No hurry," he said. "We'll talk presently, over the coffee. I never knew before that potatoes could be luscious."

"Gnocchi," said Lily indistinctly, with her mouth full.

Her naïve enjoyment confirmed Roger's first impression that she seldom had quite enough to eat. That was hardly surprising, he reflected, if she really lived on what she earned by teaching English.

"Well, thanks for that," she said presently. "It's been lovely. I'm rather a pig really. I often think about food." She accepted a cigarette from his case and leaned back contentedly to look out of the window at the crowds strolling about the piazza in the white glare of the electric standards while the band played the intermezzo from *Cavaleria Rusticana*.

"Isn't that column beautiful soaring up into the darkness. Rome is full of beautiful things all mixed up with tramlines and butcher's shops and dreadful little cabs drawn by worn-out horses with sores under the harness."

Roger, looking at the worn face, with its brittle gaiety that could not hide the lines of anxiety and fatigue, wondered how old she was.

"Why don't you go back to England?"

"No. I made my bed, as they say. I'm lying on it. Don't be sorry for me, Mr. Fordyce. I'm all right. Lots of work—except in August. I admit things have been difficult lately."

"You might call me Roger," he suggested.

"Very well. And you can call me Lily. Now about the fat Frau and her boarders." She stirred her coffee and added another lump of sugar. "Her new place in the Via della Croce is at the top of the house. An old house, of course, and no lift. She opened the door to me herself and I didn't get past the mat. I had not seen her close to before. She's intimidating. Fat and red, with hard beady eyes and a mouth like a trap. I asked about rooms and she said she had not any vacant and was going to shut the door in my face, but I got my foot in. I said I thought a friend of a friend of mine, an English woman artist, had been staying with her lately. She said I was mistaken. She seldom took English people. They gave too much trouble. So I had to thank her and come away."

"Well—that disposes of our theory," said Roger.

"I suppose so," she said slowly. "But I wasn't really satisfied. I think she recognised me as a tenant in the house she had left. I'm in and out a lot, going to my pupils."

"That is possible," he said, "but what of it?"

"I don't know. But she gave me the idea that she was unpleasantly surprised to see me, and suspicious of my motives."

"She must have heard of the accident. I suppose she has not been back to the house since she moved out," he said idly.

"I wonder," said Lily thoughtfully. "She may have been. I was told that her lease had not expired. She was trying to sublet."

They looked at each other. After a moment he said: "We must not imagine things. No one has suggested that it could have been anything but accidental. For anything else there would have to be a motive. It was just rotten bad luck. Only we've got to find out what the hell he was doing there on the top landing outside what used to be Frau Haussman's flat." She knocked the ash off her cigarette. "You needn't really, you know. I've heard your story. Gale isn't a relative of yours, or even a friend. You could call it a day, and go back to England to-morrow."

He shook his head. "I can't, because of Anne. She's no older than my sister Penny. I have to find her, or make sure she isn't over here."

"The very parfit gentle knight," she said, smiling.

He reddened. "Not at all. I'm a bit of a rotter actually. I told you about that. But one's got to look after children."

"Very well," she said. "You know the next step."

"Yes. I've got to go back to Sant Andrino."

"That means that you'll have to get up early. And I have to give a lesson at half-past seven to a pupil in the Via Quirinale. Bother, my hair's coming down." She fumbled indifferently for loose hair pins and pushed them back into the untidy mass at the nape of her neck. "Hair's a nuisance. I'd cut it off, only people would stare more than ever. They always stare. One gets used to it."

Roger paid the bill and they went out into the street. He would have taken a cab, but she would not let him. They could get a tram. He could get out at the Piazza dei Termi, and she would go on.

"You've got to be careful," she warned him. "Knight errantry costs money nowadays. You've got my address. You'll let me know how you get on?"

They parted like old friends.

The next morning he caught the early train to Vallesca.

It was the same journey that he had taken not quite three weeks earlier, but with very different feelings. Then, as he looked out of the carriage window at the wild pasture lands of the Roman campagna giving place to sun-baked vineyards and fields of maize, he could think of nothing but the woman he was going to meet. Now—it was strange how quickly the image of Nina had faded.

The same omnibus was waiting in the station yard, and the same driver greeted him with a flourish of his whip, but this time there were several other passengers, two nuns, a woman carrying a live sucking pig in a bag, and an old man burdened with a small child whose huge black eyes, sad as those of a sick monkey, stared out from a white mask of bandages.

"It's my daughter's boy," he explained. "He fell in the fire. Poverino. He has been in the hospital, but he is better now."

"N'e vero, Anacleto? Stai benone adesso?"

His clumsy work-worn fingers fumbled over the baby's tiny frail hands with a touching gentleness.

Anacleto said nothing. He was staring hard at Roger. But he leaned back confidently in the crook of his grandfather's arm.

The woman with the sucking pig said: "The best remedy for burns is a plaster of cow dung. That's how they treated my husband's sister, but she died all the same, poveraccia."

When the driver came round to collect the fares before starting Roger found that he was the only one who was going all the way to Sant Andrina. The two nuns were the first to get out, and the next was the woman with the pig. Left alone with the old man and the burnt child, Roger tried to amuse the baby by showing him the luminous dial of his wrist watch, but was unable to divert him from his fixed contemplation of his face.

Roger was embarrassed. "Why does he look at me like that?"

"I don't know, signore mio." But when Roger turned his head away he saw, out of the tail of his eye, that the old man had crossed himself.

The omnibus stopped soon afterwards at a farm gate and the last of his fellow passengers prepared to get out. But first he cleared his throat. "Signore—excuse me—"

"Certainly. What is it?"

"In the signore's place I would be careful in case of accidents—"

Roger was startled. "Why? I don't understand—"

"It is—this child sees more than we do. We have proved it more than once. He sees the malore. That is why I warn you. Addio, signore mio."

Roger, left alone in the omnibus, tried, not altogether successfully, to persuade himself that the incident had no significance. No doubt the people in these remote mountain districts were steeped in superstition. The younger ones might have acquired a modern veneer, but fundamentally they were still very primitive. But the warning gave some kind of shape to an uncomfortable feeling that had been latent in his mind. Was it possible that if he persisted in his search for Anne Gale he might be in some danger?

The mules were toiling up the last long hill with its hairpin bends. The driver pulled them up as they reached the town gate and the customs officer, in his gaudy uniform, lounged forward to receive his dues. They drove up the narrow street to the dusty open space where a few old men sat drowsing on benches in the shade of the planes.

Roger was in time to waylay the driver, who was hurrying off to the nearest wine shop.

"One moment. Did an Englishman come here a week ago? A tall man with white hair?"

The driver looked at him for a moment before he answered.

"It may be. If my passengers pay their fares that is all I ask of them. It is not my business to remember their faces."

Roger pulled out a handful of silver from his pocket and turned over the coins in his palm.

The driver licked his lips and seemed to hesitate before he drew back. "Mi dispiace, signore. I am sorry. I am a poor man, ignorant. I have a very bad memory. I know nothing. Nothing at all."

Roger was disappointed, but the driver's recollections were not essential. He would get what he wanted to know from Mario.

He crossed the square and walked round to the back of the church, past the steps where the blind beggar lay asleep in the red light of the setting sun, and down the lane between high garden walls to the hotel.

As he entered the entrance hall Mario came out of the dining-room where he had been setting the tables.

"Mr. Smith? You have come back—so soon? This is a pleasant surprise. But where is madame?"

He spoke hurriedly and with less than his usual assurance. It struck Roger that he must have arrived at an inconvenient moment. Mario was doing his best, but the note of welcome rang false.

He thought: "He's no more glad to see me than I am to be back in his damned hotel."

He said: "She's not with me this time. I've come to join a friend. He should have got here about a week ago. Gale is the name."

"Mr. Gale is a friend of yours? It is strange that he did not mention you when he was here. He must have seen your name in our book."

"There are a great many Smiths," said Roger, annoyed with himself because he felt his ears burning. "Are you telling me that he has left?"

"Yes. He only stayed one night."

"Do you know where he went?"

"No."

"He and his daughter left together?"

Mario uttered an exclamation of regret. "Pardon me. I am keeping you standing here when you must be tired after your journey. Will you have wine, asti spumanti, wine of the Castelli, or tea? I can serve it on the terrace. Or I can show you to your room. Will you have the same one as before?"

"No. A smaller one. But you have not answered my question."

"I am sorry. The young lady had left before Mr. Gale arrived. You will excuse me now. The fact is my fidanzata is here to-day with her parents. Naturally I have to give them as much of my time as possible. There are no other guests in the hotel at the moment—"

"All right. I won't keep you now. But I want to talk to you later. Meanwhile I'll have tea."

Roger chose a table as far as possible from that at which he used to sit with Nina, and lit a cigarette. He turned his back on the long white façade of the villa, with its rows of shuttered windows, to look down, past the tangled growth of the neglected garden and the cypresses of the Campo Santo, to the plain beyond.

Mario seemed a bit bothered, he thought. He turned his head presently to watch him escorting his betrothed and her parents to a table farther along the terrace.

Mario's prospective bride, a plump little person, whose round olive skinned face was heavily powdered, clung to his arm, twittering with excitement and emitting affected little shriek's of laughter, while he gazed down at her adoringly. The parents who followed them were a stout and prosperous looking couple. The father was poisoning the evening air with a black Tuscan cigar, the mother rustled in a silk dress and wore heavy gold bracelets and rings on her fat fingers.

Roger moved his chair round an inch or two so that he could observe the family party without seeming to do so. The parents, who were evidently very proud of their child, looked on admiringly while she wriggled and giggled. Roger thought that she must be extremely silly, but she was undoubtedly pretty, and Mario was either genuinely in love with her, or he was a very good actor.

Roger's tea was brought out to him by Maddalena. She looked handsome but sullen. He smiled at her as he thanked her, but she set down the tray without meeting his eyes, and went back to the house. It was pleasant on the terrace and he was tired so he sat on watching the sunset glow fade to a greenish pallor over the darkening earth and the fireflies flickering among the briars in the neglected garden.

He heard Mario's beloved suggest that they should walk about down there and the young man reply that there were snakes in the undergrowth.

"Per carita!"

Her father cleared his throat importantly. "You should have it all dug up and planted with vegetables for the hotel. What is that building among the bushes, with white walls and an outside staircase leading to a flat roof?"

"An old summer-house, but it is closed, disused, filled with rubbish."

The stout mother yawned. "Isn't it nearly time for dinner?"

Mario was very attentive and deferential, and Roger, looking on, guessed that he hoped that his well-to-do future parents-in-law would put some of their capital into the enterprise in which he and Maddalena and her husband had invested their hard earned savings. Later, in the dining-room, he was waiting on the usual habitués from the town who came nightly to the hotel as well as on his Laurina and her father and mother, who had their table near the service hatch, and Roger saw no chance of engaging him in conversation. He asked for his coffee on the terrace, but again it was Maddalena who brought it.

He said: "Are your brother's fidanzata and her family staying long?"

"No. They leave to-morrow."

"She is very charming. They will be a good-looking couple."

"Yes."

She was turning away when he said: "One moment, Signora Maddalena. Was Miss Gale's mother here when she arrived?"

It was dark on the terrace and he could not see her face. She stood quite still by his table and was silent for so long that he had time to notice the croaking of the bull frogs farther down the hill. He wondered if they were in the water tank whose cover he had displaced, in the green scum under which the body of the black dog had floated. He shivered involuntarily. It was as if the air had turned suddenly cold.

She said: "No. She had been gone some time. The signorina was very disappointed. She stayed one night, and left the next morning."

"Did she say where she was going?"

"No."

"Did she go in the omnibus or did your brother drive her down to Vallesca in his trap?"

"I am not sure. I think Mario took her."

"I'm sorry to bother you with this again," said Roger, trying to placate her, for her manner showed that she resented his questions. "No doubt when her father arrived last week he wanted to know all you could tell him. You saw her, so you must know that she is far too young to be going about alone. It was most unfortunate that her mother left no address. The girl must be found. You see, I happen to know that she had not enough money with her to pay her fare back to England."

Maddalena said: "First the signorina came, and then a man, an Englishman, who said he was her father. There was very little that we could tell him. We do not concern ourselves with the private affairs of our guests. If they pay what they owe us that is all we care about. They went away, and we know nothing. We do not want any trouble or any scandal."

"But the mother—she called herself Miss Shandon—she was here for some weeks—didn't she ask you to forward letters?"

"No. You must excuse me, signore. I have work to do." There was a contained fury in her voice that startled Roger so much that he was silenced.

He sat a while longer on the terrace, disliking the prospect of going up the vast staircase to his solitary bedroom to undress by candlelight. He could hear a cheerful babble of conversation in the dining-room and squeals of laughter from Laurina, and presently the tinkling of a mandoline, Mario's fruity tenor singing "Margherita", and the others joining in. They all seemed happy enough. Carefree. And yet—

It was a warm night, too warm to sleep, and Mario was sitting by his open window smoking a cigarette when his sister came into his room. She set down her candlestick on his chest of drawers where an incongruously fine pair of tortoiseshell-backed brushes lay among a litter of collar studs, cigarette-ends and nutshells.

"She gave you those?"

"She did."

"If Laurina saw them she might ask some awkward questions. She may be a fool, but she knows the price of such things."

"I can always tell her some story to account for them," he said easily. "Don't fuss, Maddalena. I think we've convinced old Antonelli that this place will prove a good investment. It is a pity we have no local saint or miracle-working Madonna to bring pilgrims, but we must make the best of things as they are. An omnibus of our own to bring people from the station, and a good publicity campaign. There is a sketch she made of the hotel looking across the ravine from the Campo Santo that will make a fine coloured poster."

Maddalena sat down, with a sigh, on the foot of his bed. She had been on her feet all day and she was tired. "Yes. But meanwhile there is this Englishman wanting to know this and that. He came here not a month ago, with a woman not his wife, and with initials on their luggage that were not those of the names they signed in our book. That may give us some hold on him. Otherwise I am afraid he may be troublesome."

When Mario scowled he looked much more like his sister.

"What was he saying to you out on the terrace? I saw him through the dining-room window, but I could not leave the others."

"He knows they were here. All three, one after the other. It is useless to deny that. I told him I did not know where they had gone. He will be at you to-morrow."

"Benissimo. I shall tell him that I drove them to the station at Vallesca. Where they went from there is no affair of ours."

"And if that does not satisfy him?"

"You think he might become dangerous?"

"I don't know," she said slowly. "These young Englishmen—he has a foolish habit of laughing when there is nothing to laugh at, and those blue eyes seem as candid as those of a little child—but I would not rely too much on that."

"You mean that he is not such a fool as he looks. You may be right."

"He comes here from Rome," she said. "I noticed the labels on his valise when I was putting sheets on his bed. Why hasn't he mentioned the accident to us? He must know of it. That looks to me as if he was trying to trap us. We shall have to be very careful, Mario," she said anxiously.

"Leave it to me. When Laurina and her parents have gone. To-morrow."

"I didn't mean that," she said hurriedly. "There has been enough of that. Too much."

Roger was so tired that he slept soundly in spite of the heat. It was past nine when he came down to the terrace. Maddalena brought him his coffee and rolls, and announced with ill-concealed satisfaction that Mario had gone off for the day and might not be returning until the following evening. He was seeing off his fidanzata and her parents at the station and then he was going on to Orvieto where he had business.

"Is the signore staying on?"

Roger said that he thought he would be. He wanted a word with Mario who might be able to give him some indication that would enable him to find Miss Gale. "I don't want to have to go to the police," he added, "except as a last resort."

Maddalena said: "We know nothing." Her face looked very lined and sallow in the morning light, but it struck him that she must have been almost as handsome as her brother when she was younger. He blamed himself for not having got hold of Mario the evening before. Even now he could not feel sure that these people were deliberately obstructing his attempts to find out where Anne had gone when she left the hotel. After all, he argued, it was no part of an hotel-keeper's business to furnish a stranger without credentials with information about his former guests.

He went for a stroll, wandering about the steep, narrow streets of the little town and finding himself eventually in the church, a large, dark building smelling of tallow and stale incense, but agreeably cool after the glare of the sunbaked piazza.

A low mass was just over and the congregation of five or six old women was dispersing. Roger had been looking at a fresco representing the martyrdom of Saint Sebastian on the wall near the door of the sacristy. He stepped back to allow the priest to pass in. He remembered having seen him when he was staying at the hotel with Nina. He was a tall, thin old man with bent shoulders, straggling grey hair and a look of great gentleness. The priest acknowledged his movement with a faint smile and paused.

"You wished to speak to me, my son?"

"No. At least, not exactly," said Roger, hoping he was not being rude. "I'm not a member of your church—"

"I realised that."

"I was admiring this fresco."

"Yes. It is attributed to Pinturicchio. A countrywoman of yours, who was herself a painter, often came in to look at it."

"Would that be Miss Shandon?" asked Roger eagerly.

"I never knew her name. We exchanged a few words when we met. She was always working. She made a sketch of Benito, the blind beggar. It was very clever, I thought," the priest said, but with an air of reserve, as if he could have said more but refrained.

"I think you could help me," Roger said.

"Perhaps you will come into the Presbytery. It is next door. You cannot miss it. I will be with you in a moment."

CHAPTER VII
PORTRAIT OF THE ARTIST

DON Vincenzo's house was small and clean and bare.

There were a few books on a shelf, and on the whitewashed walls a wooden crucifix and a gaudy oleograph of a bad picture by a modern artist representing the Holy Family. The stone floor was uncarpeted and the window uncurtained. The deaf old woman who had opened the door to Roger had brought in a fiasco of wine and two glasses.

The wine was thin and very sour and Roger had to force himself to drink it. He saw that the old priest would be hurt if he did not seem to enjoy it.

He said, "I can speak to you in confidence."

"You wish to make a confession?"

Roger looked alarmed. "Oh no. Nothing of that sort. The fact is—I can tell you why I'm here in a few words. I'm trying to find a young girl, a school friend of my sister's, to take her back to England. Her parents were divorced some years ago. She spent her holidays with her father. He had been given charge of her. Last month he married again without telling his daughter—her name is Anne, by the way—when she found out she decided to run away and join her mother, who is rather a well-known artist and spent some weeks here earlier in the summer."

"Divorce," said Don Vincenzo, "is an evil thing. The children suffer, the innocent for the guilty."

"I expect you're right," said Roger, "though it isn't much fun for the children if the parents go on living together and quarrel all the time. Her father came out here to fetch her home only to find that she had been here for one night and had gone again. The mother had left previously."

"Are you telling me that the mother is the woman painter who was here making sketches and of whom I spoke to you just now? We all supposed she was unmarried, a rich woman, travelling for amusement and making her art her pastime. There was—" he hesitated—"there was some talk in the town. I don't encourage gossip, but I hear things through my housekeeper. Mario Laccetti is a very good-looking young fellow and it was said that this foreign woman was infatuated. Your pardon, signore, if she is a friend of yours. There was probably nothing in it. She must be a good deal older than he is."

"And he is engaged to be married," said Roger. "His fidanzata and her family have been staying at the hotel. He seems very much in love with her."

"I have heard that also," said the priest. "People were saying that if they came while the Englishwoman was there it would be awkward for young Laccetti. Fortunately for him she left some time ago."

"Do you know when exactly?"

"No. It was about the end of last month, I suppose. I had not seen her about with her paint-box and stool and her little folding easel, and I was told that she had gone."

"What was she like—in appearance, I mean?"

"I am not a judge of women's looks," said the priest, with his faint smile, "but I should say decidedly una bella donna. Everyone said so. She was dark, with fine features, bright brown eyes, a clear skin. Not very young, but well preserved. But you know all this if she is a friend of yours."

"I have never seen her. I knew her husband."

Don Vincenzo looked at him thoughtfully. "And you are assisting him in his search for his daughter? I do not understand why you have come here. You told me he had already been to the hotel and gone again."

"He went from here to Rome. He was found the next morning dead at the foot of a lift shaft in an apartment house in the San Lorenzo district. It seems to have been an accident, but I don't know why he was there."

"You have made enquiries on the spot?"

"Yes. I went directly to Rome. I saw someone at the British Consulate who had made the necessary arrangements for his funeral, and I visited the house. He had fallen from the top landing, and the flat there was unoccupied. In spite of newspaper publicity neither his wife nor his daughter have come forward. Don't you think that is strange?"

"Perhaps," said the priest slowly. "But you say the couple were on bad terms. The child left her father to join her mother. Legally he would have the right to take her away?"

"I think so. Yes."

"It may be that the mother is hiding because she wishes to keep her daughter with her. With that object in view she might go to great lengths. At this moment they may be on a ship on their way to India, South America, Australia."

"I never thought of that," said Roger. "It is possible. Eve Shandon is a great traveller. She has been all over the place, painting. But Gale said that though she sent Anne beautiful presents she didn't really want to be bothered with the child. I fancy a girl of that age would be in her way."

"I will not pretend to misunderstand you," said Don Vincenzo. "But he may have been mistaken. Not in her moral character. I could see what she was. But about her feeling for her daughter."

"I suppose she could have her now," said Roger doubtfully. "I don't know much about the law. Gale had no near relatives, and no means beyond what he earned as a journalist. Eve Shandon had money of her own and got good prices for her work."

"It may be the intention of Providence to bring this woman back to a better way of living by means of the unconscious influence of this young girl," suggested Don Vincenzo. "I think you might do more harm than good by any interference, however well meant."

"It might work the other way," said Roger. "My sister told me that Anne idolised her mother—she had not seen her for years—if she's the sort of woman you say she'll get a shock some time, when she finds her out. Her father had let her down and she seems to have reacted violently."

"You know her well?"

"I've never seen her. She was at school with my sister. Here she is—"

He took the photograph he had brought with him from his letter case and laid it on the table. Don Vincenzo produced a pair

of steel-rimmed spectacles, wiped them on a red bandana handkerchief, and adjusted them carefully.

He was silent for a minute. Then he said, "Such beauty is
unusual. I understand better now. You are perhaps right to be
uneasy. That face is exquisite. One would say that the spirit that
inhabits such a tenement must be exquisite too, but as fragile
as blown glass. This world is too rough—but what can one do?"

"I don't know," said Roger simply. "I've got to find her. That's
the first thing."

He replaced the photograph in his case, and slipped the case
into an inner pocket.

"I still think that she and her mother are most probably on
their way to some distant part of the world."

"You may be right. I still have to talk to Mario. If he and Eve
Shandon were such good friends she may have told him her plans
for the immediate future. If he can't help at all I suppose I shall
have to give it up. I'm afraid I rubbed his sister up the wrong way.
She's rather grim. I suppose you know them very well?"

"No. I am not a native of Sant Andrina. I have been here
twelve years. They were born here. Their father had the chemist's
shop, but he had a long illness and when he died there was no
money. They both left the town and they worked in hotels. Mario
was in England for a time, I believe, and they have both been
on the French and Italian Riviera and in Naples. Maddalena's
husband was chef in the hotel where she was a chambermaid.
They all worked hard and they saved their money, and nearly
two years ago they came back here. The Villa Sant Andrina had
been standing empty ever since anyone can remember. It was
young Laccetti's idea to turn it into an hotel. He persuaded the
lawyers at Orvieto who manage the estate to let them try. He is
to pay for it by degrees. It seems that he and his sister had this
scheme in their minds years ago. They set their hearts on it and
worked and planned and scraped and saved with that one object
in view. They had just enough money to furnish a few rooms on
the ground floor and the floor above. But there. Maddalena's
husband is quite under her thumb, but I hear he is a good cook,
and a few of the townsfolk go there regularly for dinner, so that

is something. But, so far, there are very few visitors. Laccetti had hoped to get foreigners, artists, and others living in Rome who find the city too hot in the summer months. But for that they will have to advertise, and advertising costs money."

"I'm afraid it is too out of the way for many people," said Roger.

The old priest shook his head. "I hear Mario talks of buying one of these new machines, horseless carriages, to take people to and from the station. He is ambitious, full of ideas, ready to try anything that will bring prosperity to his beloved hotel. I think—" he hesitated and lowered his voice, "I think the English woman gave him money. I do not know. I look on from a distance. Neither he nor Maddalena come to mass or to confession." He glanced at the cheap alarm clock ticking on his bookshelf. "I have to visit a sick woman—"

Roger took the hint and rose to go.

"Come and see me again," Don Vincenzo said cordially as he went with him to the door. "I do not know your name—"

Roger, off his guard, said, "Of course. I'm sorry. My name's For—I mean Smith—"

He flushed with embarrassment. The old priest, he was sure, had noticed his slip. It could not be helped but it reminded him disagreeably of the difficulties he would have to face if he asked the police to help him in his search for Anne. It would put him in the wrong from the beginning that he was using a name that was not his own. In any case, he felt, the police must be a last resort. He did not think they would be inclined to pursue the enquiry. They would assume, as Don Vincenzo had assumed, that Anne had joined her mother, and that everything had happened for the best. He had no standing. He could claim no tie of blood, or even of friendship, with the vanished girl, to justify any further expenditure of time or money.

"Better go home," he thought. "What's the use?"

The blind beggar was sitting patiently on the church steps, his dirty wrinkled face and sightless eyes turned up to the sky. Roger dropped a coin in his extended hand.

The blind man said, "God will reward the signore who comes here for the second time, for his kindness to the poor."

"How do you know that I am here for the second time?"

"I sit here day after day and I listen to the footsteps of those who pass by, going up the steps to the church, or following the lane that leads to the Villa which is now an hotel. Some of those who go that way have not come back. You do not depend on your hearing, signore, to tell you if a man is young or old, happy or unhappy."

"The days must seem long to you," said Roger with compassion.

The old man seemed harmless and he was evidently glad to have someone to talk to. He was a picturesque figure with his shaggy white hair and beard as he sat swathed, in spite of the heat, in his faded blue cloak.

"You come from the presbytery. You have been talking to the parrocco. Did he tell you that the Englishwoman who was here painted my picture? It was good. She was pleased with it. She said it was one of the best things she had ever done. I was sitting here as I am now. Keep still, she said. It was easy. And she gave me ten lire. She told me she meant to stay here all the summer and through the vintage. There was so much that she could paint. And then she went away very suddenly. I miss her. She always had a pleasant word for old Benito. Have you seen any of her pictures, signore?"

"Only one sketch of a broken statue in the hotel garden."

"Ah," said the old man, "she told me she was using the summer-house there as a studio."

As Roger walked on he thought that it was odd that no one had told him that before. He had heard Mario say that the summer-house was used to store lumber. Perhaps they had let Eve Shandon work there after much persuasion, and as a great favour, and did not want to create a precedent. He remembered the screw top of a tube of paint that he had found lying on a path.

There was nobody about when he entered the hotel, but he must have been seen, for he had hardly established himself on the terrace, in a patch of shade, when Maddalena brought out his lunch. He enjoyed the excellent minestrone, the veal cutlet with artichokes fried in batter, the ripe green figs.

"If they knew how good the food was you would get half Rome up here," he told her when she came to clear the table.

She looked at him, her black eyes cold and unsmiling.

"The signore is very kind. I will tell my husband. He will be pleased."

"When did you say your brother was coming back?"

"Not before to-morrow evening." She moistened her lips before she added, "I hope the signore will wait for him. It is possible that he knows more than I do."

Roger had been so sure that she wanted to get rid of him that he was taken completely by surprise. Why had she changed her tune?

Was she trying to make amends for her rudeness the previous evening? If so, it was a curiously reluctant and ungracious performance. Roger looked after her uneasily as she went back to the house. She had been trying to get rid of him, and now she wanted him to stay. Why?

He glanced up at the huge façade of the villa with its long rows of shuttered windows. It was like a dead face, he thought: or perhaps a face pretending to be dead, which would be worse. He rose abruptly, throwing away his half-smoked cigarette. He told himself he was getting liverish from lack of exercise. A long walk over the hills was indicated.

CHAPTER VIII
DEATH IN THE GLASS

1

MARIO would have liked to have driven his Laurina down to the station in his two-wheeled trap, but the Antonellis would not allow it, so the whole party had left together in the omnibus. Mario accompanied his fidanzata and her parents to Orvieto where Signor Antonelli kept a small stationery and book shop, but he left them at the door. He had business to transact and would not be able to dine with them before he left. He told his future father-in-law that he was going to pay an instalment on the money the lawyers had advanced for the purchase of the Villa.

Antonelli shook his head doubtfully. "These grandiose schemes of yours."

"By degrees we will furnish more bedrooms. We shall do three this autumn. In the early spring we shall launch an advertising campaign. A coloured poster with a picture of Sant Andrino, showing its unique position, in all the railway stations and travel agencies."

"That will cost a great deal, Mario mio. Don't expect more from me at present."

"Maddalena and I are putting by as much as we can."

He kissed the giggling Laurina's plump little paw with fervour. He was not allowed a moment alone with her. The Antonellis were prudent parents and knew that young men were not to be trusted.

Mario did not go home immediately. He had a good deal to do, and it was not until the following day that he climbed into the omnibus waiting in the dusty station yard at Vallesca. As he happened to be the only passenger he lay down on the seat and went to sleep. He was asleep when they met the other omnibus coming from Sant Andrina at the foot of the last long hill.

The drivers cracked their whips and yelled greetings and the two clumsy vehicles went lumbering on their respective ways.

Mario woke up as the driver pulled up his mules in the piazza, lit a cigarette, took the carnation Laurina had given him, and which was beginning to fade a little after twenty-four hours, from his lapel, and stuck it behind his ear, and strolled leisurely along the lane between the high walls to the hotel.

It was hot in the kitchen where Maddalena was ironing. Her husband sat in his shirt sleeves reading a two days old copy of the *Roman Messagero*. They both looked up as Mario came in.

He said: "Where is he? On the terrace?"

Maddalena answered: "He's gone. He went less than an hour ago. A telegram came for him. I did not see it. The postino went through to where he was sitting smoking and drinking his coffee. He came in at once and ran up the stairs. I heard him moving about in his room. In five minutes he was down again with his bag. I told him his bill had not been made up, but he is staying here en pension, as you know. He could reckon how much it would come to. He gave me something over and told me to keep the change. He was going to catch the omnibus that leaves the piazza at half-past three. You must have passed him on the road."

Mario frowned. "If he is going back to England, well and good. But is he? You should have kept him until I came back."

"Easy to say that. But how could I? He told me he meant to stay. In any case"—she put the iron she had been using back on the stove and took up another—"I am glad he is gone. It is the best thing that could happen."

Maddalena's husband spoke without raising his eyes from his newspaper. "I don't understand you two. You want visitors, and when they come you wish them gone. I don't know what you have been up to and I don't want to know, but Maddalena groans and mutters in her sleep. I find it disturbing."

Mario shrugged his shoulders. "Indigestion," he said.

"It may be," said his brother-in-law in the same flat tone, "but I think she has something on her mind. I am sorry we came here. I am wasting my talent cooking for at most ten or twelve people." He turned to another page and relapsed into his habitual silence, he had said his say.

Roger, meanwhile, was still in the omnibus on his way to Vallesca where he would catch a train, piccola velocita, which, after stopping at every station, would reach Rome about midnight. The question then was whether he should go directly to his hotel for the rest of the night, or make his way at once to the house in the Via Romeo Poldini. For the telegram had been sent by Lily Oram.

Please come back I am frightened—Lily.

It had meant missing Mario, who might have given him some clue to the present whereabouts of Anne and her mother, but that could not be helped. The little English teacher was experienced, competent, used to taking care of herself in a hard world. She would not send for him, he felt sure, without very good reason. As to what could have happened he was utterly in the dark, but he was increasingly certain that there was more in this mystery of

Anne Gale's disappearance than appeared on the surface. There was danger, though he still did not know who was being threatened, or why. Gale's death might have been an accident, but Roger found that he was more and more inclined to think of that dingy landing at the top of the house in that rather doubtful quarter of the city as the scene of a very cunning and well planned crime. But what could be the motive? Gale was a poor man, depending on what he could earn by free lance journalism. His former wife would gain nothing from his death, and the girl he had recently married was on her way to Australia with a theatrical company. He had come out to find Anne. Was that why?

Was Anne the key to the riddle? Roger, sitting alone in his dimly-lit compartment as the train chugged its way across the Roman campagna, resisted an impulse to take her picture from his pocket book. There was really no need to refresh his memory. Lovely and fragile as blown glass.

The old priest's description had been apt. It was not, perhaps, strange, that Gale should have fathered such a child. There was something brittle, defenceless, about him too. He was dreamy, unpractical, predestined to make a mess of his marriages and his financial affairs.

A bubble, a bright glass bubble, floating on a dark stream.

The train stopped. Doors slammed. Roger, who had been half asleep, roused himself and got out. He had decided that he must go to Lily at once, in spite of the late hour. He took his bag to the left luggage office. The last tram had gone and he thought it unwise to draw the attention of the other tenants to his arrival by driving up in a cab. It was not a very long walk from the Central station. He set off at a brisk pace, turning down the wide modern thoroughfare that leads to the Porta San Lorenzo. He had forgotten that after twelve the main door would be closed and that he would have to ring the porter's bell to obtain admission, but his luck held, for he was immediately preceded by a cheerful and rather noisy party who had been to *Il Trovatore* at the Teatro Nazionale and who were still humming their favourite airs and disputing over the merits of a new tenor. The father of the family had a latch key. Roger slipped by unnoticed while they argued at the tops of their voices, and made for the stairs. The lights were out, but he remembered the general direction. He heard a door close below as the disputants entered their flat. A profound silence ensued as he moved up in the darkness, feeling his way along the handrail. On each landing as he came to it he was uncomfortably aware of the cage door that shut in the black lift shaft. If that door stood open it would be easy—but it couldn't happen twice, not by accident, for he was forewarned—and the murderer, if there was a murderer, would not make that mistake.

Surely this was the floor. He struck a match and saw Lily's card attached to the door with drawing-pins.

Miss LILY ORAM,
Lezione d'Inglese.

He rang the bell.

Almost at once he heard someone moving and Lily's voice said: "Chi é?"

He answered in English: "It's me, Roger. I got your wire."

He stepped in quickly as the door was opened, and stood by while she turned the key in the lock.

He saw that she was fully dressed.

"You were sitting up."

"Yes. I didn't feel sleepy. I—I rather hoped you would come. It's good of you. I hope it didn't mess up your plans."

He followed her into the stuffy, over-furnished little salotto.

"What happened?"

"Sit down, won't you, and smoke if you want to, but try not to make a noise because of the woman downstairs."

"The woman?"

"I have evening pupils," she explained, "but never so late as this."

"Of course. I wasn't thinking. Sorry. I'll be careful. I say—" he exclaimed involuntarily as he saw her face in the light. "You do look tired."

"I couldn't sleep last night, and naturally I had to run round giving my lessons just the same. So do you if it comes to that. I'll make some tea. Could you eat anything?"

"I certainly could. I haven't had a bite since lunch at the hotel and that's twelve hours ago."

"What a shame. Just wait—I'll see what I've got." She went into the tiny kitchen to put a kettle on the stove and came back with the heel of a loaf, a lump of ricotta cheese, a few salted anchovies in a saucer, and a dish of ripe black figs.

"I haven't had any supper myself. I didn't feel like it. That queer sickish feeling. Sheer funk. But I'm all right now."

"I'll lay the table while you make the tea."

He took off his shoes and crept about in his stockinged feet, and when one of them forgot and spoke above a loud whisper the other pointed anxiously downward. Lily's spirits rose perceptibly.

"This is fun," she said as she sipped her tea. A little colour had crept into her thin cheeks. She pushed the untidy mass of dark hair back from her forehead and rammed a few loose pins back into their places.

"Why did you send that wire?"

"It's rather a long story. A new pupil turned up yesterday evening. He said he had been recommended to me by the people at the grocer's shop round the corner. That was all right. I've given their little girl lessons. They pay in groceries. He spoke a little English, but wanted to improve himself. He offered very good terms, more than I usually get, and he wanted to start there and then, but I was too tired and I told him so. I had my supper set out on a tray and I was just going to have it and turn in when he arrived. He seemed disappointed, but just then the door bell rang and I went to answer it. When I opened the door there was nobody there, and I thought that was queer as I had gone at once. I could hear the lift going down. I looked in the letter box but there wasn't a note. Then I came back here. I had left this door partly open. There are several old faded photographs in frames hanging in the passage and one, rather a large one of the Colosseum, faces the door. As I came along I saw a part of the salotto reflected in the glass. I saw that man, my new pupil, leaning over my supper tray, his clenched hand over my jug of lemonade. It looked as if he was pouring something in. I had not made a sound. I was wearing my old bedroom slippers. I started humming a tune and when I went in he was standing some distance away from the table with his back to it. He said: 'If you are so tired, signorina, I will not trouble you to-night. Another day.' He seemed in a hurry to get away so I let him go. He had not even told me his name, or offered his card.

"I looked at the lemonade and thought it seemed cloudy. There were a few white specks on the tray that might have been sugar that I had dropped when I was making it. It was a hot night and I was very thirsty, but I didn't drink it. I got myself some water from the tap, and then I found an empty bottle and poured the lemonade into it and corked it, and this morning I took it round to the father of one of my pupils who has a chemist's shop in the Corso Vittorio Emanuele. I asked him to find out if there was anything wrong with the stuff. He told me to come back at twelve. When I called at the shop again I saw his son, he's the one who had some English lessons, a very clever boy, studying to be a doctor at the Santo Spirito. He was very excited. He said: 'Miss Lily, what does this mean? That liquid is lethal—it is—how you say?—noxious.' He will look up words in the dictionary and it makes him sound so stilted, and then he went on in Italian and said he had made some tests and had wound up by pouring about a wineglass full of the stuff down the throat of an old cat they wanted to get rid of. 'We thought of taking it to the Pantheon in a bag and leaving it,' he said. 'But this was an opportunity.' I tried not to let him see how I felt about that because he only meant to be kind, and they don't feel as we do about animals. He said it died in about ten minutes with—with all the symptoms of strychnine poisoning."

"Good God!"

"He didn't ask me any questions. I think he didn't want to get mixed up in anything. I asked him what he had done with the rest of the stuff and he said he had poured it down the drain. So I thanked him and I went to the nearest post office and sent off that telegram."

"You did quite right," said Roger emphatically. "I got you into this. At least—I suppose you think there is some connection—"

"I haven't any enemies that I know of," she said. "Life hasn't always been easy here, but nobody has tried to murder me before."

He was silent for a moment. Then he said: "What was the fellow like? Would you know him again?"

"I'm not sure. Probably not. I did not look at him very closely. He had a black beard, and his eyes were weak, I suppose, for he wore tinted glasses."

"It sounds like a disguise."

"It might be. I never thought of it. Lots of Italians wear beards. I—I—It's so horrible."

He saw that she was trembling.

"You can't stay on here," he said.

"I suppose not. But it was lent to me until the end of September. It is convenient, and rent free."

"Never mind that. I'll see you don't lose by it. That's only fair. Do you want to go to the police?"

She shook her head. "No. What could I prove now? And it would not do me any good. I should lose my pupils."

"I can't imagine what possessed your medical student friend to throw the stuff away."

"I told you. He only tested it to please me. He wouldn't want to be involved in any sort of trouble. Italians don't feel friendly to policemen as we do at home. If they are called to be witnesses it may start a feud, and trials hang on for months and months and waste everybody's time. You must not blame Aristide. He's a good boy, one of my favourite pupils."

"He sounds a cold-blooded brute to me," growled Roger. "Look here, Lily, I'm not going to leave you alone here. That's flat. You'd better go to bed now. You look all in. I'll get a few hours sleep here on the sofa. And in the morning we'll make plans."

"That's good of you," she said gratefully. "I didn't like to suggest it, because I'm afraid you'll be very uncomfortable, but I was dreading the moment when you'd say you must be going. I—you see, I can't help feeling that when they realise that I did not drink the lemonade they'll come back and—and try something else."

"Don't worry. If that bearded blighter calls again I'll be here to dot him one."

When she had left him he went to the door of the flat to examine the fastenings. The lock was weak and there was no bolt, but he wedged the back of a chair under the handle so that it would be impossible for anyone to enter without making a good deal of noise.

The sofa cushions were lumpy and smelt of dust, but he slept well enough and woke to hear Lily moving about in the kitchen.

"Hullo? Are you all right? Do I smell coffee?"

"You do. Are you having a cold bath? There isn't any hot water."

"I could do with one."

Ten minutes later they were sitting down to breakfast. Lily explained that she never had anything but a slice of bread with her coffee, but she had made an omelette for her guest and there were three figs left.

"You'll have half the omelette," said Roger firmly, dividing it. "You must keep yourself up. You've got to do your packing."

She sighed. "I thought I was in such luck getting this place rent free."

"You're leaving," he said, "but there's no violent hurry. We can have a talk first. We're up against something. The question is—" he hesitated. "You think there's some connection between this lemonade business and the accident to Gale?"

"Yes. You see—if it wasn't an accident—it happened on the landing just over mine. They might think I knew or had seen something, that I may be dangerous. I may be wrong, but I believe I aroused suspicion when I called on Frau Haussman the other evening and asked if Miss Shandon had been staying with her."

"I've been thinking the same thing," he said. "I could kick myself for letting you go there."

"No," she said. "It was my own fault. I was clumsy. She was too clever for me."

"I could bear to know more about that dear lady," he said thoughtfully. "There must be some way of finding out. She couldn't have disguised herself with a beard, I suppose?"

Lily giggled. "Hardly, with her figure—"

"And she won't let her rooms to the nasty English. That makes it difficult. We may be wrong, you know. She may be a tough old party with bad manners, and an unconcealed dislike for hardy islanders, and yet be innocent of any knowledge of how Francis Gale died, or what has become of his wife and daughter."

Lily was grave enough now. "It's all guesswork so far," she admitted. "And you learnt nothing at Sant Andrina? You haven't told me how you got on there."

"They weren't pleased to see me," he said slowly. "Why? You'd think they'd be delighted. So much depends on their getting visitors. They admitted that Anne Gale came expecting to find her mother there. She left the following day. Then Gale arrived. He, too, left after one night. Beyond that they say they know nothing. Not one of the three left any address, or let fall any word about their future plans. That may be so, of course. But the woman was sullen and resented my questions more than she need have done, I thought, and her brother was elusive. His fidanzata and her people were there and naturally he was very occupied with them, and when they left he went with them. He had not returned when I came away. I was waiting for him. I thought I might be able to extract something. He—the people in the place had been talking. I gathered that Eve Shandon had taken a violent fancy to him and had made him presents. He's very good-looking."

"So many Italians," said Lily, "are good, honest, and very hard-working people. So many have been kind to me. Faithful friends. But there are others. Was there anything else?"

"Well—an old man whom Eve Shandon used as a model told me that she had occupied an old summer-house in the hotel garden as a studio. Mario had gone out of his way to explain that the summer-house was used to store lumber and was kept locked up. Of course, it might be that Eve was allowed to work there as a special favour and that they did not want other guests to butt in, but there was no need to lie about it."

"Is that all?"

Roger opened his mouth to speak and shut it again. He had not forgotten the incident of the black dog, but he felt a curious reluctance to speak about it. Nina had been annoyed with him at the time, and he had felt that he had made a fool of himself, but that was not the real reason. That glimpse he had of black hair floating just below the viscous surface in the old stone water tank had given him a shock and he wanted to thrust it away and shut it out of his mind. If he had allowed himself to think about it he might have realised, its possible importance, but the time for that had not yet come.

"I'm helping you to move," he reminded Lily. "You must not be alone after this. Haven't you any English friends who would take you in?"

"No. There aren't many left in Rome in August. They go home, or to Switzerland, or up in the hills, or to the sea. Of course, there are a few derelicts, but we don't know each other. The British colony—in case you don't know it—is divided into three layers. The top is the Embassy crowd and women who have married into the great Roman families, and rich people who like Rome, or who are Catholics. They have expensive flats or villas or stay in the best hotels. Then, in the middle, there are the elderly widows and spinsters who drift here from Florence, and stay in cheap pensions near the Piazza di Spagna, and attend the English church in the Via Babbuino. The people in the lowest layer are a very mixed lot, jockeys and their wives, old women who used to be variety or circus artistes, girls who came over to take posts as governesses and got thrown out when the father of their pupils made love to them. That's what happened to me, by the way. You may as well know it. I was very young and very silly. He told me he was desperately unhappy, that I was the one gleam of light—and all the rest of it. When his wife found out he simply denied everything. She offered to pay my fare back to England, but I wouldn't take it. That was six years ago, and I've lived here ever since and kept my head above water. And—I'd like you to know this, Roger—I haven't earned a soldo in the easy way. I'd rather starve or make a hole in the Tiber. I—it isn't that I'm specially virtuous. He put me off it for good. You see—I was in earnest, terribly, and he was just amusing himself."

She dropped the end of her cigarette in her coffee cup and stood up. "I know a woman who has a little flat off the Piazza Barberini. She might let me have a room. She wouldn't mind my having pupils. She gets a good many people herself coming for consultations. She's a palmist. I'll get my things together."

"Will it be all right if I come with you and see you settled in, or would that make a bad impression?" he asked.

"I had better go alone," she said. "I'm not afraid in broad daylight. Luckily I haven't any pupils coming to me just now, but I have two lessons to give in different parts of the city this afternoon. Where will you be staying?"

"Where I was before. At the Albergo del Rio near the Central station. When can I come and call on you?"

"Any time after six." She wrote the address on one of her cards and gave it him.

"I'm not leaving this house before you do," he said. "I'll wait while you pack."

She was ready in little over ten minutes. Her belongings were pitifully few. They went down the stairs together, meeting nobody on the way. Roger called a cab.

CHAPTER IX
LOOKING FOR TROUBLE

ROGER, having disposed of Lily Oram for the time being, went into a barber's shop for a shave and a haircut, and had an excellent lunch in a small trattoria a few doors farther on. Then he took a cab and had himself driven to the office of Messrs Thomas Cook in the Piazza di Spagna, where he had arranged with his aunt to have his letters forwarded.

The spruce young man who gave them to him asked if he wished to arrange for any excursions. A coach was going that afternoon to Hadrian's Villa and Tivoli, and there were two places unfilled. Roger thanked him and declined, and then, yielding to an impulse, asked him if he had ever heard of Sant Andrina.

"No. At least—" The young man's bland indifference had annoyed him, but he unexpectedly became more human. "It's funny you should ask that. Sant Andrina. I believe somebody was in here a few days ago to try to induce us to boost the place. Up in the hills somewhere, isn't it?"

"Yes."

"They left some cards. Apparently there's an hotel there. I don't know what's become of them. Naturally we couldn't recommend it without finding out something more about it."

"You said a few days. Was it the day before yesterday?"

Roger tried to keep his voice steady. He was excited. There was a possibility that Mario Laccetti had been in Rome, and he found it disturbing.

"The day before yesterday? Yes, I think it was. I wasn't here myself. I had gone out to my lunch. I heard about it afterwards. Graves, you were here when some chap came in and asked you to recommend his hotel?"

Another young man came forward. "Yes. He was very persistent. I had a job to get rid of him. It sounded all right, picturesque and all that, but too out of the way."

"Was he Italian?"

"Oh, definitely, though he spoke English well. A good-looking bloke. I gathered that he was the head waiter and part owner. It sounded a hopeless proposition to me. He left some cards, but I think they were thrown away."

Roger had no further questions to ask. He was now convinced that Mario had been in Rome a few hours before the stranger had called at Lily's flat. His could have been the hand she had seen reflected in the glass of the picture in the passage, clenched over the jug of lemonade on the supper tray. He pondered this new development as he walked slowly, without noticing where he was going, up the hill to the Pincian gardens. There he sat down on a bench under a tree, and stared with unseeing eyes at the stout, swarthy Roman nurses gossiping together while their charges played, running races round the fountain.

After a while he remembered his letters. There was one from a friend of his aunt, living at Warwick, asking him and Penny to come over for tennis, the bill from his tailor for the suit he had ordered, and a letter from Miss Fordyce.

"If the first Mrs. Gale is in Italy, and has heard of her husband's death, she will have got into touch with the authorities if she has any natural feeling at all," wrote Aunt Polly. "In that case you have probably met her by this time to talk things over. I wonder what sort of impression she will make on you. I heard about her, quite by chance, yesterday evening. Penny and I were spending the evening with the Gwilts—round games for the young people, and whist for the old fogies. We are none of us up to this new game of bridge. A woman who is staying with them, a friend of Moira's, is a painter. She does miniatures, I believe. I asked her if she knew the work of Eve Shandon, and it turned out that she had once shared a studio with her in Chelsea. She said, 'Eve is brilliant. She has a touch of genius. But she's erratic. She seldom really finishes a picture, but her sketches are marvellous.' I said, 'Apart from her work, did you like her?' She turned that off, but I got her away from the others and told her I had a good reason for asking, and she admitted then that they had parted company because, though she flattered herself she was not narrow minded, Eve's goings on were a bit too much for her. I won't go into details, but it's evident that she is not a fit person to look after a young girl. Of course, Roger, if she wants to keep Anne with her, and the child is of the same mind, we can't do anything about it. But I think she won't be at all keen on having a daughter in tow, giving away her age, so will you tell her from me that we shall be delighted to have Anne here during the rest of the holidays if she will allow her to come home to England in your charge. Penny sends her love. You know how lazy she is about writing. Take care of your-self, my dear boy. Don't drink unboiled water, and be careful not to become involved in any dispute with porters or cabmen. I have heard they all carry knives. But, of course, after your years in Malaya you can hardly need advice about that sort of thing,

"Your affectionate Aunt Polly.

"P.S. I have invented a new cake with an orange flavouring that is going very well. The Americans seem to like it, and of course Stratford is full of them just now."

Unboiled water! Roger laughed aloud, to the great astonishment of a small child clasping a large doll who had been gazing at him for some time. It was just as well, he thought, that Miss Fordyce did not know what he was up against. He did not know himself, definitely, but he was beginning to realise that he would need all his wits and a good slice of luck as well if he was to come out of an ugly business unscathed. He had to find Anne, and he had to take care of Lily Oram. He still blamed himself for having let her go to the Pension Haussmann. But for that unfortunate visit she might never have been suspected, as she evidently was now, of knowing what had really happened on the top landing the night Francis Gale fell down the lift shaft. As it was, he felt responsible for her safety.

It wasn't only that. He liked her. She had helped him by listening to him, and by her eager interest. He had felt that she was as anxious to find Anne as he was. He thought he could understand that better now that she had told him something of her own story. She had been young and defenceless once in a hard world. Even now, after years of struggle, her hold on the life line was precarious. She was used, he supposed, to her hand to mouth existence, but it horrified him. She was plucky too, she had tried hard not to let him see how badly her nerve had been shaken by her narrow escape from death, but he had seen how her hands shook as she said: "I wish Aristide had not shown me the cat's body. Its fur was all staring, and it was quite stiff and arched like a bow, and there was foam on its lips. I thought, 'I should have looked like that, if—'"

He took a cigarette from his case and lit it. He had to decide on his next step. It was comparatively easy for the detective heroes of the thrillers he most enjoyed. They usually had the resources of New Scotland Yard at their disposal, or, if they happened to be amateurs, they had a faithful, though thick-headed, friend in attendance, or a valet who was also a boxing champion and an expert photographer.

He was alone, and the circumstances of the case were such that he could not expect any help from the police even if he had felt any desire to ask for it. He had no evidence that Francis Gale had been murdered, that Eve Shandon and Anne had not vanished of their own accord; no evidence even of the attempt to get rid of Lily, since what was left of the lemonade had been poured down the drain. "Yes," he thought, "and if they'd succeeded with her it would have been called suicide, and if they get me it will look like an accident."

He got up and walked slowly back the way he had come through the Pincian Gardens towards the Villa Medici and the Spanish Steps. At six he was going to call on Lily in the Piazza Barberini, but meanwhile there was the Pension Haussmann. It seemed to Roger that it was time he made the acquaintance of the Frau.

The Via della Croce is not the most esteemed of the many streets leading out of the Piazza di Spagna. It is a quiet street, but it has a furtive and slightly raffish aspect. Roger found the house he was looking for without any difficulty. There was no porter, and the entry was dark and dingy. There was no lift. He met nobody on the stairs. There was a doctor's plate on the door of one of the flats on the fifth floor. The name was Donati. He went on to the top floor.

Someone was playing the piano. The music ceased abruptly as he rang the bell, but he had to wait some time before the door was opened by a stout woman whose small grey eyes were like pebbles set in the red granite of her broad flat face. Her scanty fair hair was dragged back from her forehead and fastened in a tight bun at the back of her head. Her blue cotton overall was spotlessly clean. A faint steam was rising from her large red hands.

"So?" she said harshly. "I was washing. What do you want?"

She spoke Italian fluently, but with a strong German accent.

Roger gazed at her with that deceptive air of boyish candour that was apt to mislead strangers, and said: "The music has stopped. I hope it isn't my fault. It was lovely."

The hard face relaxed slightly. He had been fortunate enough to find the only chink in Frau Haussmann's armour.

"That was my son, my Siegfried. He is a musician. He would be studying in Germany, but his health is not good so he stays here with me. What do you want?"

"It was Schubert, wasn't it. Beautiful. I think you let furnished rooms?"

"I have nothing at present." She hesitated. "Next week perhaps, if you care to call again. My rooms are not cheap, but they are well furnished and very clean."

He could believe that. If she had any virtue beyond that of being a devoted mother it was obviously cleanliness. An aroma of soap and furniture polish hung about her. He wondered as he went down the stairs, if she had taken him for an Italian. It was lucky, he thought, that he was good at languages and had exchanged lessons with a clerk in an Italian shipping office during the six months he spent in Singapore.

He had not heard the door close. Though he did not turn his head he knew that she was watching his descent. That, he felt, was not in character. Normally she would have gone back at once to her wash tub. It was a little thing, but it went to show that she was uneasy. Something, though not much. On the whole his visit had been unproductive. Had it, though? He had learned that she had a son, and that she was supporting him while he was studying music. In spite of this she seemed unwilling to let her rooms. Roger did not believe they were all occupied. There was a wineshop opposite. He might pick up something there. But it was already past six o'clock, and Lily was on his mind.

The church clocks were striking the half hour as he rang the bell of the mezzanino flat in a house whose windows looked down on the fountain in the Piazza Barberini. He was hot and tired, and the sound of falling water was pleasant. He knew that it was unlikely that Lily's friend would reach the German woman's standard of cleanliness, but he was hardly prepared for the concentrated odours of drains, joss sticks, and garlic, that met him on the threshold.

"Signora Nefert?"

The signora was short and fat and wore so many bangles that she jingled as she moved. Her dark greasy skin was thickly powdered. She was decidedly plain but she looked good tempered.

"Lily has not come in yet, but she will not be long. I am so pleased to have her here with me," she said as she led the way into a stuffy little room furnished with two armchairs upholstered in shabby red brocade and a rickety little table on which a crystal was lying on a black velvet cushion.

"This is where I receive my clients. But I have finished for the day. You will excuse me. I am making a frittata. You will stay to supper with us?"

"I shall be delighted."

She laid a plump, beringed hand on his sleeve. "I am so glad that one of the signorina's English friends has come to see her at last. She is too much alone here. It is not right. I do what I can, but it is not much. She taught my little girl English, and she helped me nurse her when she fell ill, when she died last year. I do not forget that. And now I must run, or the frittata will be burnt."

Lily came in a few minutes later. Her worn face lit up when she saw Roger. She sank into one of the chairs, pulled off her hat, and threw it on the floor.

"All right so far?" she said. "I don't mind admitting I've worried about you."

He was smiling at her as he took the chair facing her. "Same here. But I like your friend. She seems a good sort, and she's evidently devoted to you. How much have you told her?"

"She knew about the accident where I was staying. It was in all the papers. When she heard what happened the night before last she said at once that probably someone was afraid I could give evidence that would prove a murder had been committed. She's very quick—you have to be in her profession. I warned her that I might be followed here. I said I'd find some other place if she felt at all nervous, but she wouldn't hear of it."

"She has asked me to stay to supper."

"She said she would. She thinks we are old friends. You don't mind—"

"Time is no measure for friendship," he said.

He looked down at the crystal, glimmering in the gathering dusk.

"Can anyone foresee the future? I wonder—"

"Do you want Nefert to look for you?"

"No. Do you?"

She shook her head. "She has offered to more than once. I won't let her. What are you going to do, Roger? Give up the search? What more can you do than you have done? It seems hopeless."

He said, "I think Mario Laccetti was in Rome the day before yesterday. He took the opportunity to try to interest the staff at Cook's Agency in his hotel. I discovered that almost by chance."

Her eyes widened. "It might have been he who—"

"It is possible." He told her of his visit to the Pensione Haussmann. "She said she had no rooms vacant, but I had a feeling that she was lying about that. She wasn't abusive as she was to you. I don't think she realised that I was English. I got round her by admiring her son's playing. Do you know anything about him?"

"Oh yes. I heard about him from some of the other tenants. They said he's consumptive, but his mother won't admit it. She idolises him. Nothing is too good for him. He's about nineteen."

"I see."

Looking at him it seemed to her that he had changed in the very short time that had elapsed since they first met. His pleasant, fresh-coloured face had hardened in some way she could not have described. He was wearing what his Aunt Polly called his mulish look. As a boy he had been so good-natured and easy going that only the few people who knew him best had been aware of the stubborn streak in him.

He said, "I believe I've got most of the pieces if I only knew how to put them together, the people and the motives and all. A plan of sorts has been forming in my mind. I'm not going to tell you what it is. I shall be away for not less than three days. It may be more. But if you haven't heard from me at the end of a week I want you to deliver a letter I'm going to write to the English consul. After that it will be out of our hands and up to him."

"You are going to do something dangerous?"

"Well—it may be, but I don't see any other way. And I've got this."

He took an automatic from his coat pocket and laid it on the table between them beside the crystal.

She said, "Dear me. You're very unexpected. You're not at all the sort of man one imagines might be carrying a gun."

"I've been four years out in Malaya, assistant manager on a plantation. Actually I've never had occasion to use it, but the other chap who was with me and I used to get a lot of practice shooting rats. I'm not quite so harmless as I look."

She sighed. "That's a comfort. Put that thing away before Nefert comes in. You—you'll keep on the right side of the law, I hope."

"I don't know much about Italian law. In any case I shall try not to be found out," he said gaily. His spirits were rising since he had decided on a plan of campaign. "That frittata smells good."

She said urgently, "Don't go. Give it up and return to England. You don't know what it's like here. They keep you in prison for months without a trial. I've thought you may be up against something more than you realise. I told you how Aristide poured the poisoned lemonade away. People don't ask for trouble here. Witnesses are threatened. It's not like England where the police can't be bribed."

He said, "I know all that, but I'm going to find Anne. Don't worry, my dear. I'm much tougher than I look. Take care of yourself while I'm gone."

Before she could answer Nefert called to them that supper was ready.

CHAPTER X
BOOMERANG

DINNER had been served to the habitués of the Albergo del Castello, the doctor, whose wife was away staying with her mother, the dentist, who was a widower, the two clerks from the local branch of the Banca Commerciale, and the two very old men who spent most of their days dozing on a bench in the shade of the planes in the piazza. By ten o'clock the last comers had finished and gone back to the town, passing along the lane in twos and threes, smoking their black Tuscan cigars, and at peace with the world after an excellent meal.

"That fellow Mario away again. He's always gadding nowadays."

"Gone to see his fidanzata at Orvieto. I don't blame him. She's a pretty girl, carina assai, and they say her father has a pocketful of soldi, and that she is the only child. Mario's fortunate."

"It's lucky for him they haven't heard about the English-woman."

All the men laughed loudly and nudged each other.

"Lucky for him she left when she did, before Antonelli brought his wife and daughter."

The doctor did not agree. "She would have been discreet. She would have effaced herself. She was staying at the hotel. E basta. A fine woman like that, and no longer young. She would know very well how to deal with a delicate situation. She was amusing herself with Mario. There could be no question of rivalry between her and the Signorina Antonelli."

"I think you are wrong," said the dentist. "She had reached the dangerous age, the age when a woman clings desperately to a lover, feeling that he may be the last. Venus toute entière a sa proie attachée." He was proud of his French.

"She might have done, but she didn't," his friend reminded him. "She was sensible and left. Probably she felt that it would be painful to look on while Mario paid the required attentions to the future Signora Laccetti."

There was a chorus of good nights as they reached the piazza and separated to go to their homes in the town. The two young bank clerks lingered to look across the valley from the parapet of the terrace where, during the day, the women spread their linen to dry. The few scattered lights in the plain might have been stars reflected in water.

"A night for love."

The other said, "She gave him some handsome presents. He showed me tortoise shell backed brushes. But that was at first. I don't know what went wrong, but latterly he wouldn't talk. What is that light moving on the hillside?"

"Where? I don't see anything?"

"In the hotel grounds. Not the gardens. Farther down. It's gone. Mario coming home perhaps. He uses that short cut a good deal."

"Why not? He keeps his horse and trap in a shed at the foot of the hill, and saves three miles of road."

"He is ambitious. He dreams of the day when Sant Andrina will be a fashionable resort, and his precious hotel full of tourists."

They both laughed. "There is no one staying there now?"

"No. The rush has not begun."

In the hotel kitchen Maddalena was washing the dishes while her husband, sitting at the table, read to her tasty snippets from the *Messagero* about laundry girls who drank sublimate after being crossed in love, and men who knifed each other during a quarrel over a game of Morro. Sometimes he broke off to attend to the wicks of the brass lucerna. The table was strewn with the little scorched bodies and blackened wings of moths that had fallen into the flames.

Maddalena listened sullenly. When Mario was at home he sometimes helped her with the washing-up, but she would not ask her husband. He was so patient and uncomplaining, and he took as much trouble over the dinner he cooked for the pack of nobodies who came to the hotel every evening as he had when he was chef at Monte Carlo. He was an artist, she thought proudly, and when one is an artist—They both looked up when the door opened, expecting to see Mario. As Roger Fordyce moved forward Maddalena dropped the plate she was holding. She had hoped they had seen the last of the Englishman they knew as Mr. Smith.

Roger closed the door carefully behind him. He looked dusty and tired, and his face was very white.

"Where is your brother, signora?"

"He is away. What do you want here, at this hour? How did you come?"

"Never mind that. I must talk to you two." He looked at Maddalena.

"What is your husband's name?"

"Luciano Olivieri. But you can have nothing to say to him."

"You are mistaken. I shall have a great deal."

Olivieri folded his newspaper. He glanced in a puzzled way at the young foreigner who spoke such good Italian, and then at his wife. He said, "There is something here that I do not understand."

Roger kept his eyes fixed on the woman. Mario's absence perturbed him. It might wreck his plan. Everything now depended on how far his sister was in his confidence. Her face told him nothing, it might have been a mask moulded in yellow wax.

He said, "I have nothing to do with the police. I have already told you why I am here. I want to find the young girl who came to this hotel to join her mother. You told her that her mother— whom you knew as Miss Shandon—had left. The girl stayed one night here. You admit that?"

"Certainly."

"Where is she now?"

"I have told you before that we do not know. If people staying here leave an address for the forwarding of letters we attend to it. Otherwise—" she shrugged her shoulders.

"We are hotel keepers. It would not do for us to be too curious. Would you have us peep and pry and make enquiries about the married couples who sometimes come here because it is quiet and well away from all their friends? It might turn out that they are married—si—but not to each other. And what then? It is not our affair. Unless, of course, they give us too much trouble."

So they guessed that, thought Roger ruefully. But it did not really matter so long as Nina was not recognised. That could only happen through sheer ill luck.

He said, "Miss Shandon was here for nearly three months. She must have had some correspondence to be sent on."

"No."

"She gave you no address? You had no idea where she was going?"

"None. I advised the young girl to return to England."

"You speak a little English?"

"A few words. Enough for that."

"Didn't she tell you that she had not enough money to pay her fare home?"

"She said nothing to me about money. She paid her bill. We did not overcharge her."

"Mario took her down to the station in his trap?"

"I do not remember. He may have done."

Roger saw a pulse beating in her throat and the involuntary twitching of her hands. There were beads of sweat on her upper lip. It was not only that she resented his questions: she was afraid. He waited a moment before he resumed.

"I think you know where she is. I am prepared to buy that."

Olivieri intervened. "What is all this, Maddalena?"

She snapped at him, "Be quiet—you—" and turned again to Roger.

"We know nothing. I tell you again for the hundredth time. Nothing. Dio mio! Are we to have no peace—"

"Then I must ask you to be patient while I lay some of my cards on the table. The Englishwoman who was here last year came again in May. She was out all day painting in the town and on the hills. She worked very hard. But she found time, unfortunately for her, to fall in love with your brother. That is, at first she amused herself. He was twenty years younger. She had had numerous affairs. But gradually he acquired great influence over her. She gave him presents, she gave him money. He persuaded her to give, or perhaps only to lend, quite a large sum to enable you to carry on here. To do that she had to sell out some stock. In return she demanded his undivided attention. She was exacting, fiercely possessive, and he was growing tired of her. Moreover, he was expecting a visit from the girl he hoped to marry and her parents. There was money in that quarter too, and he had already got all he could hope to get out of Eve Shandon. So he killed her."

Roger paused again. Neither of his hearers moved or uttered a sound. Olivieri's jaw had dropped. A large moth blundered into the flame of the lamp and fell on the table.

"It may have been premeditated. I don't know. More likely it was during a quarrel. He did not know what to do with the body. He pushed it into a water tank and replaced the lid. Before he could do anything more about it we arrived. I think that he took his sister into his confidence, and that she helped him by hiding the clothes and other possessions of the victim, and that his brother-in-law was told that she had left at a moment's notice.

"Mario's troubles were not over. I showed an inconvenient interest in the remains of the old castle walls, and went down the garden to look at them. The summer house which Eve had used as a studio was locked. It was not likely that I would lift the lid of the old tank, but I did, and I saw something floating just under the surface of the water which I took to be long black hair. I said nothing at the time and I tried to persuade myself that I was mistaken, but later I spoke about it to—to my wife, and Mario overheard me. He had been annoyed by the howling of a dog, a stray mongrel that had attached himself to Eve. Like most English people she was fond of dogs and she had been kind to the poor beast, and he had followed her when she went sketching on the hills. He had missed her and had taken to coming into the grounds at night to hunt for her. I heard him myself. Mario lay in wait for him, gave him a piece of poisoned meat, which the half starved brute wolfed down quickly enough, and when he was dead, threw a bucket of water over him. When I came down to breakfast I was taken to see his body and told that it had been found in the tank. The dog, a cross bred retriever, had black curly hair. It was near enough. I believed the yarn. I wanted to believe it, even if it made me look a fool. It was clever. And we were leaving anyway. When we had gone there was time for Mario to dig a grave. But it was not quite deep enough. I know. I've been looking for it, and I found it an hour ago."

"Santissima Madonna," muttered Olivieri. "No. No, it can't be."

"Lies. All lies," said Maddalena harshly.

"She was wearing a dress of white muslin with little white embroidered flowers, an all over pattern, I think, but I have only seen a little piece of it. It is still damp, but the earth over it is dry. There had been no rain for a long time."

"Madonna mia. She had such a dress. Maddalena, say that it is not true."

"True"—her voice cracked—"This man is mad. All the English are mad. She was a mad woman. Whatever happened was her fault. Why couldn't she leave the boy alone—"

Roger said: "Tell me where the girl is—Anne Gale—and I will forget what I have seen."

Maddalena stared at him for a moment. Then she said more quietly.

"You would make a bargain. But why should we trust you?"

"You would have to take my word. I am not a policeman. I have not undertaken to find Eve Shandon, or to avenge her murder. My job is to find the girl. You understand? I am not here to set the law in motion. Let me have her, alive and unharmed. That is all I ask."

"What makes you think that we can do that?"

Roger hesitated. So far he believed that he had made no mistake, but the absence of Mario was a serious disadvantage. He said: "Never mind that. I know more than you think. I could find her—in time—without you. But in that case, of course, I should feel bound to advise the police to dig in your garden."

She said: "I cannot decide anything to-night. You had better stay here. Mario will be returning to-morrow. You had better talk to him. See, it is past eleven. We are working people, and we are tired. If you will come upstairs I will show you a room where you can spend the night. Come."

She lit another lamp and led the way out of the kitchen and up the great staircase. Roger followed her. It was an odd ending to their interview, and he was puzzled by the abrupt change in her manner. She stopped at the door of the room he had occupied before.

"You can sleep here. There are sheets on the bed, matches and a candlestick on the night table. Felice notte."

She turned and left him. He stood staring after her. What did she mean to do? Would she and her husband dig up the body and try to hide it somewhere else? Somehow he thought not. Olivieri had either known nothing of the murder, or he was an extremely good actor. He was obviously devoted to his wife and very much under her thumb, but she might find him difficult to manage.

He lit the candle, but its tiny flame did little to disperse the shadows. Mechanically he removed his collar and tie. He needed sleep, for he had had a long and wearing day. It had been a part of his plan to approach Sant Andrina from a fresh angle, and that had meant leaving the train at the next station after Vallesca and a twelve mile tramp across rough country, with the thermometer at about eighty-five in the shade. And then, after night had fallen he had carried out his investigations.

He had broken into the summerhouse, and there he had found proof that when Eve Shandon left the Albergo del Castello she had taken nothing with her. There was a heap of clothing, dresses, underwear, shoes and hats, thrust into a corner behind some canvasses. A palette set with colours that had gone dry lay on the table beside an open paintbox, and the walls were covered with sketches.

The sinister implications of that close and airless room had been almost too much for Roger. He had been glad to get out of it.

And then, only a few minutes later, he had found the patch of freshly turned soil not fifty feet away from the old water tank. The earth was loose and dry, easy to move, and the body which he knew must be that of Eve Shandon was scarcely a foot below the surface. When he had made quite sure he had leaned against a tree for a while, feeling faint and sick.

He had the necessary knowledge, the problem was how to make the best use of it. He believed that Mario would be prepared to buy his silence by helping him to find Anne. That the young man should be absent from the hotel that night was a stroke of bad luck. He had expected to find him in the kitchen with his sister and brother-in-law. There had been nothing for it but to carry out his plan, but he had an uneasy feeling that, in the end, Maddalena had got the better of him.

And yet it was quite possible that she had spoken the truth, and that she knew no more than he did what had become of Anne. He still thought that Mario knew, but he might not have taken his sister into his confidence. The discussion would have to be resumed in the morning Or—was this all wrong? Should he do his obvious duty and go to the police?

It would mean a life sentence for Mario—there was no capital punishment in Italy.

There was water in the jug. He poured some into the basin and rinsed his face and hands. As he dried them on the towel he noticed how quiet the house was. All those rooms, empty and silent. He wondered if Olivieri and his wife had gone to bed, or if they were still sitting in their hot, lamp-lit kitchen, facing the ugly facts he had put before them, the man still horrified and bewildered, the woman defiant, intent only on saving her brother from the consequences of his crime.

And then, suddenly, he realised that he had forgotten what was to have been his safeguard. He had meant to tell them that he had written out his statement of what he believed to have happened to Eve Shandon and made arrangements to have it sent to the English consul in Rome if he did not reappear within an agreed time. That was his life insurance. Without it they might try to get rid of him as they had of Francis Gale. He would have to be very careful. He went over to the door and found that there was no key in the lock. He turned the knob and made a fresh discovery. He had been locked in. Had they thought that, on reflection, he would understand that he was in imminent danger, and try to get away?

He wedged the knob with the back of a chair and went over to the window. As he opened it and leaned out he fancied he could hear a murmur of voices in the room beneath. There was a glimmer of light, too, shed on the stones of the terrace. Evidently he was just over the kitchen. There was, of course, no chance of getting out that way. He did not fancy a thirty foot drop. In any case he believed that when morning came he would be able to make them see reason. He lay down on the bed, half dressed, and slipped almost at once into the deep and dreamless sleep of physical exhaustion.

He woke refreshed, but feeling both hungry and thirsty.

He had left the shutters partly open and a shaft of sunlight I pierced the shadows of the room and lay like a sword on the marble floor. He washed as thoroughly as he could without soap, used his pocket comb on his hair, and put in his collar and tie. He looked at his watch. It was twenty minutes past nine. He wondered if Maddalena would provide him with any breakfast, and if he could trust her not to poison his coffee. He tried the door and found that it was still locked.

He removed the chair and rattled the knob impatiently. They could not imagine that they would gain anything by keeping him a prisoner. Unless—he experienced a very unpleasant qualm as he remembered that he had taken a great deal of trouble to arrive at the hotel unseen. Not even Lily had known what he was about to do. He had, in fact, staged his own disappearance, and if it proved to be complete and permanent he would only have himself to blame. It was a relief to hear voices and footsteps in the passage. He stepped back a pace as he heard the key turning in the lock, and he kept his right hand on the handle of the automatic in his coat pocket. But when the door was thrown open he was almost too surprised to move. The corridor seemed to be full of people.

There were several men in some kind of uniform, two wearing the cocked hats with red and blue cockades of the carabinieri. One of them stepped forward and said, "In the name of the law. I arrest you for the murder of Eva Sandoni—the Englishwoman known as Eva Sandoni or Smith, who was supposed to have left Sant Andrina in your company on the 5th of August."

Roger swallowed hard. "But—this is absurd—I—"

"You can say what you wish to say to the Prefect. You will be able to engage a lawyer to look after your interests, but it is useless to deny the facts. The body has been found buried in the garden of this hotel. Basta—"

He was handcuffed. His arms were gripped on either side. He was being taken to the police station. He had passed it once when exploring the maze of winding streets in the old town. A dark and dingy building with windows heavily barred. He had hurried by because it stank.

CHAPTER XI
HALF TRUTHS

"YOU are accused of killing this woman by stabbing her, and attempting to conceal the body by burying it in the garden of the Albergo del Castello at Sant Andrina."

"It is ridiculous. I did not know her. I never saw her alive."

"We have the evidence of several witnesses that you were together at the hotel for five days at the beginning of August.

You had joined her there. She was alone before. You occupied adjoining rooms."

"No. Not Miss Shandon. There was another woman who arrived the day before I did. The bus driver can tell you that. I admit that we stayed at the hotel as husband and wife. She left when I did. Laccetti drove us to the station in his trap. We never saw Miss Shandon. I think her body was then in the water tank. She had probably been dead only a few hours. I thought I saw a body in the water. I spoke to Laccetti, and he made me believe that it was that of a dog."

"Not a very likely story. But if you can produce this other woman perhaps we can believe it."

"Ask the bus driver."

"We have examined a large number of witnesses. The bus driver is one of them. It is an undisputed fact that an English or possibly American woman came to the hotel the day before you. But she only stayed one night. Laccetti took her down to the station the following morning."

"She was there with me. There were several men dining at the hotel every evening. They must have seen her."

"They saw you dining on the terrace with a woman dressed in white. For some weeks before that they had seen the Signorina Sandoni dining there alone at the same table. It was dark on the terrace and the candles were shaded. They are not prepared to swear that your companion was the Signorina, but they assumed that it was. On the other hand the witnesses Mario Laccetti and Maddalena Olivieri fu Laccetti, who knew her well, maintain that this woman in white was Eva Sandoni and no other."

"But—Good Heavens! If I murdered her, as you suggest, how could I have got away with it? How was it they did not suspect that there was something wrong when she disappeared, and go to the police?"

"I must remind you that that is what they did, and that in consequence you are now under arrest."

"Yes. Weeks after. Why didn't they at the time?"

"You informed Laccetti that you would be driven to the station in his trap. He went down the hill to harness his horse.

You came alone and told him that the signora Smith had changed her mind and was going by the omnibus. You said that she would be returning in the autumn and that she was leaving her painting materials and some of her clothes in the summerhouse which she had been allowed to use as a studio. Laccetti agreed to that, and said he would see that nothing was disturbed. This evidence is borne out by the facts."

"Signore Pretore, I assure you that their story is a pack of lies. These are the very people by whom she was done to death. For God's sake—there must be some way of proving it—"

"It is very simple. You can have a lawyer to defend you. If there really is another woman in the case, and if she is the one who admittedly came to the hotel the day before you did you have only to produce her. If her story agrees with yours it will throw a different light on the whole affair."

The prisoner leaned forward, resting his hands on his knees. His collar was grimy and his hair dishevelled. Compared with the magnificent carabiniere in his blue and red uniform who stood on guard by the door of the pretore's office he looked dingy and insignificant. His eyes, very blue eyes, the pretore noticed, the eyes of a northerner, were red-rimmed with want of sleep.

He did not speak at once. He seemed to be thinking. At last he said dully, "I see. I can't produce her."

The pretore glanced at his cancelliere, who was writing busily. "Then I am afraid—" his voice was not unkind. In the Latin countries the crime of passion is always regarded with a certain amount of sympathy. He was thinking that with a good advocate the prisoner might get off with a fairly light sentence.

"Can't I prove my innocence without that?"

"Why did you come to Sant Andrina the second time?"

"I was trying to find Eve Shandon's daughter—"

"I thought you said you did not know the Signorina Sandoni?"

"I didn't. I knew her husband. He was killed in Rome a fortnight ago. He fell down the shaft of a lift."

"That is very curious. Was his name Sandoni?"

"No."

"This woman was not a donna per bene? She took lovers?"

"I have heard so."

"You were jealous. That is why you killed her."

"I did not kill her."

"Why did you come back to Sant Andrina the third time, secretly, on foot?"

"I suspected the people of the hotel of having committed a murder. I wanted to make sure."

"Luciano Olivieri saw a light some way down the garden and thought someone had come in to damage his vines. He went down and found you, and you told him that you were coming up by the short cut from the valley through the hotel grounds and had missed your way in the dark. He thought it strange and after you had been shown to your room he went down again with a lanthorn. He found several spent matches on a patch of ground that had been recently dug. He turned over the soil and found a body lying a few inches down. He informed the police early the next morning, and you were arrested."

"A part of that is true. The rest is lies. He did not see me down the garden. I found the place where she was buried and went on up to the house. Olivieri and his wife were in the kitchen. I told them what I knew and what I guessed about the whole black business. They denied everything, of course. Then—I was dead beat—they offered me a room—I was going to lock myself in. I thought I wasn't too safe—but I never dreamed they'd have the audacity to accuse me. Do you really suppose I would be mad enough to come back once I had got clear away if I really had murdered her?"

The pretore shook his head. "It was foolish. But it does happen. They are drawn back to the scene of the crime. Fascinated. The psychologists are agreed that it happens. And perhaps—Mario Laccetti has propounded a theory that you wanted to find and destroy a sketch she made of you which might identify you if ever the body was found. You broke into the summerhouse, and you may have taken it and burned it. That would account for the numerous spent matches. No tinder was found, but that would be blown away. You know best if this happened, and if this was your reason. It seems not unlikely."

"Very ingenious," agreed the prisoner. "Not a word of truth in it, though."

The pretore looked at him gravely. "Signor Smith, mere denials will not help you. You will be taken back to your cell. Writing materials will be supplied if you wish to get into touch with friends and relations. Further enquiries will be made before you are brought to trial. You need have no fear that justice will not be done here as it would be in your own country. I understand that your defence rests—depends—on the existence of another woman. If there is such a person and she has any affection for you she should come forward, even at the sacrifice of her reputation. There is no capital punishment in Italy, but a sentence of fifteen years' reclusione—solitary confinement—is, I have always thought, worse than death. I would advise you to give her the opportunity to save you—if there is such a person."

"I can't do that. It would be—No, I can't."

The pretore shrugged his shoulders.

"Think it over," he said. "I shall be seeing you again to-morrow."

Roger had heard that this was the Italian method. The prisoner was examined over and over again, taken through his story, faced with discrepancies, reminded of what he had said before, led on to contradict himself. The pretore was obviously an honest man, anxious to find out the truth, but it was only too clear that Roger had failed to convince him.

He was handicapped from the start by the fact that the Olivieris had gone to the police, and that he, admittedly, had not done so.

His version of the facts was involved, with gaps which he would not be able to fill in. He could not bring Nina into the affair, and without her—his heart sank as he faced the fact at last—he was not likely to be believed. Looking back on those five days to which, before he had lived through them, he had looked forward in a fever of delight, he saw how Nina's nervous fear that she might be seen and recognised played into the hands of his opponents. It was true that the men who came to the hotel for dinner could only have seen her indistinctly and from a distance, a white blur on the starlit terrace, and after the first day, when she had been alone, she had never gone beyond the hotel grounds. At first he had thought they must be all in league against him, but now he realised that need not be. Maddalena and her brother had been too clever for him. Their lies had been well thought out. They had only had to persuade Olivieri to support them, and apparently they had succeeded in that.

Whatever the consequences to himself he must keep Nina out of it. He owed her that. It was no question of high-flown chivalry, but of common decency. If her husband divorced her what had he—Roger—to offer? He had nothing but his salary as assistant manager on the plantation of the Copthorne syndicate; and they weren't even in love with each other.

It seemed to him that he had two alternatives. One was to put forward as his defence his search for Anne Gale, with all that had led up to it and that had happened since he undertook it after hearing of her father's death in Rome, only suppressing Nina's name and any detail concerning her that might by any chance lead to her identification.

The drawback to this course was that if his name was mentioned in any report of the case that might appear in the English papers, one of his fellow passengers on the *Meopham Castle* might connect it with Nina's. Their flirtation during the voyage home from Singapore had been harmless enough, and they had not taken much trouble to avoid notice. Another point was that Aunt Polly and Penny would have to suffer for his folly, being pointed out as the relations of the Englishman who was being tried for murder in an Italian court. They would be loyal, he knew. They would stick up for him. But it would be hard on them.

The second alternative was to allow the authorities to go on calling him Smith, and to refuse any information regarding himself. In that case, he supposed, the verdict would almost certainly be guilty. But there was one advantage. When he came out of prison, if he ever did come out, he could resume his own name and make a fresh start, and Penny would not have to feel that people, when they were introduced to her, were wondering where they had heard the name of Fordyce.

No capital punishment. That was one comfort. He felt glad that he was not in France. The idea of being guillotined sent a cold chill down his back in spite of the close heat of his cell. A quick death, but messy.

It was difficult to realise that all this was really happening to him. It was like a nightmare from which he must wake presently. His ankles were itching. He turned down his socks and several fleas sprang out. There was a dark greasy mark all round the walls where they had been polished by the shoulders of former prisoners, leaning against them when they grew weary of sitting on the hard planks of the bench that served at night as a bed. The window was high up, out of his reach, and heavily barred, but it gave him a glimpse of a sky intensely blue. He thought of grass, of trees. Why hadn't he grasped before how lovely the world was? He remembered, the spring before he left England for his job in the East, picking primroses with Penny in the hedgerows of a field beyond Shottery. The scent of primroses. In respect of stinks there was nothing to choose between the prison at Sant Andrina and the more important one at Vallesca where he supposed he would be kept until he was brought to trial. Unwashed clothes, human excrement, rank tobacco and frying oil. He began to worry over what might happen to Lily Oram. He had been offered writing materials. Perhaps he should get into touch with her. If he decided to carry on as Smith it was going to be difficult to explain matters to his aunt. If he simply disappeared she would institute enquiries. Then there was Anne. He had failed there, too.

He asked the man who brought his supper, a bowl of pasta and a glass of unexpectedly good red wine, for some paper. He still had his fountain pen in his pocket. His jailer was civil and friendly. Roger was to discover that to be accused of stabbing a woman did not put a man outside the pale. It might even be regarded as a social asset in some quarters. He said, "I want to write to a friend. Will my letter be read?"

The other grinned. "It may be. I'd be careful what I said if I were you. Can I get you anything?"

"Yes. A tablet of soap. I want to wash."

"One sees that the signore is English. Vede, signore, if you will give me your shirt my wife will wash it and you shall have it, well starched and ironed, in the morning. She is a lavaindaia. Any day you can see her down by the river, under the bridge, beating her linen on the stones. We both have to work to make ends meet. I am very badly paid." Roger took the hint and produced a lira. The jailer's eyes brightened, and he said his old mother would pray for the signore to the Madonna. He went off, carrying the shirt rolled up in a bundle, and came back presently with a packet of cheap stationery and a bottle of ink.

Roger had finished his supper. It was turning chilly in his cell now that the sun had set. He buttoned his coat over his bare chest before he settled down to write his letter to Lily.

Three days after the arrest, Don Vincenzo, instead of going back to his presbytery after saying mass, put on his shabby beaver hat and grasped his old cotton umbrella, which was green with age and splitting at every seam, and climbed into the omnibus which was just about to leave the piazza. Three hours later he had presented himself at the municipal offices in the town of Vallesca, and was asking to see the pretore.

Don Vincenzo seldom left his parish, and then only on business connected with the church. He was nervous, and his fine face twitched a little as he waited patiently until the pretore should choose to receive him. Government officials were sometimes anti-clerical, and he was not sure that he would be given a hearing. The pretore, however, was civil. He bowed, though he did not offer to shake hands, and he asked his visitor to be seated.

"What is your reason for coming here, Reverendo?"

"I am from Sant Andrina. Signor pretore, I have seen and spoken to the young Englishman who is accused of killing the signorina Sandoni. He was in my church one morning. I invited him to come into my presbytery. He drank a glass of wine with me. He talked to me frankly and openly, asking me various questions regarding her. It was plain to me that he had never met her. He told me he had come to Italy to find her daughter—she was the divorced wife of a friend of his. To me his story rang true.

Appearances may be against him, but I do not believe that he committed this crime."

The pretore rubbed his chin. "You find him simpatico? So do I. But that does not prove his innocence. He is at an age when almost any man who discovers that his woman has been unfaithful will draw a knife. We are men of the world, reverendo. We know it is so. The blood boils—e pam!"

"In this country perhaps," said Don Vincenzo, "but not in England. It is a question of climate."

"Ah, the fogs. One has heard of them," agreed the pretore.

"But in this case—" he shook his head. "We have the evidence of the people of the hotel, Laccetti and his sister and his brother-in-law. Why did he return the other night, secretly and after dark, to break into the summerhouse, if it was not to destroy something that would prove his guilt, and perhaps to move the body to a safer hiding place or to dig a deeper grave? She was lying only a few inches under the surface—"

Don Vincenzo shuddered. "Poor creature. May Heaven have mercy on her soul. But I am sure the Englishman did not commit this crime. You must look elsewhere, signor pretore."

"Where?"

"That is not for me to say. I have nothing to do with human justice. I have said what I came to say." He rose with unimpaired dignity and took his leave. The pretore, though actually inclined to anti-clericalism, was so far impressed that he went with him to the door and watched him trudge off down the street.

CHAPTER XII
THE STOLEN LETTER

THE sun had set in a blaze of glory behind Monte Mario, to the usual jangling of church bells, and Lily Oram, who had been teaching all day, hurrying from one house to the next, correcting exercises, giving dictation, trying to concentrate thoughts that were inclined to wander, was looking forward to sitting on the loggia of Nefert's flat in the cool of the evening, with her shoes off to rest her tired feet, soothed by the splash of water in the fountain and the ceaseless flow of Nefert's conversation. But the palmist's broad swarthy face was too expressive to be ignored. She seized Lily's hand and drew her in.

"Cara mia, cara mia—"

"What is it?"

"They entered my flat. This morning, while I was out marketing. I bought salad and anchovies and cheese for a salad, and half a yard of silk to match that flowered material I was showing you, and then, as I was near Sant Agostino, I went in to say a prayer to the Madonna. She has always been good to me, but she wasn't this time. They must have been here then. Not another candle does she get from me. I came back and found the door ajar. The lock had been forced. I have had a man to mend it since. And your room—well, see for yourself—"

Lily said nothing. She had turned very pale. She went into her room. The drawers had been pulled out and their contents thrown on to the floor, the cupboard door was open, the bed had been stripped. Her books were on the floor too. She stooped to pick them up, one by one. After a moment she looked up at Nefert who was standing in the doorway watching her.

"It has gone," she said.

"Money?"

"No. The letter. I was to take it or send it to the English consulate if I did not hear from him at the end of the week. I must have been followed here. I should not have come. It was not fair to you."

"You think it has something to do with that lift accident?"

"Yes. He had some plan. He hoped to bring it home to them. He would not tell me how. I suppose we have been seen together. They know I have tried to help him. I put the letter he gave me between the pages of this book—Browning's *Men and Women*. It's gone. And they have taken all the papers and letters I kept in my writing-case."

"Were they important?"

"Only to me. Letters from my father and mother, who died when I was a child, letters from parents of pupils recommending

me. Odds and ends that I have kept to remind me of old times. I
will find a room somewhere else to-morrow, Nefert. Forgive me—"

"Nonsense," said the palmist vigorously. "You will stay here.
They have got what they wanted, so we shall not be troubled again.
Via! I will help you put the room to rights and then we will have our
supper. And afterwards you shall tell me more about this affair."

"You would be wiser to let me go, Nefert."

"I shall not do that, cara."

"Very well."

And so, when the supper had been cleared away, and they were
sitting together in the dark on the loggia, where Nefert grew carnations and chives in old pots and pans and a small lemon tree in a
tub, Lily told her the whole story as she had heard it from Roger.

Nefert, usually so voluble, heard her out in silence. When she
had done, she said: "It is worse than I thought."

Lily's heart sank. She respected Nefert's judgment. Her clients
came from every class of society, and from their more or less
unconscious revelations she had learned a great deal. She was a
woman of little education, but she knew her world.

"You mean that he is not likely to find this child—Anne Gale?"

Nefert drew at her cigarette and expelled a cloud of smoke.

"This young man—he is very chivalrous—and very foolish. Ask
yourself what would happen to him if he walked into a factory and
tried to stop the work by sticking his finger into the machinery?
Flesh against steel, and not one piece of steel but a complicated
arrangement of wheels and cogs and pistons. Steel wins."

"I don't understand."

"Cara, it is evident that these people, the young fellow at the
hotel, the German padrona of the pensione in the Via della Croce,
are only parts of a much greater whole. If he gets in their way, if
he threatens them, other parts will come into action and eliminate him so that the machine can go on running smoothly. That
is why his plan, whatever it is, is bound to fail. When he comes
here again you must persuade him that his search for this girl is
useless, and that he should go back to England."

"I don't know," Lily said doubtfully. "He won't like letting go.
We don't as a nation—"

"So I have heard," said Nefert rather drily. "By not letting go you have gained an empire. But you must try. I like him. He is simpatico. I should be sorry if anything happened to him." Lily shivered. Nefert touched her bare arm. "You are cold? Let us go indoors. I bought a *Messagero* but I have not yet had time to look at it."

She lit the lamp and Lily fetched her work bag and a pair of stockings that needed darning. Nefert put on her spectacles and unfolded her paper. Lily sat frowning over her work and starting at every sound. Her nerves were on edge.

The older woman's comments had been far from reassuring. She was afraid, not so much for herself as for Roger. Nefert was probably right. He was over confident. In some ways, she thought, he was young for his age.

Their friendship had ripened very quickly under the stress of the events that had thrown them together, and she felt as if she had known him for years instead of for less than a week. They were both twenty-four. She had guessed from something he let slip that he believed that she was much older, probably in the late thirties. It was not flattering, but she tried to be philosophical about it. Hard work, and not enough to eat, and no time or energy left at the end of the day to take care of her appearance. All very well for women with very little else to do to spend ten minutes brushing their hair, and another ten rubbing skin food into their faces and wiping it off again. Besides, the plainer she looked the less likely she was to be worried by the embarrassing attentions of the fathers and brothers of her pupils. It was really lucky for her that Italians did not care for thin women. And yet, though she knew it was inconsistent, she could still be hurt by their audible criticism. "Brutta secca—"

She said: "They came here hoping to find out how much he really knew about them. I think the letter must have been a kind of statement for the consul to take to the police—"

Nefert interrupted her. "Aie! What was the name of that place up in the hills?"

"Sant Andrina."

"Listen to this. 'A foreign woman, believed to be English or American, stabbed to death, and body buried in the garden of an hotel at Sant Andrina. The woman, who had signed the hotel register in the name of Eva Sandoni, had been joined by a compatriot. The couple appeared to be on terms of the greatest intimacy. They left abruptly. The hotel staff did not witness the woman's departure but were informed by her companion that she had left by the omnibus that plies between the town and the nearest station, and that, as she would be coming back quite soon, she had left most of her luggage in a garden room which she had been allowed to use as a studio. Nothing has since been heard of her, but the man returned last week. He left after one night. Late on Tuesday evening the proprietor of the hotel, Olivieri Luciana, aged forty-two, saw lights in the garden, and fearing that thieves had come to strip his vines, went down to investigate. He found the Englishman, who told some confused story of having come up the hill by the short cut through the hotel grounds and missed his way in the darkness. He thought it prudent to accept this explanation and the unexpected visitor was given a room, but later Olivieri returned to the spot where he had met the other. He saw, by the light of a lanthorn, some freshly turned soil strewn with spent matches, and a garden spade, the property of the hotel, which was kept with other implements at the foot of the terrace, lying near. Olivieri, horrified by the sinister implications of these discoveries, lost no time in informing the local authorities. A body which was identified as that of Eva Sandoni was found in the place indicated, and so near the surface that it is to be assumed that the murderer had taken the appalling risk of revisiting the scene of his crime to dig a deeper grave. The suspect, who gave the name of Richard Smith, and refused his age or any other particulars and had no papers on him that would assist in his identification, was arrested, and removed, after a preliminary examination, to the prison of Vallesca, where he will be detained pending further enquiries.'"

"Oh, dear—" said Lily distractedly.

"What did I tell you? This Smith—"

"It must be Roger. Of course it is all lies."

"Sicuro. But they have been clever. There is some truth in it. He called himself Smith? Why? You did not tell me that."

"He stayed there on his way home from the Malay States with a woman whom he had met, I think, on the boat. I gathered that he had been desperately in love with her, but that it was very soon over. But she is married, and her husband has an important position. This is confidential, Nefert. He only told me because I had to understand why it was so difficult for him. I am trusting you—"

"Love," said the little palmist with a gusty sigh. "At my age one has corns and indigestion and worries about paying the rent. The young ones have love. The line of the heart—"

Lily was not listening. She said. "Eva Sandoni is the newspaper version of Eve Shandon. That's Anne's mother. When Anne came to the hotel and then her father, they had to be stopped. There's the motive. What can we do, Nefert?"

"For the moment, nothing. Your hands are tied. If you come forward, if you go to the consul, the first thing to come out will be that the prisoner's real name is not Smith but Fordyce. That will lead to more questioning. His family would be involved. Come, cara," she patted the girl's thin shoulder, "we shall not help him by sitting up all night. Coraggio."

Lily rose obediently. She knew that Nefert was right. Nevertheless she lay awake for a long time, worrying. The letter. What would she do if he sent her a message asking her to deliver it? She had thought it would be safe between the pages of her Browning. She should have carried it about with her as she did her money, in a linen pocket pinned to her stays. It was past three when she fell asleep.

When she woke it was broad daylight, and Nefert, in her white cotton wrapper and with her greasy black hair in curl papers, was standing by her bed.

"There is a letter for you just come. The postmark is Vallesca. Read it while I make the coffee."

She came back presently with two cups on a tray. "I haven't much time. I expect a client at ten. What does he say?"

"He says that I am not to make any use of the letter he left with me. I am to tell his aunt not to worry, and that owing to unexpected complications he may remain abroad for some considerable time. Tell her, he says, to leave things alone, so far as he is concerned. Nothing to be gained by making a stink. He signs himself Richard Smith."

Nefert looked at her quickly and looked away again. "Drink your coffee," she said. "It's hot and sweet."

Lily blew her nose, and replied with determined cheerfulness that she was getting up at once. She had a pupil in the Via Sistina and she would have to run if she was not to be late.

"And after that?"

"Carmela Marucci at eleven."

"Any relation of Commendatore Marucci?"

"His daughter. What do you know about him? Carmela lives with her grandmother. The Commendatore is nearly always in Naples. I have never seen him."

"He is one of my clients," Nefert said. "That is, he has been to me two or three times. He is a rich man. He has some interest in a shipping line. He wanted to know if a name he had chosen for a ship was lucky. I looked in the crystal for him, but the clouds did not disperse."

"What do you do then?"

"I do my best. I can't afford to disappoint a client. I say something about proceeding with caution and looking both ways—"

Lily swallowed some coffee and hooked up her blouse. "Carmela is a sweet little girl," she said, "not clever, but she tries hard." Most of Lily's pupils were boys and girls of lower middle class families who needed a smattering of English to help them to get jobs as hotel servants or shop assistants. She had lived down her initial disaster, but it had not been forgotten, and the doors of the great Roman families were closed to her. But the Marucci came from the South and did not belong to the magic inner circle of the old nobility. Marucci's father had made money in building speculations. Nothing was known of his origin. He had married the daughter of an impoverished member of the Calabrian aristocracy who was always known as the contessa though her husband had no title. She had been a widow for some years, and when her son's wife had died she had undertaken the upbringing of his little daughter. The Commendatore had built a villa for her in the new Prati di Castello quarter of Rome, on the banks of the Tiber, across the Ponte Margherita. It was dazzlingly white, and decorated with cupolas and balustrades so that it looked like an expensive wedding cake and it was handsomely furnished and had all the modern fittings, electric light, and a bathroom with a shower, but not a telephone, because the contessa disliked them, and, in any case, there were very few at that time in private houses.

It was cool and pleasant when the awnings were out and the electric fans working, and Lily found the Marucci ménage, consisting of the old lady and her granddaughter, and a staff of well-trained servants, a restful change from the stuffy over-crowded flats smelling of frying oil and cheap scent, where the unmarried aunts and elder sisters and cousins of her pupils were always lounging about, half dressed, interrupting the lesson with their gossip or their disputes.

The contessa was tall and thin and very upright, with a ravaged face that had once been beautiful. She always dressed in black and wore a scarf of fine black lace over her silvery white hair. Twice a week she drove in a hired victoria through the Borghese Park and the Pincian Gardens, with Carmela sitting beside her in a frilly silk frock and a hat wreathed with daisies. Carmela was sent to hear mass with one of the maids, but her grandmother never went out on foot. She suffered from some form of rheumatism, and walked slowly about the house, leaning on an ebony stick with a gold handle made like a hand with fingers extended to avert the evil eye. Being a Calabrian from the far South she still believed in sorcery. She did not think it necessary that girls should be educated. It only made them restless and put ideas in their heads. But the Commendatore had given his orders, and visiting mistresses were duly engaged for Carmela.

Lily was always a little afraid of the contessa. She came into the room sometimes while the lesson was in progress, to ask if Carmela was doing well, and she would look searchingly at the child, and at the teacher as if she was seeing her through the wrong end of a telescope. But though she was frigid she was always very polite.

Carmela was a pale and rather sickly little girl, with a soft voice and a timid manner. She had been shy with Lily at first, hut had soon become attached to her, more fond indeed, than her grandmother realised, for she was always very quiet when the old lady was present. She had everything that money could buy, but no companions of her own age. Lily often felt sorry for her. This morning she was excited and her attention wandered.

"You are to be asked to stay to lunch to-day," she told Lily.

"That is very good of the Signora Contessa," said Lily. The food would be good, and she would not be expected to pay for what she ate by talking English to her hostess.

"Il Babbo is here, and he wants to meet you."

"That is very kind," said Lily, and now she wished she could make some excuse to get away. She had a nervous dread of encountering any of the male relatives of her pupils derived from her unhappy early experience. Outwardly of course, she knew how to behave. She listened respectfully, answered in monosyllables, and only smiled when civility required it. When they were pompous she was bored and irritated, when they meant to be kind she was afraid they might become familiar. She could be natural and even charming with every other member of the family, but not quite with uncles and brothers, and not at all with fathers. Fortunately nobody noticed or understood what she felt and she hoped herself that she might in time overcome what she regarded as an annoying weakness.

Carmela went on chattering gaily about her father. He had brought her a necklace and a brooch of pale pink coral.

"You have a great many presents, Carmela."

The little girl nodded, smiling and fingering her necklace. When they went into the cool darkened dining-room for lunch the old contessa was there, sitting at the head of the table, with her son facing her at the foot.

"Here is the English Miss, Rinaldo. Miss Oram, Signor Commendatore." Marucci rose and bowed. He spoke unexpectedly, in English, with a strong American accent. "Pleased to meet you, Miss Oram." He was tall, like his mother, but, unlike her, inclined to corpulence. His face was handsome, but spoiled and jaded. He looked as if he had had too much of everything but sleep. Carmela ran to him, and he stooped to kiss her. It was evident that he idolised his little girl. Throughout the meal he encouraged her to talk and gave her his whole attention, putting out a big dark beringed hand now and then to touch the little bunch of soft fair curls tied with black ribbon at the nape of her slender neck. It was like a bear trying to play with a white butterfly, thought Lily. No, not a bear, a panther. Large as he was there was nothing clumsy about the Commendatore Marucci. He moved, as so many southerners do, with an animal swiftness and grace. The contessa observed them both indulgently.

After coffee had been served the Commendatore looked at his watch. "It is time for you to rest, tesoro mio, and for you too, mamma mia. I shall be taking you both for a drive later, perhaps. I would like a word with you, Miss Oram, before you go."

He frowned as Carmela went to give Lily a hug, before she left the room with her grandmother, but he said nothing more.

Lily, who had risen from her chair, waited while he lit a cigar.

"I will not keep you long," he said. "I just wanted to ask if you were satisfied with her progress?"

"Yes. She works hard."

"Good. I noticed just now that she was inclined to cling to you. She has an affectionate disposition. But children soon forget."

He had his mother's knack of making the person he was speaking to feel very small and far away.

Lily realised that, for some reason, he did not like her. But he went on very smoothly. "You will not find it too hot crossing the Ponte Margherita at this hour? There is no shade."

"I am used to it."

Rather to her surprise he held out his hand. She was obliged to take it. He gripped her fingers so hard that she cried out.

"I beg your pardon," he said. "I do not always remember my own strength."

"Something pricked me."

"Surely not. I see—forgive me—there is a drop of blood. It must have been the setting of my ring. I noticed the other day that the edge was sharp. I will have it attended to. Does it hurt?"

"Not at all. It is nothing."

"I am very sorry."

"It is nothing," she repeated.

He rang the bell. The manservant was waiting in the hall to show her out.

Marucci went upstairs to his own room. There had just been time for him to open his wall safe and close it again when he came out, Carmela was standing at the landing window. She called to him excitedly. "Babbo, I think there has been an accident on the bridge. There is quite a crowd, and it looks as if somebody was being lifted into a cab. Now the cab is driving away. The vetturino is whipping his horse as if he was in a hurry."

"If it was an accident," said her father, "he may be taking someone to the hospital."

He smiled as he drew her to him. She took his hand and rubbed it against her cheek, crooning to it. "Babbo mio, babbo mio—"

"My little bird," he said.

"Where is that ring you wore at lunch? I wanted to ask you—I have never seen it before and now you have taken it off."

"It does not fit me. I shall take it back to the jeweller and change it."

"Do you like the signorina Inglese? She is carina, n'e vero?"

"You will not be seeing her again for a while," he said. "It is too hot in Rome at this season and you need the sea air. I have taken a villa at Sorrento."

"For all of us?"

"For you and your grandmother and the servants."

"When shall we go?"

"To-night."

Chapter XIII
A CASE FOR ELIMINATION

THE new bridge, named after the dowager queen, the widow of the murdered Umberto, was still so white that it dazzled the eyes. Lily, holding on her hat as a puff of wind, hot as the breath from an oven, blew grit and dirty scraps of paper towards her, thought the Tiber, flowing under the arches, looked as yellow and viscid as oil. She looked across the river towards the Pincian Hill and the obelisk in the Piazza del Popolo which had once been a place of execution.

She was half-way across when she felt obliged to stop and lean against the balustrade. She felt very queer. Her heart was thumping and there was a mist before her eyes. Behind the mist the figures of people going to and fro on the bridge, of an old man pushing a handcart, and of a little Roman cab drawn by an emaciated horse, expanded and contracted in the most extraordinary way, shrinking to the size of pin points and swelling up again like balloons filling with gas.

Voices rose and fell in the same way, so that a complete and terrifying silence was succeeded by a deafening clamour in which only a few words could be distinguished.

"Poverina—It is the heat. It is the sun."

It seemed that someone had been taken ill and was lying on the dusty pavement, the centre of a circle of sympathetic but not very helpful strangers.

Lily had an instant of complete clarity, during which she knew that she was being lifted into the cab which had drawn up by the kerb. Then the mist formed again, and the pendulum swung from silence into a cataract of sound and back again, and, when she opened her eyes, everything within her field of vision shrank and expanded so that she felt sick and dizzy.

"Perhaps," she thought, "if I keep quite still, if I hide in the dark." She kept her eyes shut and relaxed her muscles, and felt herself sinking through miles of space.

She tried, feebly, to push away a hand that fumbled at her dress over her heart. Someone laughed so loudly that she thought her ear drums would crack. The sound ceased abruptly. She forced her eyelids up—they were strangely heavy—and saw a vast face bending over her. The face disintegrated in a red fog, leaving only two lambent eyes.

A voice said: "What is the effect of the drug?"

Another voice which she knew she had heard recently answered. "It is very uncertain. That is why it is seldom or never used by the medical profession. They don't care to take risks. It induces a kind of temporary paralysis which, in a case like this one, is more convenient and looks better than any form of restraint. Can you keep her here for the time being?"

"I have only this surgery and the room at the back where I sleep and have my meals. Patients may come. If the effect of the drug passed off while there was somebody here it might be awkward."

"That is not very likely. I will give her another injection before I go."

"Can't she be taken upstairs as they always are until it is time to take them away?"

One voice was tremulous, husky, and uncertain, the other deliberate and confident to the point of arrogance. It was the latter speaker who had laughed, and who now laughed again contemptuously.

"You don't imagine this one is for export. Look at her arms, look at her neck. Skin and bone."

"Then why—"

"She knows too much."

The husky voice grew sharp with fear. "I don't do anything outside the routine. This surgery is a junction, not a terminus."

"An epigram. Excellent, signor dottore. But the circumstances are exceptional. An unfortunate chance has put this woman in possession of information which might be dangerous to us. I do not say she could do very much, but she might oblige us to divert the passage of the goods into other channels and that would mean loss of time and money to all concerned. We had been waiting, as you know, to take the top floor flat over your surgery. You and the Frau between you can do all that is necessary to prepare the travellers for their voyage."

"It is a damnable traffic," muttered the doctor.

"Caro amico, it is too late to develop scruples of conscience. Take her into your back room and lock the door between. Perhaps she can be carried upstairs after dark."

*

Frau Haussman was sitting on the flat roof where, in the shade of a chimney stack, she and Siegfried had made a little garden of herbs in old pots and boxes. It was pleasant there, high above the traffic in the streets, and there was room to hang out the washing to dry in the sun and the wind.

Siegfried was playing his violin. His mother sat listening, her gross heavy body at rest, her broad red face beaming with satisfaction.

"Ach, schön—" she murmured. "Ach, schön—"

The front door bell rang in the flat below, two rings, and another after an interval. The music stopped. The young man looked at his mother uneasily. "Someone for you again?"

She nodded without meeting his eyes. "Yes, meine Liebe. Business. You stay here. I will go down."

She showed the visitor into her dining-room, a bare spare room, scrubbed and polished to satisfy a northern conception of cleanliness. He sat down, unasked.

"She was kept in view? Have you had a report?"

"Yes. Beppino saw her leave the Piazza Barberini. She went to a house in the Via Sistina and stayed an hour and a half."

"So long? She has a pupil there, but the lesson lasts an hour."

"Beppino thinks she was kept waiting, that the pupil had not come back from hearing mass. He had been watching the house nearly half an hour when a young girl went in with an older woman. He heard one of them say that they were late."

"Good. What happened then?"

"She walked slowly through the Pincian Gardens and sat for ten minutes on a bench."

"Waiting until it was time to give her next lesson. Very satisfactory. And what then?"

"She went down the hill, crossed the Piazza del Popolo, and went over the bridge. He saw her enter a certain house. He had been told that he need do no more beyond reporting to me."

"Precisely." Marucci was smiling. The Frau, looking at his clean-shaven jowl, was reminded of the bloom on a black plum. His smile faded. "It is strange. I expected her to take some action. She must have seen the account of the Sant Andrina affair in yesterday's papers. I thought she might go to the consulate. Beppino was to prevent that at all costs. Whatever she knows must go no farther."

Frau Haussman's florid colour had changed and gone patchy. "You will not bring her here," she said.

"She is below, in the room behind the surgery. The doctor says he cannot keep her, and it is evident that there is more room for her here. We have to consider what is to be done," he said harshly. "That fool Laccetti has landed us all in a fine mess. His sister had the Englishman arrested. A clever move, but a desperate one. A breath-taking audacity. I don't like it. We have had nothing to do with the law before. As it is Laccetti will have to give evidence at the trial. Who knows what he may not let slip when he is examined and cross-examined. We have the letter the Englishman left with the Oram woman. He seems to have guessed pretty well what happened at Sant Andrina, but he knows nothing about the Rome end, our end. When we have finished with her we can feel fairly safe."

Frau Haussman moistened her lips. "She posted a letter."

"What?"

"I said that she posted a letter. In the Piazza del Popolo. Beppino could not have stopped her. He was not near enough."

Marucci glared at her. "Why didn't you say so before?"

"I was going to tell you. Perhaps it has no importance," said the Frau submissively.

"We shall have to find that out. But for that we must wait. She has been drugged, and she will not be able to talk until to-morrow or the next day. The doctor will bring her up here after dark."

"There is a boat sailing at the end of next week. Will she go by that?"

"She would be useless. It seems a waste of money to pay the freight charges just to get rid of her." He sat for a moment frowning and gnawing his lip. "Have you a bath?"

Frau Haussman answered hurriedly. "No. No, please. We wash in basins. We have nothing like that."

He was looking at her as if had not heard. "Why travel half round the world to the harbour at Rio when we have a river here? I will buy you a bath, a portable affair. You can put it in one of the empty rooms. Your boarders will be glad of it, and you can charge them extra."

"Mein Herr, mein Herr," she said imploringly. "I cannot because of my son. In August there are no classes and he is always here. I know that even now he is not easy in his mind. When he asks questions I put him off as best I can, but it is difficult. It would be impossible if his head were not so full of music that there is no room for anything else."

"It is your own fault if you have brought him up to be finicking," Marucci said impatiently. "It is for his sake that you engaged in the business, wasn't it? So that he might grow stronger in a warmer climate than that of Hamburg and have a musical education. Does he really believe that you earn enough to keep the pair of you out of your pension? Do you ever have any boarders that are not sent to you by the organisation?"

"Sometimes." She sighed deeply. "I don't want him to know."

"Well, you have a day or two to think it over. She must be allowed to recover from the effects of the drug, and persuaded to talk. It is a pity about your son. He is a good-looking young fellow, and he might be useful to us if he was sensible. We pay our agents well as you know."

Frau Haussman shook her head. "I have served you, and I will go on serving you. I need the money. He hardly coughs at all now. But if he found out how I have earned it he would kill me."

"Romantic notions, eh?"

The German woman was wounded by his unconcealed contempt for her boy. She said: "Had you no illusions, mein Herr, when you were his age?"

"What age is he? Nineteen? At nineteen I was working, in Chicago. Mine wasn't a sheltered youth." He looked at his watch. "I must be going. Don't worry. I will arrange everything. You have nothing to fear if you do your part. The doctor will bring her up to you during the night. She is ill, but not ill enough to be sent to an expensive nursing home. You are taking her as a favour, out

of kindness. Tell your son that. You don't want to be sent back
to Hamburg, do you, with the winter coming on? Those icy fogs
drifting in from the North Sea, eh?"

"No, mein Herr," she said humbly. "I will do my best."

"I will see that you get a bonus when it is all cleared up. These
English are a pest. Always poking their noses where they are not
wanted. Why, even in Naples there is some ridiculous society
financed chiefly by them that tries to prevent a man from beating
his own horse. And their—merchandise—is difficult to handle.
Their stuff fetches a good price, and so one is tempted—but you
see what it has led to in this case. This young man, Smith or whatever his name is—why, he isn't even related to the girl. He has
nothing to gain. Yet he comes here, busying himself. How is one
to deal with such people? They're without sense, when you offer
to buy they will not sell, they are hard when you expect them to
be soft, and soft when you think they will be hard, and somehow
by accident, they have acquired an empire."

"It will fall to pieces at the first blow," said the German woman
comfortably. She relished this sort of talk. It helped her to forget
what she had promised to do. She waddled back quite cheerfully
to the roof where Siegfried sat on an old packing-case looking
across the other roofs towards the dome of St. Peter's where it
seemed to float, light as a bubble, on the horizon.

She said: "One of the doctor's patients. She can't afford a nurs-
ing-home. I have agreed to take her in for a few days. And we were
going to-night to *Aida* at the Nazionale. You must go alone, meine
Liebe. I must be here to receive her." He said, without turning
his head to look at her. "Young and pretty?"

"Not in the least."

"You have seen her then?"

"No. But he told me she was middle-aged, and suffering, I
gathered, from some wasting disease. You must keep away from
her, Siegfried. There may be some danger of infection."

"Was it the doctor you were talking to down there? I heard
your voices going on and on."

"No. A relative of the patient."

He moved away from her and picked up his violin. Frau Haussman relaxed and sat down with her basket of mending in the lengthening shadow cast by the chimney stack. Her broad face assumed an expression of bliss that verged on imbecility as Siegfried began to play Schubert's "Serenade". She thought. "Ach, schön. Ach, schön. My child is a genius. Nothing else matters."

CHAPTER XIV
DEATH IN THE CRYSTAL

IT WAS characteristic of Miss Fordyce that she chose one out of the row of yelling blue-bloused facchini waiting on the platform before the train stopped, and that presently that facchino and no other was carrying her small valise out of the station. The choice of a vettura followed. Miss Fordyce picked out a vetturino who looked good-natured, and whose horse seemed to be well cared for, and she kept both men waiting while she examined the animal under the collar for hidden sores. Satisfied, she gave the facchino an adequate tip, and told the cabman to drive to a small hotel in the Via Sistina. When she reached the hotel she paid off the cabman and walked in, carrying her bag.

The porter came forward. "Madam is expected?"

"No. Can I see the manager?"

She looked about her, recalling the past. When the manager arrived she asked for room number fourteen.

"Certainly, madam. As it happens to be disengaged at the moment. The season has hardly begun. May I ask why—"

"I stayed here with my mother thirty years ago, and we shared that room. I am glad to see that everything looks much the same."

"We have installed a lift and electric light."

"I shall use the stairs," said Miss Fordyce firmly.

The manager rang for a chambermaid. "Show madam room fourteen."

He looked after her with a half smile.

"It is a type," ventured the porter. "The British spinster."

The manager nodded. "Yes. There are sub-divisions. The help-less, and the efficient. This one, I think, is efficient. Who would think to look at her that she had spent two nights in the train? Not a hair out of place."

Miss Fordyce's Italian was rusty from disuse but adequate. She established friendly relations with the chambermaid. "When is lunch served? From twelve onward? I will be down in ten minutes." She unpacked her bag, changed her blouse, and refreshed herself with cold water. Though she contrived to survive a long train jour-ney and a Channel crossing without looking noticeably dirty or crumpled, she was tired, and she would have liked to lie down on her bed for an hour or two after lunch; but she had to see the writer of the letter that had brought her to Rome as soon as possible.

She had the letter with her, and she had re-read it several times while she sat in her corner of the second-class compartment of the Paris-Rome express. It was a hurried pencilled scrawl covering several pages that had evidently been torn from an exercise book.

DEAR MISS FORDYCE,

Your nephew may have mentioned me when he wrote. I am Lily Oram, and I live here and earn my living by giving English lessons. I was in the flat below when his friend, Mr. Gale, fell down the lift shaft, and that's how we met when he came to make enquiries. I don't know how much he has told you, and that makes it difficult. There's not time to explain everything, even if I could make it clear in a letter. I'm writing this while I wait for my pupil. The sooner it is posted the better. He told me he had come over to look for Mr. Gale's young daughter Anne, who had disappeared. I wanted to help, because I was young and silly once and there wasn't anybody to give me a hand when I most needed it. Never mind that. The point is that we were up against more than we realised. I'm sorry I haven't the time to break the bad news gently. They have arrested your nephew on a charge of murdering Mr. Gale's divorced wife—Anne's mother—her body was found buried in the hotel garden where she had been staying. He was arrested under the name of Smith, which he used when he went there the first time. He does not want you to intervene, or do anything, that would connect him with you. I had better tell you what he told me. I hope it won't be a great shock to you. He spent a few days at this hotel at a place called Sant Andrina, with a married woman. He didn't say, but I think she is English and that he met her on the boat coming home. He will want to keep her out of this at any cost, and I'm afraid that is going to make his defence difficult. We have not found Anne, and I'm afraid we never shall now. He showed me her photograph. Such a lovely little face. I can't bear to think what may have happened. We have really found out very little, but we think a German woman who keeps a pension, 822, Via della Croce, may be mixed up in it. She had the top flat over me in the house where Mr. Gale met with what looked like an accident, but she has moved since. At least, she had moved before, and the flat was empty, but I'm sure she still had the keys as her lease was not up. Please write to me, if you answer this, presso Signora Nefert, 99 B. Piazza Barberini. I am staying with her at present, but I may have to move again. I hope you can read this, and that you will understand. I have to stop now.

Yours sincerely,

LILY ORAM.

On receiving this letter Miss Fordyce had packed her bag and caught the next train to London, leaving her devoted assistant, Miss Briggs, and Penny to carry on the business in her absence. Obviously if Roger was in a mess she would have to get him out of it. She was not exactly surprised to learn of his sentimental entanglement. She had suspected something of the kind. His reason for leaving the boat at Naples and lingering on his way home overland had never been made clear. He would have to safeguard the woman's reputation, naturally. The question of whether she was worth the sacrifices he might have to make on her account did not arise. "He made his bed," thought Roger's Aunt Polly grimly, "and he'll have to lie on it. But if I had known I would never have let him come back to Italy."

She had half a bottle of Chianti with her lunch, and a cup of coffee afterwards. So far, she thought, she had been lucky. The hotel was just as she remembered it, still under Swiss management, unpretentious, but clean and comfortable. Thirty years is a long time, but she thought she could still find her way about Rome. She stood for a moment on the sunbaked pavement outside the hotel, adjusting her smoked glasses, a small, neat, grey figure, obviously a tourist, though she was not carrying a Baedeker, and turned to the left. The Piazza Barberini was not far away.

Rome had not changed. The same deep umber shadows under the eaves, the same golden light, the same intensely blue sky, the sound of running water in every courtyard; and scraps of broken carving, satyr heads, and acanthus leaves, and capitols of vanished columns, built into modern walls.

She ignored a small boy who trotted beside her begging for soldi.

She remembered the piazza on the slope of the hill, with its central fountain, and the Barberini palace, with the famous bees and the papal tiara on the escutcheon, at one corner. All the English went there to look at Guido Reni's picture of Beatrice Cenci on her way to execution.

The small boy tugged at her sleeve and pointed excitedly across the square to where a small crowd had collected before the door of one of the houses. "Dicano che hanno ammazzatto una donna—" "They say a woman has been killed—"

Miss Fordyce said sharply, "Run across and find out the number of the house, and I will give you two soldi."

Her Italian would have shocked a purist but it was sufficiently intelligible. The boy darted off and came back almost at once.

"The number is ninety-nine. They are waiting for the hearse to take her to the mortuary. What is the matter, signora? Sta male?"

"No, I'm not ill," she said faintly. She looked down at the eager little brown face. "Here are your soldi. You can do something more for me. Go over there and listen to what is being said. Find out what happened, and I will give you a lire. I will wait here in the shade."

"Sta sicura. Faccio io," he said importantly and ran off again. Miss Fordyce stood unnoticed on the other side of the square and saw him edging his way through the crowd. She could see two men in the uniforms of the municipal police standing in the doorway. This time the boy was longer away. Her heart sank while she waited for him. She thought, "Too late. What shall I do now?"

He came back at last.

"It is a woman who told fortunes by reading hands," he said. "A sort of witch, but the neighbours all liked her and said she did no harm. She was found lying on the floor in her sitting-room with the table overturned. They think it was one of her clients, that she was bending over—so—looking at his hands, and that the hands went up—so—as quick as a whip lash, and gripped her throat. It was for money. Her purse was there beside her, open and empty."

Miss Fordyce shuddered. The boy had enacted the scene with all the unconscious dramatic force natural to his race. She could almost hear the flat voice of the palmist. "You have a strong will. You could be ruthless. I see indications of a change of fortune. A profitable transaction—" breaking off with a stifled cry for the help that would not come. She could almost see the wretched woman's last client, his work done, backing away to the door.

She said, "Have they any idea who did it?"

He shook his head. "The pretore came. I heard them say that he questioned many people. But the flat above is empty, and she had many clients. No one noticed."

"Did she live alone?"

"They said there was a woman staying with her, a foreigner, but she has not been seen for some days. Perhaps it was her," he hazarded.

Miss Fordyce took a lire from her purse. In those days a lira was worth tenpence in English money. She dropped it in his small and grubby palm. "You are a very intelligent boy."

She was touched to see that he glowed with pride at her commendation. He said, "The signora is too good. Is there anything more I can do?"

"Nothing more, thank you. What is your name?"

"Amleto."

Shaken as she was she contrived to smile at him.

She walked on to the nearest cab rank, where she picked out a vettura. She gave the driver the address of the English consulate. "And if you beat your horse or use a goad I shall know how to deal with you."

The driver grinned.

At the consulate Miss Fordyce was shown into a small room furnished as an office where a young man sitting at a desk rose at her entrance.

"Sit here, won't you? What can I do for you? I say—aren't you well? Can I get you anything?" he asked anxiously. "Brandy? A glass of water?"

"I should like a drink of water," she said. "I'm sorry to be troublesome—"

"It's fearfully hot. Hardly the time to come to Rome—"

"It isn't that. I've had a shock." She sipped the water he had brought her and looked over the edge of the glass at his pleasant boyish face. "Are you the consul?"

"Well, actually I'm the acting vice consul. A sort of understudy of the understudy." He smiled disarmingly. "You see, in August, there isn't much doing. The British colony is dispersed. Gone home, or to the mountains or the sea. The consul is on holiday, and the vice is ill, unfortunately. But I expect I can do anything you want done."

"I wonder," she said. "You are English?"

"Well, actually," he said again, "I'm a Scot. Ronald Guthrie, at your service."

"Do you know the country and the people well?"

He looked rather surprised, but he answered as amiably as ever. "That's rather a large order, but—well, I've stayed here quite a lot. My sister, who is older than I am, married a Roman a few years ago. Mixed marriages aren't always a success, but hers is. My brother-in-law is no end of a good chap, one of the best. May I ask why—"

She said, "I think my nephew called here about a fortnight ago. No, less than that. Ten days. It was about the death of an Englishman who fell down a lift shaft."

"I remember the case," said Guthrie, "and I remember hearing that someone had called to ask if we had any knowledge of his daughter who might, or should have been with him at the time.

We had no knowledge of a daughter. I did not see your nephew, Miss—"

"Fordyce."

"One of our clerks saw him and took down some notes. He has not been here again."

"It is difficult," she said, "because for some reason, which may be a good one, my nephew does not want to apply to the police. And yet this girl—she is little more than a child—has disappeared, and we have to find her."

"I think your nephew said there was no relationship," said Guthrie. His manner had cooled slightly. Miss Fordyce noticed it.

"Don't get it into your head that we're criminals trying to get hold of her," she said. "We are perfectly respectable. We're not related to poor Francis Gale and we didn't even know him very well, but his child was at school with my niece, and we happen to know that she's very alone in the world, so we've taken over. I hope that's clear?"

"Quite," he said. He laughed, and after a moment she laughed too.

She said, "You are quite right to take nothing for granted. I can give you plenty of references, and I will. I really need help and advice very badly."

"Your nephew—"

"My nephew is not with me. For the moment he is out of the picture," she said, carefully. "He made a friend while he was in Rome of an Englishwoman who lives here, a teacher of languages. She was living in the block of flats where Francis Gale met his end. She has since moved. I had a letter from her the other day. That is why I am here. I came at once. I lunched at the hotel where I have taken a room and went afterwards to call on her. There was a crowd outside the house. I learned that the tenant of the only flat that was occupied had been murdered. Strangled. A woman who was staying with her, a foreigner, has not been seen for some days. I took a cab and came here."

"Good Lord!" exclaimed Guthrie. "Do you mean that it has only just happened?"

"I don't know when it happened. The body had just been found. She was a palmist. They seem to think the murderer was having his hands read—"

"Did she live in the Piazza Barberini, opposite the Trittone fountain? That was Nefert. Lots of people went to her. My sister did. She said she was quite good. A little fat woman reeking of garlic, but she told my sister several things. Lucky shots, I daresay. She was supposed to be partly Egyptian. Strangled, did you say? How horrible."

Miss Fordyce glanced at the young man's shocked face. She said: "The question seems to be, what has become of Miss Oram?"

"Is that the woman who wrote to you?"

"Yes. I rather gathered from her letter that she believed herself to be in some danger."

"May I see the letter?"

Miss Fordyce sighed. "I am afraid not. Some of it is private."

"I don't see how we can be of much use to you if you can't take us into your confidence."

"I know," she said, "but there it is. I can't. It isn't the Anne angle, it's this scrape my nephew has got into. It is worse than that. He seems to have fallen into a well-laid trap. I don't know the details, but I am afraid it is serious. The point we have to remember is that he is extremely anxious not to involve another person, and that if we interfere we might bring about that result." She stopped for a moment to steady her voice, which had faltered for the first time. "That is why, though he means so much to me, I have to leave him out of this. He came to Italy to find Anne Gale. He can't carry on, and I have come to take his place."

Guthrie said, "Had he traced her at all?"

"Yes. She arrived at the Albergo del Castello at Sant Andrina, expecting to join her mother there. The hotel people told her that her mother had left some time previously. They had no forwarding address. She seems to have told them she had not enough money to pay her fare back to England. They advised her to go to Rome and apply to the consulate."

"She did not come here," said Guthrie. "If I wasn't here myself I should have been told."

"Your clerks are all entirely trustworthy?"

"I believe so."

She said: "Forgive me, but when my nephew wrote he said he was beginning to feel that he could not trust anybody. You see, he was convinced that Francis Gale was murdered."

"The police made enquiries, Miss Fordyce, and came to the conclusion that his death was accidental."

"I know. And he did not tell me why he was so sure."

"It is all so vague," he said. "What do you want me to do?"

She answered promptly. "I would like you to find out as much as you can about a German woman who keeps a pension at 822 Via della Croce. I don't know her name, but Miss Oram seems to think she may be involved in some way. And I would like to hear what is known about Miss Oram herself. I liked her letter, and Roger seems to have complete confidence in her, but a young man isn't always a good judge."

"Well, that's something definite, anyway," said Guthrie, "though, frankly, I've no idea how I'm to set about sleuthing after these two females. This isn't a detective agency. Look here, Miss Fordyce, would you mind if I consulted my brother-in-law? He's very brainy, and I'm a bit of an ass actually. And he's absolutely straight."

"I should be most grateful," said Miss Fordyce. "Perhaps you could both dine with me this evening at my hotel? I can engage a private sitting-room so that we can talk undisturbed."

"Thank you. I'm pretty sure he will be able to come. My sister is at Anzio just now with the children, and he and I are leading a picnic existence, with dust sheets over the drawing-room furniture."

She gave him her card with the name of her hotel written on it.

"I shall expect you at eight. I am going back now to rest."

CHAPTER XV
MISS FORDYCE IS WARNED

THE marchese Luigi de Sanctis was a man of about fifty, slightly built and delicate in appearance, with melancholy brown eyes, and a small black beard trimmed to a point. He might have stepped out of a picture by Velasquez, thought Miss Fordyce, as they shook hands. She was relieved to hear that he spoke English.

"But of course you would, with an English wife."

He smiled. "Ours is a bilingual household. The children speak an extraordinary mixture of both languages."

The manager had made no difficulty about letting her have a private sitting-room for one evening. It was out of season, and the hotel was half empty.

"Are you going to help me?"

"I hope so," he said. "Shall we dine first, and then when the coffee is served and we are no longer subject to interruptions—"

She agreed. "You are quite right."

Miss Fordyce had been lying down and she felt rested, but she had had a shock, following a period of acute anxiety, and its effects had not quite passed off. She left the two men to make conversation, only putting in a word now and then. She noticed that Ronald showed a rather charming deference to the older man, whose manner to him was amused and indulgent.

"You know," he said, "you English look matter of fact, and are romantic; and we look romantic, and are matter of fact—"

Miss Fordyce wanted to say that he certainly looked romantic, but she felt that would be too personal. "The barnyard hen clucking at the moon, while the nightingale lays a breakfast egg," she suggested.

Ronald laughed loudly, and de Sanctis looked at her with increased attention. "How rare—and how delightful—to meet a witty woman."

"That isn't wit, it's the Chianti," said Miss Fordyce. "I'm not used to it. We drink cocoa for supper at home." But she was not ill-pleased.

The waiter had cleared the table and left them. They all three lit cigarettes and sat for a few moments quietly in the gathering dusk.

The marchese was the first to speak. He said, "There is an account of the murder of the palmist Nefert in the *Corriere della Sera*. They seem to think it unlikely that the murderer will be found. No one saw him—or her."

"They don't suspect Miss Oram?"

"They don't mention her. I should not think suspicion could fall on her. They say considerable force was used."

"Do you know anything about her? Miss Oram, I mean."

The marchese shrugged his shoulders. "She is—forgive me—a déclassée."

Miss Fordyce looked at him thoughtfully. "What do you mean by that exactly? No morals, or easy morals?"

"No. I don't want to do her an injustice. She made one slip, and since then, from what I hear, there has been nothing at all of that kind. She coaches young men for their exams, but they are not allowed to take liberties. The scandal in which she was involved is about six years old. She came over from England to take a post as nursery governess to the children of Prince Stefano Cavalcanti di Segno. Cavalcanti was a poor man with expensive tastes, and he had married the only daughter of a rich manufacturer from Milan. I forget what his father-in-law makes, bicycles or lavatory seats, it does not matter. It was not a happy marriage. Stefano was bored and irritated by his wife, who really was an impossible person, and either out of sheer ennui or because he was really attracted, he made love to the governess. She was very young, about nineteen, and inexperienced, and she took him seriously. I daresay if he had suggested it she would have consented to die with him. Probably he was embarrassed by her fervour, but that's only a guess. When the wife found out what was going on she turned the girl out of doors. I mean that quite literally. Some say it was the middle of the night and that she poured a bucket of water over the unfortunate creature from an upper window. What is certain is that she carried Stefano off to Milan. He was dependent on the allowance made him by his father-in-law so he could not do much, but he wrote to a friend begging him to find out what had become of the girl.

"The chaplain at the English church in Via Babbuino had found her a room and offered to pay her fare back to England, but she refused to go. They say Cavalcanti pawned his watch and his dress studs and sent her the money. She took it, but only as a loan, and subsequently she paid it back. She was befriended by a fellow countrywoman, an eccentric but kind-hearted person who earned her living by teaching English, and went to the Pantheon every evening with a bag of scraps begged from her pupils, to feed the stray cats there. She kept the girl with her. There was a child, but luckily it did not live. Miss Oram remained with her protectress until the old woman died, when she took over most of her pupils. Of course many doors were and have remained closed to her, but it is said that she is a conscientious and hard working teacher, and very patient with slow and backward children, and the fees she asks are very small. I imagine that she is rather lonely as, outside her work, she cannot have many friends. It would have been easier for her if she had gone gay after the Cavalcanti affair, but I suppose she hasn't the temperament."

"I see," said Miss Fordyce. "I liked her letter. I hope nothing has happened to her. If it is a coincidence that the woman she was staying with has been murdered it is a strange one. Have you formed any theory about this case, marchese? I assume that Mr. Guthrie has told you what I told him at the consulate this afternoon?"

"Yes. He said you were keeping something back."

"That is true, but it concerns my nephew. It is his affair. I mean this disappearance of Anne Gale."

The marchese knocked the ash off his cigarette in the saucer of his coffee cup and took his time about answering. "She is young, very young?"

"Barely sixteen."

"And unusually attractive?"

"I have never seen her, but judging from her photographs she is a very beautiful girl. My niece raves about her. They were at school together and great friends. That is why her father came to us—"

"I should say that there is very little doubt what has become of her," said the marchese quietly. "She has almost certainly fallen into the hands of a gang engaged in what is called the white slave traffic."

Miss Fordyce drew a long breath. It was her own fear, but it had not before been put into words. She said: "Would it be any use going to the police?"

"None, I should say. These people are very well organised. They are probably camorristi, or pay tribute to the camorra."

"That's a secret society, isn't it?"

"Yes. It operates chiefly in Naples and Calabria, but it almost certainly has ramifications all over Italy. In Naples they work openly. Elsewhere they have to be more careful. This chapter of accidents to people who have engaged in the search for the vanished girl looks like their doing."

"Then—what do you advise?"

"I should advise you to return to England at once. You have no cause to reproach yourself. It is not your affair, and you can do nothing; while, if you persist, you will certainly be in danger of something very unpleasant."

"Thank you," she said coolly, "but I shouldn't dream of going back just yet. I'm not easily frightened."

De Sanctis laughed. "I thought you wouldn't be, but I had to warn you. I meant it, you know. You really will be in danger. I should lock my bedroom door, if I were you. Of course you may be safe enough so far, but you will never know when their agents connect you with the previous searchers for the lost girl. Perhaps the cabman who drove you to the consulate, perhaps a waiter at this hotel. You will have to be on your guard. Don't leave letters about, or talk of your affairs with strangers. That is just what you have been doing, by the way."

"What do you mean?" she said indignantly. "I have done nothing of the kind—" she broke off in some confusion.

For the first time a doubt assailed her. Had she been incredibly foolish in trusting these two men? But Guthrie was her compatriot, employed at the consulate. She got up quickly and switched on the light. They were both looking at her, Guthrie with surprise, and his brother-in-law with a smile.

"Let me reassure you," he said. "I am not a member of the camorra. But I might have been. They will be very likely to approach you to find out, if they can, how much you know."

"Can't you give me some constructive advice?" she asked. He was silent for a moment, stroking his beard reflectively. He said at last: "I confess I am puzzled by their activity. Normally the girl should be well on her way to Buenos Aires by now. What have they to fear? It looks as if there had been a hitch, a bit of grit in the workings that may throw the whole machine out of gear. Why do they have to use such violent measures to get rid of enquirers? They don't stick at murder, and their people get protection, but they don't kill for the sake of killing. Even they must realise that some day they may go too far. Our Government is well meaning, but unfortunately weak, and perhaps in parts corrupt. The camorra is a cancer in the body of my country, Miss Fordyce. Some day, perhaps, we shall produce a surgeon with the skill and the courage to cut it out."

He rose and closed the shutters over the windows. "The night air is pleasant, but it is not wise for us to sit in a lighted room in which we can be seen from the houses across the street. Ronald told me that Miss Oram, in her letter to you, mentioned a German pensione in the Via della Croce. I have sent my servant Pietro to find out what he can about the place. It will be easier for him. He can talk to the porter at the door, the cobbler across the road. I told him to report to me here so that you can hear what he has to say without delay."

"It is very good of you—" said Miss Fordyce.

"Not good at all. I do not like these people. They give my country a bad name. Most of us are decent, law abiding. Our peasants especially. They work so hard, they are so patient in adversity, they are magnificent, the salt of the earth—"

"I believe you," she said gently. "I think you must know how much the English have always loved and admired Italy and the Italian people. I hope our countries will always be friends as they are now."

"I hope so too."

There was a knock at the door and a waiter came in.

"The servant of the signor marchese."

"Tell him to come in."

Ronald Guthrie said to Miss Fordyce. "Pietro was Luigi's fosterbrother. He comes from the family estate. He is quite trustworthy."

The waiter had gone out, closing the door after him. Pietro came forward, he bowed to Miss Fordyce, but he looked at the marchese as a dog looks at his master. He stood before him, turning his hat about in his hands and began what appeared to be a long narrative.

Ronald Guthrie edged his chair nearer to that of Miss Fordyce.

"Can you follow?"

"Not a word."

"It's the dialect of his native village," he whispered. "They jabber away like that together sometimes. Luigi will translate it all for us presently."

De Sanctis was listening, only occasionally intervening with a brief question. After a while Pietro seemed to have said all that he had to say, and the marchese turned to the others.

"There is a wineshop in the Via della Croce, nearly opposite the house in which we are interested. Pietro could not get the landlord to talk, but after a while he was called away, and he had better luck with the young woman who came to serve the customers in his place. She told him there were foreigners who had taken the top flat in the house across the way. They have only been there a few weeks. They did not appear to have many boarders, but she thought they sometimes received pilgrims on their way to one of the wonder working shrines, because two or three times she had seen women heavily bandaged and apparently hardly able to walk being helped into cabs and driven away."

"That sounds rather sinister," said Ronald.

"I thought so, too, but there may be nothing in it. She said there was a doctor living in the same house, and they might have been his patients. She said the foreigners were a mother and son, and that the son was bello, biondo, like an angel, but that he was always coughing. She said that two days ago a large portable bath was brought on a handcart late at night and taken into the house. She would not have known, but she was awake with toothache, and she heard voices and looked out of the window. She said she had heard that foreigners are mad about baths, but why bring it at such an hour?"

"A bath," said Miss Fordyce blankly. "It doesn't make sense."

"It might not be used for washing," said de Sanctis.

Ronald opened his mouth to say something and changed his mind after catching his brother-in-law's eye. Miss Fordyce, glancing at him, noticed that he had turned very white.

She said: "I think I will go there to-morrow and ask if they have a vacant room."

The marchese agreed. "But not alone. Ronald and I will be with you. We will meet you to-morrow morning at nine at the foot of the Spanish steps." He laid his hand over hers with a reassuring pressure. "You need a good night's rest. Don't forget to lock your door."

"I don't know how to thank you—"

"There is no need."

"Before we go—does this door lead into your bedroom?"

"Yes."

"Is there another way out?"

"Yes. A door into the corridor."

"Will you allow me to examine the room, just as a precaution?"

"Certainly."

She followed him as he passed into the next room and watched him as he looked under the bed and into the cupboard.

"You did not bring much luggage."

"As little as possible."

"You will lock both these doors. I would suggest moving a piece of furniture so that they cannot be opened without making a noise."

"Dear me," said Miss Fordyce. "You'll make me quite nervous if you go on like this. This is a most respectable hotel. I stayed here thirty years ago with my dear mother. They were most obliging then, and we felt quite at home. Naturally they haven't the same manager, but it seems just the kind of place it used to be. Still, I'll do everything you say if it makes you any happier. It's the least I can do since you have been so kind."

Guthrie and his brother-in-law had left the hotel and were walking down the Via Sistina, with Pietro following a few paces behind, when the marchese stopped to laugh.

"I can't help it," he said presently. "When I think of her response to my efforts to frighten the good lady almost out of her wits, it was characteristic, I am sure, but at the same time it was deliciously unexpected. The French have a word for it. Impayable. She has promised to lock her bedroom doors to please me. A gracious gesture."

Ronald looked puzzled. "I don't quite get you. You did frighten her, though she took it very well. When she shook hands with me I noticed that her hand was trembling. I suppose you thought it was necessary."

"Caro mio, it was most necessary." De Sanctis was quite serious now. "I meant every word I said to her. In England, with your habeas corpus and your policemen, you do not understand. You and I have to bring her to the point where she will consent to leave Rome. I don't want anything to happen to her. I like her. She has never been sexually attractive, she has never learnt any feminine airs and graces, but she is intelligent and kind-hearted. An agreeable combination. I have an aunt, about her age, and unmarried, but she is narrow-minded and pious, and we have always detested her."

"She is very mysterious about her nephew," said Ronald.

"I think we will wait until we get home to discuss that aspect of the case. Are we being followed, Pietro?"

"I do not think so, padron."

The long street was deserted but for one or two indefinite figures lurking in the shadows. One, as they approached, proved to be a harmless householder in carpet slippers, taking his dog for a run. It was past eleven and except in some quarters Rome has no night life. When they stopped to listen there was no sound but the sound of running water.

Presently, in the marchese's own room, lined with books, in which he spent much of his time working at his history of Etruscan civilisation. ("He will never finish it," his wife said, "but it keeps him amused."), he returned to the subject. It was late, but neither of them were inclined for sleep.

"You must have seen the accounts in the papers of the murder of an English woman artist at an hotel, not in the Castelli, some place more remote."

"Yes. Eve Shandon. At least, I think it must be her. They call her Eva Sandoni, but that's not English. I've seen her work. She had a show in Bond Street with another woman two years ago. Her stuff was good. I bought a sketch of an Algerian donkey boy for a wedding present to a friend of mine. I don't think the English papers can have got on it to yet or they would give it some space. She was fairly well known. She'd been mixed up in some case in the Courts too. Good Lord! Wait a minute. I remember now. She was divorced. I was at school at the time and just the age when one is curious about that sort of thing. There were two or three co-respondents and some juicy details. And her husband's name was Gale. I think he was a journalist. Gale!"

De Sanctis nodded. "I felt sure there was some connection. A young Englishman has been arrested and charged with having murdered her. He says he had never even met her, but declines to give any account of himself. The hotel people say he spent some days with her and registered in the name of Smith."

"Sorry if I'm dense," said Ronald, "but this does not help me at all."

His brother-in-law lit another cigarette. "I always smoke too much when Jean is not here to stop me," he said regretfully. "It will affect my heart, and she will be left a widow whose only consolation will be that she looks very charming in black."

"Don't talk like that, Luigi. It's unlucky. What about this Smith?"

"He is the nephew of our Miss Fordyce."

"But he's called Fordyce too—oh, I see. At least, I think I do."

"There are ways and means of getting rid of people who pry about and ask awkward questions. In America I believe they call this particular method a frame-up. We can't do anything about it for the moment. It is our function—self-imposed—to attend to this end of the business, and for that we have to meet the aunt of this young assassin at nine o'clock." He yawned. "Perhaps we should go to bed."

Ronald Guthrie said uneasily, "Maybe I shouldn't have brought you into this. Jean will never forgive me if—"

"If what? Caro mio, you cannot stop me. My self-respect is involved. I have to prove that not every Italian is a Cammorist or a Mafioso."

"As if that needed proof—"

"Not to you, perhaps. Besides, I am interested. My life has been too secure, uneventful."

"Nonsense."

"Very well. I will give you another reason that you will find unanswerable. Do you remember the last glimpse we had of your niece and godchild, Simonetta, when we left Anzio last week after taking Jean and the children down to the sea? A small chubby child busily engaged in filling her bucket with sand. Much too busy, I'm sure, to notice the incoming tide. But she was in no danger. Her mother and her nurse were close at hand. But the time will pass, and a day may come when she will not be so well guarded—"

Ronald nodded. "You're right. I can't answer that one. But is it any use, Luigi? I mean—is there any hope of getting the girl back? Isn't it—too late?"

"I am afraid it may be. But one cannot be sure. Look at the time. Good night, Ronald."

The younger man looked at him anxiously. "Luigi, I can't help wishing you know, you can't stand up to the Camorra. I've been here long enough to know they're too strong to be tackled by any individual."

"You need not come with me to-morrow, Ronald."

Guthrie flushed to the roots of his fair hair. "I don't deserve that."

The marchese laid a hand on his shoulder. "Caro mio, I did not mean it. We shall both be there. And perhaps I have been looking too much on the dark side. It may not be so regrettable after all."

Ronald shook his head. "I don't think we should delude ourselves. I can't help thinking of the account we read in the evening papers of the murder of Nefert. A cold-blooded, callous crime—"

"I know."

Chapter XVI
THE HOUSE IN VIA DELLA CROCE

AT NINE o'clock the following morning Miss Fordyce was standing at the foot of the Spanish steps, gazing reflectively at the yellow-stuccoed walls of the house in which Keats died. Even in August there are usually a few foreigners to be seen in the vicinity of Cook's office, which was just across the piazza. An old man came up and tried to sell her picture postcards. She had just succeeded in getting rid of him when Ronald Guthrie joined her.

"I say, I hope I'm not late," he said breathlessly. "Are you all right?"

"Quite, thank you. I expect you overslept yourself," she said, smiling.

"As a matter of fact, I did. Luigi and I sat up late talking things over."

"He has not come with you?"

"He thought it might be best to meet us there. We should attract less attention if he were not with us."

"I carried out his injunctions. Luckily I woke in time to take down my barricades before my nice chambermaid brought my breakfast. I don't know what she would have thought."

"There were no—no excursions and alarms?" he said gaily.

In broad daylight their elaborate precautions seemed unnecessary and a trifle absurd.

She answered slowly, "I am not sure. I woke once, fancying I heard something that might have been the turning of the doorknob. A small, stuffless sound. I confess it startled me. But I may have imagined it. After all, how can these people be aware of my coming to Rome?"

"We are hoping they aren't," he said, "but we can't be certain. If they know that Miss Oram wrote to you they might expect you to take some action and prepare to counter it."

"I am very worried over her disappearance," said Miss Fordyce, as they crossed the piazza together in the direction of the Via della Croce.

"So is Luigi I can see, though he hasn't said much."

"Have you seen this morning's papers?"

"I just had time to glance at the *Popolo Romano* while I was wolfing my coffee and rolls. Nothing fresh about the murder in Piazza Barberini. No arrest. One can't blame the police. All sorts of people went to her to have their hands read. Here we are."

They passed from the shade of the narrow street into what seemed at first almost complete darkness. After a moment, as their eyes grew accustomed to it, they saw a dingy stone-paved entrance hall and a steep staircase with an iron rail. It was an old house, and there was no lift. De Sanctis was waiting for them at the foot of the stairs. He bowed over Miss Fordyce's hand.

"All well so far," he whispered. "Pietro will be watching from the other side of the street. He knows what to do if we do not come out within a specified time."

"Surely they wouldn't—" began Ronald.

His brother-in-law checked him. "The first and second floors are unoccupied. The doctor on the third floor has a very dubious reputation. The German woman whom we are going to see has the flat above. That means that there are no tenants who might give an alarm or come to our assistance if we required any. Anything may happen here—or nothing."

Ronald looked at Miss Fordyce. "I say—I wish you'd go back to the hotel and let us carry on," he urged.

"Nonsense," she said briskly. "I'm going up."

She was breathing hard when they reached the top landing.

"I'm not used to so many stairs. Just a minute. I am to begin by asking about rooms. Now—"

She pressed the electric bell. They heard it ringing inside, but there was no other sound.

"Try again," said de Sanctis curtly when they had waited several minutes.

Miss Fordyce obeyed, but again without result.

"Well, that's that," said Ronald at last. "They may be out. It's a nuisance though, holding us up. What do we do now, Luigi?"

"Pietro has been watching the house since six o'clock. He told me just now that no one answering to the description of the

German woman or her son had come out. They must be here. Unless—"

"Unless what?"

"I don't know, but I mean to find out."

He had produced a piece of wire and was bending over the lock. Ronald looked shocked. "I say, old chap, you can't do that."

"What do you say, Miss Fordyce?"

She was watching the thin delicate clever hands manipulating the wire. "You could have had one of my hairpins," she said.

De Sanctis chuckled. "You see, Ronald, as your poet says, the female of the species is less law-abiding than the male. But seriously, caro mio, we can't afford to be scrupulous in this affair. Ecco—"

The lock clicked and the door swung open, revealing a small bare entrance hall, very light and spotlessly clean.

The marchese stepped inside and the other two followed.

"Is there anybody in?"

There was no answer. The doors along the passage were closed. The passage ran the whole length of the house and turned at right angles at the far end. De Sanctis went down it and looked round the corner. "There is a short flight of stairs there leading up to the roof," he told them when he came back. "They may be up there, but they would have heard the bell. We'll have a look round—"

There was a small dining-room, and four bedrooms furnished with cheap modern stuff and smelling of soap, varnish and carbolic. The floors were so highly polished that they had to be careful to avoid slipping. Another room was empty but for a grand piano with a stool, and a chaise longue of battered wicker work with some faded cushions drawn up to the window.

"I suppose the son practised and rested in here."

"Why the past tense, Luigi?"

"There's no music. There are no personal belongings in the other rooms."

Miss Fordyce, who had lingered to peep into the tiny kitchen, joined them. "They can't have been gone long," she said. "There is a drop of milk left in a jug on the pantry shelf, and it has not turned sour."

"A matter of hours then. There is one more room."

He opened the door and they looked in. There was no furniture, nothing but a large and rather battered tin bath standing in the middle of the room. It was more than half full of water. The room itself, in marked contrast to all the others, was far from clean. The floor was grimy, and tattered strips of soiled paper hung from the walls, showing darker patches where pictures had hung formerly.

"The frau cleaned the rest of the flat with Teutonic thoroughness. I wonder why she left this room untouched if they meant to use it for a bathroom. The first thing a woman with her evident passion for cleanliness would do with this object would be to scour it and give it a coat of white paint."

"This is the bath the girl at the wineshop saw arriving in the night on a handcart," said Ronald. "This water hasn't been used for washing. I mean, it's not soapy."

"The question is, has any water splashed over the edge—" said the marchese. He walked round the bath, peering at the dingy reddish brown cement of the floor. The other two watched him, puzzled and uneasy.

"Hard to tell," he said at last. "It's hot here under the roof. It would soon dry."

Miss Fordyce looked at him. She had turned rather white.

"What does it mean?"

"I can only guess," he said. "It was brought here secretly. No attempt was made to prepare it for ordinary use, and yet it was filled with water. The interior is rusty, the enamel has worn away. It does not make sense."

"I don't like it," said Ronald. "There's something horrible about this room. Let's get out of it."

"Very well, caro mio. We have seen all there is to see. I agree that there is something about it—antipatico—but at the same time curious and interesting."

He followed the others into the passage, closing the door after him. "We have seen everything?"

"There's the roof."

"Yes. We must go up there, but I do not expect to find anything. You see how it is. They have gone, leaving hardly a trace. No rubbish even, no waste paper or old letters that might have an address on the envelope. There was, you may have noticed, a good deal of fine feathery ash in the dining-room stove. The frau is a methodical and extremely efficient housekeeper. She does not go out leaving a mass of litter for the next tenant to clear up. But why did she leave that one room untouched? That room is the jarring note in an otherwise unexciting domestic piece. Two people with luggage could not have gone yesterday before night fell without being noticed by the young woman in the wineshop. The counter faces the open doorway, and when she is not behind the counter she is lounging about on the pavement gossiping with her neighbours. I have seen her every time I glanced out of a window. They must have slipped away during the night, some time before Pietro arrived at six o'clock. Why?"

"Mightn't it be that they had seen the account of the murder in Piazza Barberini in the *Corriere della Sera*?" said Ronald.

"That is a possibility. I think we will call on the doctor on our way down. But first the roof."

"I think I will wait for you down here," said Miss Fordyce. "I'm not very good at heights, and if there is only a low parapet I might feel giddy."

"Very sensible," said the marchese approvingly, "sit down and rest. We shall not be long."

Ronald hesitated. She had sat down on the only chair in the little kitchen. She looked tired and strained and old.

"Are you sure you don't mind being left?"

She forced a smile. "Not a bit." He really was a nice boy, she thought. He reminded her a little of Roger. Honest and well meaning, but, of course, not very clever.

"We'll be as quick as we can," he said, and hurried after his brother-in-law.

The door at the top of the steep little flight of stairs leading to the roof was unlocked. They emerged and looked about them, shading their eyes from the glare as they moved forward. Clothes props and lines showed that the roof had been used as a drying ground. Carnations, rosemary and other herbs flourished in a heterogeneous collection of old pots and cans in the shade of the chimney stack.

"These must have been watered yesterday evening," said de Sanctis. "The earth is quite moist."

The roof was divided from that of the next house by the fact that it was about twenty feet higher, and on the other side there was a sheer drop into an alley.

"No way out from here," said Ronald.

"No." He looked thoughtfully at a number of battered packing cases stacked in one corner. "I suppose they brought their china and glass and bed linen in these. Here is the remains of a label, badly defaced, but it looks like a shipping company. Hamburg to Naples. Did you notice the pictures in the dining-room, Ronald?"

"There was the usual cheap chromo lithograph of the All Highest in shining armour."

"The Kaiser. Yes. But there was also a view of Vesuvius. Never mind that now. Help me to shift these."

"Where to?"

"Only a few inches. I want to test their weight."

"Hot work," said the younger man presently. "The sun is broiling up here. This last one is pretty heavy, Luigi. What about it?"

They looked at one another and de Sanctis sighed.

"Yes. We had better see what is inside. Perhaps we can lever up one of these strips of wood."

"Let me try with my penknife. Oh, blast!" as the blade snapped.

"All right. The nail here is coming loose."

A long sliver of wood cracked and split and de Sanctis pried it back. His long, thin, delicate fingers plucked at the straw packing to what lay beneath. After a moment his face, which had been tense with anxiety, relaxed. He stood up, wiping his hands fastidiously on a silk handkerchief.

"Books, nothing but books."

"Thank God—" said Ronald.

"We'll try the doctor. Come on—"

They had reached the head of the stairs leading down to the flat below when de Sanctis stopped abruptly, making a sign to

Ronald to be silent. They both heard a man's heavy tread coming along the passage, followed by the opening and closing of one of the room doors.

"I'll deal with this," whispered de Sanctis. "You stop here. Come if I call you, not otherwise—"

He was quick and he made no noise. When the door of the room containing the bath opened he was in the passage, and he and the newcomer were brought face to face.

"Scusi," said de Sanctis, smiling. "I was on the roof. I did not hear you come in. The agent did not tell me he had more than one key. The rooms are large and light, and the outgoing tenant has left everything in order."

The other said harshly, "You have an order to view? May I see it?" He was a tall man, powerfully built. His dark good looks were marred by a coarse and sensual mouth and a heavy prognathous jaw. De Sanctis knew him by sight and by name. Commendatore Rinaldo Marucci was a Neapolitan. His father had made money in building speculations and had married a daughter of a noble but impoverished family in Calabria. The son had inherited his father's business acumen and had built up a very large fortune, no one quite knew how. He was said to have a controlling interest in a number of enterprises of which, ostensibly, he knew nothing. He was known to be a widower, with an only daughter who was being brought up by her grandmother. Though he had recently been made a member of an exclusive club to which de Sanctis belonged they had not, so far, exchanged a word. Marucci, knowing the marchese to be bookish, disinclined for society, and only moderately well off, had thought him negligible, and de Sanctis would have described the Neapolitan in one word, "Canaglia".

"An order to view? Naturally," said de Sanctis easily. He felt in his pockets. "I must have dropped it. I hope you have not set your heart on this place. I think it would suit my friends, and as the first comer—"

The other said, "There must be some mistake. This flat is not to let."

"Not? But in that case why am I here? And why are you?" The faint insolence was, of course, intentional, and accurately timed as the planting of the first banderillo in the bull's flank.

Marucci flushed with anger. He had grown used to deference. He said, "This house happens to be my property. I have business with the actual tenant, who appears to be out at the moment. I don't know how you got in, marchese—"

He checked himself. It was clear that he was uncertain and did not wish to commit himself too far.

De Sanctis took a cigarette from his case. He supposed that Miss Fordyce was still in the kitchen. He doubted if she knew enough Italian to follow their conversation. Was there any way in which he could get her out without being seen by Marucci?

Before he could think of anything Marucci spoke again. "Just a moment—" he said. "I had better make sure—"

He moved away down the passage, opening every door he came to and looking into the room. De Sanctis paused in the act of striking a match as he glanced into the kitchen. To his profound astonishment and alarm Marucci made no comment and merely closed the door again and passed on. She was not there, then? Could she have left the flat, while he and Ronald were up on the roof? If she had called out they would have heard her. Or would they? They had been making a good deal of noise themselves when they were moving the packing-cases. He walked down the passage to join Marucci. The Neapolitan was looking into the room that contained the bath. He closed the door as de Sanctis came up.

"You went in there just now, I think. Rather a primitive arrangement, isn't it," said the marchese, making his voice sound friendly. He had decided that he could not afford to quarrel with Marucci. "Are you waiting for your tenant to return?"

"I might," growled Marucci.

"Then I think I will too. I want to see her. She might be willing to sub-let."

"She can't do that, marchese. There is a clause in the lease. I regret—" said Marucci. He was very civil now. "I can't understand how you came to be given this address. Which agent was it?"

De Sanctis, seeing no way out of it, named a firm with an office in the Via Nazionale. "I must apologise for my intrusion," he said. "I think I'll go back to them now. Perhaps I shall find out how the mistake arose."

"You had better return the key to me," said Marucci.

"The key?" De Sanctis looked about him. "I left it in the door."

"It isn't there now."

"Are you sure?"

"Of course. I let myself in with the key on my ring. This one." Marucci jingled a bunch of keys impatiently.

"What an extraordinary thing." De Sanctis felt in all his pockets. "Cigarette case, purse, matches, my own latch key. I don't seem to have it. I feel quite sure I left it in the lock. Careless of me, perhaps. Could it have been taken by someone before you arrived? Well, as I have nothing to return, perhaps I need not go back to the agent at once."

"On the contrary," said Marucci curtly. "An explanation is due to me from these people, and I mean to have one. I am coming with you."

"But certainly, if you wish."

Ronald Guthrie, waiting at the top of the stairs leading down from the roof, out of sight of the two men standing in the passage, heaved a sigh of relief as he heard the door of the flat closed. He had been afraid that Luigi would be obliged to take his departure, leaving the other in possession. But Luigi had been clever. He had made the best of an awkward situation.

Miss Fordyce, apparently, had kept out of the way, in the kitchen.

Ronald called to her as he ran down the stairs. "All clear. We'll get out of this, pronto."

She did not reply. He looked into the kitchen. She was not there. He went from room to room. "Miss Fordyce. I say—"

He returned to the kitchen. What was he to do? Time was passing. It would not take very long to drive to the Via Nazionale and back in a vettura. That fellow who called himself the landlord might be back very soon. He took a cigarette from his case and noticed that his hands were shaking. He was not quick-witted and subtle, like Luigi. He did not really know what they were doing in this damned place. The vanishing trick. The girl had gone, that child they were all after, and Eve Shandon, whose sketch in oils of a donkey boy was hanging in his friends' drawing-room, and the little English governess, and now Miss Fordyce. She was a type, of course. Most fellows had an aunt like that, sharp tongued, upright, indomitable, a warm-hearted dragon. He liked her. Luigi liked her, she amused him.

What had happened while he and Luigi were up on the roof moving those packing cases? It must have been then, when they were making too much noise themselves to hear any sound in the rooms below. What had they done to her?

She was brave, but she was only a little woman, elderly—

The unlit cigarette had shredded away between his fingers. "Oh, damn and blast!" he said loudly.

The window was closed, the small kitchen was stiflingly hot. The heavy silence was broken by a faint scrabbling sound. A mouse nibbling behind the wainscot? It ceased and began again, and it seemed to be in or near the dresser. He looked at the wall and saw that there was a door there. It was almost invisible because it was covered with wallpaper, and the pattern of trellis and rose garlands had been well matched. There was a small knob of white enamel, rather high up. He turned it. The door swung open. He saw that it was a small dark cupboard, with two shelves above for glass and china. Below there was something like a heap of clothing. It stirred feebly, and Miss Fordyce crawled out on her hands and knees. He lifted her up. There was blood on her hands and on the floor.

He said: "My God, you've been hurt—"

She gasped. "No. Nothing. Want of air. My nose. I—fainted—I think—"

CHAPTER XVII
DOCTOR'S ORDERS

1

Miss Fordyce had lunch served in her private sitting-room. She and Ronald were half-way through their meal when the marchese joined them.

"I only want a plate of minestrone." When the waiter had left them he said, "Did you dematerialise—or what?"

Miss Fordyce was looking rather pale, but as neat as ever.

Ronald said, "She was in the kitchen cupboard. She couldn't open it from the inside and there was no air. It was lucky I heard you, wasn't it, Aunt Polly?"

She smiled at him. "I should have died. I shan't forget it, my dear boy."

He reddened. "Oh, I didn't mean that. I mean—I didn't do anything."

"You lent me a pocket handkerchief. You were most kind and considerate."

The marchese was much diverted by this affectionate interchange.

"You are what the Americans call a fast worker, Ronald."

"Don't be an ass," growled his young brother-in-law.

"I was so glad to see him," explained Miss Fordyce. "I howled. I made a complete fool of myself. After that we couldn't be formal. And he does remind me of my poor Roger. So I asked him to call me aunt."

"Very nice," said de Sanctis. "Would you extend the same privilege to me? I know I do not deserve it."

"Of course, if you like."

"And now if you could tell me what happened?"

"I heard someone letting themselves into the flat with a latch-key and I did not want to be found sitting in that kitchen, so I got into the cupboard. It was very hot and dark and airless, and I soon began to feel faint, but I couldn't get out again."

De Sanctis said nothing for a moment. He was remembering that he had been so sure that she was not in the flat that he had nearly called Ronald down from the roof so that they might leave together. He finished his minestrone. The waiter brought coffee. When they were alone again he turned to Ronald. "Did you get out without an encounter with our friend the commendatore?"

"Yes, Aunt Polly was a bit upset, naturally, but she pulled herself together very quickly, and we tottered off. Luckily there is a cab rank quite near."

"Rome," said Miss Fordyce, "is rich in cabs."

Ronald grinned. "Romans never walk if they can possibly help it. Luigi doesn't. He's a lazy devil. Lucky for him he doesn't tend to adipose deposit. Who was that chap Luigi? Did you know him? And how did you get rid of him?"

"By sight only, the saints be praised. He is a member of my club. He is a Neapolitan, and is more often there, I fancy, and I believe he has business interests in South America. Plenty of money, and does himself well. I don't know why he was made a commenda-tore. Probably he has a good deal of backstairs influence."

"And he really does own that house in Via della Croce?"

"Why not? I expect he has a lot of house property. It is considered a good investment. I think he was as surprised as we were to find the flat empty—and that is interesting. Our morning wasn't wasted."

"What happened at the agent's office, Luigi?" asked his broth-er-in-law curiously.

"They had, of course, no recollection of handing me any key or order to view, but they know me there as an entirely respectable and law-abiding citizen, and I don't think they cared for Marucci's blustering manner. They were too polite to contradict me."

"And was the commendatore convinced?"

"Marucci? I'm not sure," said de Sanctis slowly. "We parted with mutual apologies and compliments and professions of esteem, but I fancied there was still a shade of distrust. Luckily he did not see either of you. If he is what I think he must be he can have me taped. These people keep dossiers of us all, like the French police. It is a part of their job to know which sheep are worth shearing. I don't suppose he has given me a second thought until now. I am comparatively poor. I have nothing to do with national or municipal politics. I employ my leisure harmlessly, but from his point of view, uselessly, in writing a book that may never be published, and that, in any case, would only be read by one person in a thousand. I am homme rangé, with a wife and two children. He could not suppose that I would be so mad as to make myself persona non grata to his organisation without some very good reason. And what reason could I have?"

Miss Fordyce said, "The Camorra"—and paled as she uttered the name. "They—they could make trouble for you."

"I shall be on my guard," he said, "but we must work quickly."

"What can we do now?"

"You will rest in your room while Ronald and I call on the doctor."

She shook her head. "I am coming, too."

"Very well. I will go first, and you can follow with Ronald as before. How long would it take you to pack?"

"Five minutes. Why?"

"I just wanted to know. A riverderci—"

When he had gone Miss Fordyce said: "I feel very guilty. This may lead to something very unpleasant for your brother-in-law. He is going to make enemies of these people, and he has no personal interest—it isn't fair."

"Don't worry. He's enjoying himself. You can see he has the greatest contempt for this Marucci chap. To the Romans all the Neapolitans are just plain mud."

2

After parting with the Marchese de Sanctis outside the house agent's office, Marucci crossed to the shady side of the Via Nazionale. It was past noon and he wanted his lunch. There was a trattoria a little farther down the street. He went in and ordered vitello alla Milanese with fried potatoes and beans, after taking the edge off his appetite with a heaped plate of pasta which he wound round his fork and swallowed with uncanny skill and

speed, washing the greasy mess down with rough red wine. He
was not affected by the clatter of knives and forks, the clamour
of voices, the steamy heat and the smells of cooking. When he
had finished he sat for a minute or two, frowning, and exploring
his teeth with one of the picks provided by the management. The
waiter who brought his bill shrank from his intimidating glare, but
Marucci was not angry with him. His thoughts were elsewhere.
Bertha Haussman. He had always relied on her.

But that son of hers was a bad influence. How dared she leave
the flat without his permission? Had she carried out his orders?
That fellow de Sanctis, with his airs and graces, just because
he belonged to an old family. Nobili decaduti, thought the self-
made man with a sneer. A foolish busybody, flat hunting for his
friends. But seeing him safely off the premises had wasted his
whole morning.

He left the trattoria, took a cab and drove back to the Via
della Croce.

The doctor answered his insistent ringing of the bell.

"You kept me waiting," Marucci said angrily.

"Pardon, Commendatore, how was I to know it was you?" The
doctor's puffy unwholesome face was sallower than usual and a
nervous twitching of his eyelids very apparent. His black alpaca
coat and baggy old trousers were stained with grease and wine,
and looked as if they had been slept in. He wore a black silk scarf
round his neck to hide the absence of a collar.

Marucci looked him over with unconcealed distaste. "What's
the matter with you? You aren't fit to be seen."

"I have been very worried, sleeping badly," stammered the
other.

Marucci pushed past him as he stood on the threshold of his
dingy surgery. "Shut the door. I've got to talk to you. What has
been happening here? Bertha and her son are not upstairs. Did
you know?"

"She—she brought down the—the last consignment—last
night. She said she couldn't deal with it. I could see she was badly
frightened. She asked me if I had seen the—the trouble in Piazza
Barberini in the evening paper. I had. There was an account in

the *Corriere della Sera*. I said it was nothing to do with us, but she wouldn't listen. That great face of hers, like a ham, was blotched with crying. I think her son had been at her. I was angry. I had done my part. I've no—no storage room for perishable goods. But she wouldn't listen. Later I heard them carrying something heavy down the stairs. If they have gone I suppose it was a trunk."

"They'll be sorry," muttered Marucci. "I'll see to that."

"What am I to do?"

"Had they used the bath?"

"No. No. She came without the boy. She has always tried to keep him out of the business. It could be done when he was away all day at his music classes, but he's been at home lately. I think she's afraid that if he really understood he might go to the police. She said she had told you the bath was impossible. You were asking too much of her."

Marucci leaned against the doctor's desk, scowling, and twisting a ring about on his little finger. The big Brazilian diamond flashed, the only bright thing in that grimy room.

"They will be dealt with," he said. "Did she tell you where she was going?"

"No."

"Don't you fail me, Donati. You have these rooms rent free and are well paid for every patient I send you. And you are free to treat as many as you can get in the ordinary way. You might get more if you pulled yourself together, and kept this place decent. What would you do if I turned you out of here?"

The doctor shrugged his shoulders and held out his hands, palms upwards. "Nothing."

"Just so. You're too old and too rotten with drugs to make a fresh start, even if that were possible. Now I'm going to be frank with you." Marucci paused to light another cigarette and inhale. "I want this affair of the murdered Englishwoman cleared up. It must not be allowed to drag. As time passes there is always more danger of inconvenient revelations. It's Laccetti's fault. He tried to use the organisation to cover his own doings. That is not allowed. I have to go to Vallesca and find out on the spot what can be done in the matter. I may need your assistance. If I do I shall send you a telegram. It might be to-morrow. Be ready to come at once."

The doctor licked his lips. "What about—" He jerked his head, indicating the door leading to the inner room.

"I will arrange that two men whom I can trust will call with a handcart to fetch the bale between one and two to-night."

"The—the bale," stammered the other. His face was ghastly. "Aren't the goods for export?"

"No. I told you I was clearing up. Don't look at me like that," Marucci said brutally. "It should be easy enough for you. You doctors. Don't tell me you've never killed a patient."

"Never intentionally."

"Well, let it be an accident, mistake the bottle, let your hand shake as you measure out the dose. Please yourself. But it must be something she could have done for herself, you understand. Here is a note which you will leave in the pocket of her skirt." He laid a half sheet of paper torn from an exercise book down on the desk. A few words had been written on it with a purple indelible pencil.

"A last message?"

"Yes."

"Is it in English?"

"It is." The big man was complacent.

"You think they will believe she wrote it?"

"Certainly. Why not? The paper is taken from an exercise book she brought to my house for my daughter's use. The pencil is hers. She made corrections with it and dropped it only the other day. The writing resembles hers quite sufficiently."

"I do not understand English. What does it say?"

"It does not matter. It will show that she killed herself." He looked at his watch. "I must be going. Carry out my instructions, and I will see that you get a bonus."

"Listen to me—" the other said desperately.

Marucci's face hardened. "If it isn't done, and well done, you'll be turned out. You've no savings? I thought not."

He went out, slamming the door. The doctor sank into his chair and covered his twitching face with his hands. "Marucci was right," he thought bitterly: he was rotten: his mind was corroded, his will power had crumbled. His fear of any open space had increased. He went out as little as possible. The four walls of his surgery were his haven. If he was thrust out he felt that he would die as a mollusc dies when torn out of its shell. Marucci did not know that, and when he realised it he would show no mercy. His raw nerves quivered as he thought of the train journey to Vallesca, the strange faces, strange rooms, the demands that would be made upon him. "I can't bear it," he thought. "Finished. I am finished. This is the end."

CHAPTER XVIII
THE RESIDENT PATIENT

1

THE doctor had been sitting huddled in his chair, sunk in contemplation of his own misery, for barely ten minutes, when the bell rang. A patient? Well, why not? He still had a few, though most of them came furtively, after nightfall, to be treated for diseases of which they were ashamed. He got up, with a groan, and went to the door.

There were three people waiting on the landing, a well-dressed middle-aged man with a neatly-trimmed black beard, a much younger man with a round fresh-coloured boyish face, and a small elderly woman. The younger man and the woman were obviously English. The doctor, taking fright, would have closed the door, but he was not quick enough. The bearded man brushed by him without asking his leave and the other two followed. The four of them quite filled the small entrance hall.

The bearded man said very politely: "Please excuse us. You are Dr. Donati? We think you may be able to assist us. Is this your surgery?"

The doctor found himself back in his chair behind his desk. The woman sat in the chair usually occupied by his patients, and the two men remained standing. He said, rather breathlessly. "One of you is ill—or hurt?"

They looked very harmless, but he could not forget that they had practically forced their way in.

The bearded man answered. "No. We have come for Miss Oram."

"I beg your pardon? I do not understand."

"An Englishwoman. We believe that she had been left in your charge. We have come to fetch her away. This gentleman is attached to the English consulate."

The doctor raised a bony hand, sallow and not overclean, to cover the twitching nerve in his cheek. He could not hide the uncontrollable flickering of his eyelids, but his voice when he replied was tolerably firm.

"You have been misinformed, signore. I have no resident patients. An Englishwoman? I was sent for to treat a case of narcotic poisoning two days ago, a case of attempted suicide. She was a foreigner, possibly she was English. Perhaps she is the person you are looking for. I never heard her name."

"Where was this?"

"I was taken there in a cab. It was in the centre of the older quarter of the city, behind the Pantheon."

"The name of the street?"

The doctor licked his lips. "The Via Arco della Ciambella."

"And the number?"

"I did not notice."

The woman, who had been silent hitherto, said very quietly, in English, "He is lying. I could not follow what he said, but I am sure it was all lies."

De Sanctis nodded. "Maybe." He resumed. "You must forgive my insistence, Signor Dottore. This is a serious matter. You saw this patient only in a house in Via Arco della Ciambella. Are you prepared to swear that is the truth?"

"Certainly."

"By everything you hold sacred?"

"Yes."

"Is she there still?"

"I could not say. They talked of moving her into the country."

"Who were they?"

"I do not know. They—they were foreigners too."

The marchese turned to Miss Fordyce, and told her what the doctor had said. "You know it isn't impossible," he added. "She may have gone to friends we know nothing of. The overdose might have been accidental. She had been frightened and worried, and she probably would take something to make her sleep."

"Yes. But why send for this doctor, who is almost certainly connected with the woman upstairs? Wouldn't that be an extraordinary coincidence?"

"Per Dio. You're right. I had missed that point. He's simply trying to get rid of us."

The doctor had been watching them anxiously. What were they saying? He wished he could understand English. He started violently the younger man, who had not yet spoken, uttered a loud exclamation and reached out to pick up something from the dusty littered desk. The doctor, suddenly realising what it was, snatched at it too, but he was not in time. The young man held him off with a large hand flat on his chest.

"I say. Good Lord! Look at this."

I am sorry Nefert had to die, but I owed money to her and not she would wait. Now I finish altogether because life is too hard.—Lily Oram.

"Ask him where he got this, Luigi."

The doctor, losing his balance as Ronald Guthrie thrust him back, had fallen back into his chair. His face had taken on a greyish tinge and was shining with sweat, his lips moved without making any sound.

"He's ill," said Miss Fordyce. "What is that paper, Ronald?"

"It seems to be a farewell message from—from Miss Oram. Perhaps she really has—see for yourself—"

She took the paper from him. "It looks like her writing. She used a purple indelible pencil for her letter to me. But—it does not sound quite right. And not she would wait. That isn't English—"

"Not would wait. Non voleva aspettare. A literal translation from the Italian. A fake. It might be. Good for you, Aunt Polly."

"To be found on her," she said, "to make it seem like suicide. It might be that, I suppose—"

"Clever, but not quite good enough. And it's not this chap's work, is it, Luigi? He doesn't know what we're saying, does he?"

De Sanctis had been watching the doctor closely while they were speaking and he was satisfied that he had not understood one word. He said, "You're right. He's only a tool. Pietro said the other came back here. He only left a few minutes before we arrived. We thought he had been upstairs, but it's more likely that he was here. You've only to look at the poor wretch. He's sick with fright. Stay with him, Ronald, while Aunt Polly and I search the flat."

The doctor half rose from his chair as they moved towards the door leading to the inner room. "You must not, you can't—I protest—"

Ronald's hand on his shoulder forced him to sink back again.

De Sanctis hesitated before opening the door. "Perhaps it would be better if I went alone—"

Miss Fordyce was pale but resolute. "I'm going with you." The inner room was evidently the doctor's bedroom. The window was closed and flies buzzed on the panes. The heat was overpowering, and there was a sickly smell of drugs mingled with that of stale food and tobacco. The bed was unmade and clothing was scattered about, trailing over chairs and on the dusty carpet. The basin on the washstand was half full of dirty water, stained red.

"Don't worry," said de Sanctis quickly, as Miss Fordyce shrank closer to him. "Didn't you notice that he'd cut himself shaving. Hands unsteady, especially in the morning. What a wreck. And he must have been pretty good once. I looked him up last night in the register. Lots of qualifications. Bologna and Milan. There's another room beyond this. All the rooms lead out of one another."

He tried the door. "This one is locked. Wait here a moment. He will have to give me the key."

He went back to the surgery.

Ronald Guthrie was standing guard over the huddled figure.

He said uneasily, "The poor devil's got hiccoughs now. All to pieces, isn't he—"

De Sanctis bent over him and said very distinctly, "The key."

Donati did not raise his head, but after a moment his shaking fingers fumbled in a drawer of the desk. He muttered, "Here it is," and then more loudly, "I'm glad really—"

De Sanctis took the key from him and hurried back to Miss Fordyce. The room beyond the bedroom was unfurnished and had evidently been used for storing lumber. There were two large empty packing-cases and a wheeled carrying chair. The straw from the packing-cases was strewn on the floor in a corner, and something lay there, covered with a soiled cotton sheet.

De Sanctis crossed the room quickly and turned back the covering.

Miss Fordyce had followed him.

"Poor thing," she said unsteadily. "Is she—"

Lily's emaciated body was still clad in the crumpled blue cotton frock she had been wearing when she left the Villa Marucci nearly a week earlier. Her thin face was partly hidden by a disordered mass of dark hair. Her arms, bare to the elbow, were mere skin and bone. De Sanctis, kneeling by her, was feeling for the pulse. He said, "Look at the needle marks. She's been drugged. Her breathing is very slow. She wouldn't have lasted much longer. Aunt Polly, will you find the kitchen and make some coffee? It must be hot and strong. The doctor will have to help us."

But when he went back to the surgery he found that Donati was lying with his head on his desk in a state of collapse.

Ronald, looking worried, explained that he had swallowed a capsule before he could stop him.

The marchese shrugged his shoulders. "He would, just as he might have undone some of his dirty work. Leave him and come with me."

The doctor's flat was hot and airless and Ronald suggested that all the windows should be opened, but de Sanctis would not allow it. "We must not attract attention," he said.

Lily was lifted to her feet and forced to walk up and down the room, between the door and the window, while they held her up on either side. For a long time they had to support her whole weight, while her feet shuffled aimlessly and her head sagged forward. It was gruelling work, and soon even Ronald was drenched with sweat and breathing heavily. They had been at their self-imposed task for nearly two hours when the marchese, after a glance at Miss Fordyce, who was looking haggard with fatigue, decreed that they might all rest for five minutes. Lily was lowered gently on to the straw. The others sat on the bare boards, resting their backs against the wall. Nobody spoke for more than a minute.

Then Ronald said, "Aunt Polly, this is too much for you—"

She answered in a husky whisper. "I'm all right. There's some coffee left in the pot on the stove. We might all have some."

"A good idea."

Ronald struggled to his feet and went into the kitchen.

He came back with a steaming coffee pot and three odd cups on a battered tray. Miss Fordyce sipped the black bitter liquid and announced that she was ready to go on.

De Sanctis looked at his watch. "We shall have to get out of here. We're running a big risk. A little more coffee for the patient, I think."

There was less difficulty in swallowing, and she was no longer a dead weight when they lifted her. She had even tried to speak, but so far she was unintelligible. De Sanctis examined the pupils of her eyes and saw that they were almost normal.

"I think we might move her now. The air will do her good. Are you willing that she should be taken to your hotel, Aunt Polly?"

"Of course. I was about to suggest it. Ronald, you'll find Pietro waiting below. Ask him to fetch a vettura."

"What will you do about the doctor?"

"Nothing. We've got what we came for."

2

An hour later Lily was sitting, propped up with cushions, on the sofa in Miss Fordyce's private sitting-room at the hotel. She looked like a ghost, but she was fully conscious. She had grasped the fact that Miss Fordyce was Roger's aunt and that the two men were her friends, and she was ready and anxious to talk.

"I don't really remember anything much after leaving the Villa Marucci. I felt very queer when I was crossing the bridge.

It might have been the sun. Someone put me in a cab though I tried to tell them I really couldn't afford it, and after that it was all confused and horrible, like a nightmare. I say, aren't I skinny?" She began to laugh weakly as she held up a hand that looked almost transparent.

"Don't worry. You're safe with us," said Miss Fordyce. "Drink a little more milk. Now, my dear child, if you possibly can, will you tell us about Roger."

"He wanted to keep you out of it." She hesitated, frowning, trying to marshal her thoughts. "I wrote you a letter. How long ago was that?"

"A week to-day since you posted it."

"Oh—my friend I was staying with will be anxious. Could you let her know I'm all right? Nefert, the palmist. She advertises in the *Corriere*. You'll see her address there. The Piazza Barberini."

Ronald opened his mouth and shut it again without saying anything.

Miss Fordyce said: "We'll attend to it. And now, my dear, I do beg of you to tell us everything you know; everything that has happened since you first met Roger. Never mind what he said. These gentlemen, the Marchese de Sanctis, and Mr. Guthrie, who is the acting vice-consul, are trying to help us. Luckily you mentioned the house in the Via della Croce in your letter, or we might never have found you."

Lily said: "It's bigger than we thought at first. All right. I'll tell you."

The two men lit cigarettes. Miss Fordyce, who had ordered tea, refilled her cup. Lily lay back among the cushions and closed her eyes. Physically she was still very weak, but her mind was quite clear. She told her story simply and in a way that carried conviction. Her three listeners paid her the compliment of a close and undivided attention. When she had finished there was a short silence. Ronald looked at his brother-in-law, who was taking another cigarette from his case. Miss Fordyce blew her nose.

"Marchese," she said brusquely.

"Yes, Aunt Polly?"

"Is my nephew in real danger of—of a miscarriage of justice?"

"I am afraid he may be. There seems to be a considerable weight of circumstantial evidence against him, and, of course, witnesses who are prepared to perjure themselves."

"What can we do?"

"If he could produce the woman who stayed at the hotel with him the case against him would probably fall to pieces. There would be clear proof then of a conspiracy, since the people at the hotel are saying that the woman who was seen dining with him on the terrace was Eve Shandon. The people who saw them from a distance might be honestly mistaken, but not the hotel staff."

"Roger won't do that. Well—he'll have to take his medicine. A heavy price for a piece of folly," she said with a sigh.

"What shall we do now, Marchese? Advise us. Is there any hope that we might still find and rescue the child—poor Francis Gale's daughter?"

De Sanctis shook his head. "None, I think. Too much time has elapsed since she fell into their hands. I think there can be little doubt that Marucci is engaged in the white slave traffic, a very profitable business. I had heard that he had a controlling interest in a small shipping line, cargo boats carrying a few passengers and running between Naples and various Eastern ports, and others with a western route touching at Genoa and Marseilles. It would be impossible to prove. He has far too big a pull. The house in Via della Croce has been used for—shall we say storing the goods in transit. These people don't usually touch girls who are likely to have friends who may make trouble, but this unfortunate child dropped into their clutches like a ripe peach falling from a wall. She had come to join her mother—and they knew that she would never find her."

"They don't stick at murder," said Ronald. "You still think it would be useless to go to the police, Luigi?"

"Worse than useless. If they decided to hold an enquiry we should all be held as witnesses—and—don't forget our methods have been illegal. We broke into that flat this morning. We were right, mind you. It was the only way." He looked at Miss Fordyce. "Aunt Polly, may I speak to you for a moment alone? Will you come into the corridor? Forgive me, Miss Oram. We shall not be long, Ronald—"

He held the door open for Miss Fordyce to pass out before him. "Well," she said. "What is it?"

"I could not ask you before her. You know her history. Would you be willing to take her back with you to England?"

"Certainly, if she wishes it."

They were alone in the passage, but he lowered his voice. "Whether she wishes it or not I think she should go. You will both be in danger here. You know too much."

"In a few days, when she has regained her strength—"

"Signora mia carissima, is it possible that I was mistaken when I said that you were intelligent? When Marucci learns what happened this afternoon he will be like a mad dog. We don't know who saw us leave that house, or if we were followed here. I tell you frankly that I cannot think of any way of insuring that you would not meet with some accident. His organisation have ways and means. Think of the story we have just heard. Gale fell down the lift shaft. Lily Oram was to have committed suicide."

"What do you suggest?"

"There is a through train to Paris that leaves the Central station at ten forty-five. I sent a telegram to my wife at Anzio this morning. She will be there with our two children and the nurse. I am sending her home to her parents in Edinburgh. That will show you that I am in earnest about this."

She thought: "He does not belong to this century. He should be wearing a ruff. Grenville on the *Revenge*, or Raleigh. But perhaps it is only the beard." Since they had first met—and it was difficult to realise that that was only twenty-four hours ago—he had taken the lead, and she had followed. And she was used to making her own decisions.

She said: "How can I leave Italy without even trying to see Roger? The fate of that poor child is a tragedy, but he is my own flesh and blood. Surely relatives are allowed access to prisoners awaiting trial?"

He looked down at her, his dark eyes gleaming with mingled amusement and irritation.

"Aunt Polly, listen. Are all the English impervious to facts? I mean—is it a congenital, chronic, irremediable defect?"

"It's difficult, you know. At home we are so safe. Did you mean what you said now about your wife and family?"

"Certainly. I want to keep a move ahead of the Commendatore and his friends. If I have not to worry about Jeannie and the babies I can give my mind to the problem. Don't look so aghast. She would have been going next month in any case."

"Are you going too?"

"No."

She laid her hand on his arm. "Please—you must not get into trouble here on our account. We have no right to expect it."

"You have from Ronald, as temporary acting vice-consul—and I am helping him because he is my brother-in-law. Does that make it easier for you?" he asked with a smile.

"I shall never forget your kindness."

"Let us rejoin the others. You will have to persuade Miss Oram."

"To leave with me by the night train? She hasn't any clothes for the journey."

"I have thought of that. I have sent Pietro home with a note to my wife. She and Miss Oram are about the same height. He will bring back what is necessary."

Lily needed even more persuading than de Sanctis had anticipated. She was used to Rome and she had friends, hard working, poor people most of them, but always to be relied on to give a helping hand.

"I've got my pupils," she explained. "I get recommended. I can keep myself. I—I haven't anyone in England, and I shouldn't be able to earn."

"I can find you a job," said Miss Fordyce, suppressing some doubt on the subject. A girl like Lily, living from hand to mouth, eating at odd times in cheap restaurants, rushing about to give lessons, might have grown too restless for domestic work.

The marchese, who had been listening, intervened.

"Can you tell us anything about this, signorina."

He laid the note they had found on the doctor's desk on her knee.

"Why, it looks like a page torn from Carmela's exercise book—" She looked up at them. "I didn't write this. What does it mean?"

De Sanctis said, speaking more gently than was usual with him, "I think you have an unselfish nature, signorina. I noticed just now, when you were telling us all that has happened that you were thinking of the young girl, Anne, whom you have never even seen, and of the nephew of our friend here, and that you had not seen the affair at all from your own angle."

"Oh yes, I have," she interrupted, "but they only wanted to get rid of me because they thought I knew too much—"

"That motive still exists. This note—it is an imitation of your handwriting. The Commendatore would have specimens to hand in his daughter's English translations, corrected and annotated by her teacher."

This was news to Lily. She had heard nothing of their visit that morning to Frau Haussmann's flat. She looked round at the three grave faces and stammered: "Carmela's father? I didn't like him, but—"

"He owns the house in Via della Croce."

Lily shuddered. "This was the second time. Before there was the cat, with froth on its lips. You are right. I can't stay here. I can't."

CHAPTER XIX
THE NEXT STEP

IT HAD been raining all day, after weeks of drought, and there was a chill in the air. Don Vincenzo shivered as he came out of the church. The winters were cold in Sant Andrina, high up in the mountains. Snow fell, and was blown by the tramontana into deep drifts. The old women coming to the church to pray brought their little scaldini filled with embers with them to keep them warm. The priest, who was too poor to be able to afford a fire, dreaded the coming of winter.

He spoke to the blind beggar who sat on the church steps, huddled in his cloak.

The other lifted sightless eyes. "There is a stranger in your house, padre mio. He came by the omnibus."

"At my house? Who can it be—"

"He asked me the way. He speaks like a Roman. A gentleman, and charitable. He gave me a lire for my trouble, and it was no trouble, but a pleasure, as I told him."

"You talk too much."

Don Vincenzo crossed the deserted piazza to his house. His housekeeper was waiting for him at the door. She pointed mysteriously to the sitting-room. "Someone for you—"

Don Vincenzo hesitated for a moment in the tiny bare passage and crossed himself before he went in. His visitor rose as he entered. He was a man of about forty, of distinguished appearance, with fine features and melancholy dark eyes. He wore a small black beard trimmed to a point.

He introduced himself. "My name is de Sanctis, Luigi de Sanctis. Here is my card."

The priest bowed. "Please sit down. Are you the authority on Etruscan culture? If so, I have read some of your articles. I have a friend who is kind enough to send me reviews—"

"Hardly an authority," said de Sanctis, but he looked pleased. "It is not a subject of general interest, but I have devoted my time to it."

"We have nothing here, I think," said the priest, "though the foundations of the castle ruins in the hotel grounds may have been laid when that lost language was the common tongue."

"The castle grounds. That is where they found the body of a woman who was murdered while staying at the hotel, I believe." The priest's face changed. He took a screw of paper from a pocket of his shabby cassock and helped himself to a pinch of snuff before he answered. "I have taken it upon myself to say a few masses for the poor creature's soul. She was, I fear, a sinner, and she was not of our faith. A beautiful woman, though no longer very young. She was an artist. You knew that, perhaps? I am no judge, but she made a sketch of the interior of the church at the moment when a ray of light falls on the pulpit, which I greatly admired.

She told me that when she returned to England she would hold an exhibition of her work there, but it was not to be."

"What has happened to her paintings?"

"I believe they are still in the summerhouse she used as a studio. The pretore from Vallesca came over to conduct an examination on the scene of the crime. I suppose the summerhouse is locked and that he has the key."

"Do they think she was murdered there?"

"I think so. What is your interest in this painful affair—"

he glanced down at the card lying on the table, and added— "Signor marchese."

"I do not ask questions out of idle curiosity. They have arrested a young Englishman who spent a few days at the hotel about the time she disappeared?"

"Yes."

"Do you think he is guilty?"

The priest was silent for a moment. Then he said: "You have read accounts of the case in the newspapers? I hear it has been given some publicity."

"Sicuro."

"The hotel people say he joined Miss Sandoni, who had been here alone for several weeks, painting, that he was evidently an old friend and that they were led to believe, by him, that she had gone away for a time, leaving the town in the omnibus. They say he explained that she had received a telegram and had to go off in a hurry. She had left most of her luggage and her painting materials, and they assumed that she would be returning sooner or later. It has been established that there was no telegram delivered at the hotel that day. The young man himself says that he knew nothing of Miss Sandoni and that she was not at the hotel when he arrived., He admits that he had a—a female companion, and says that she came the previous day and that they left together and were taken to the station at Vallesca by Mario Laccetti, who keeps a horse and trap which he sometimes uses for station work. Both these stories cover the known facts to some extent. It is agreed that another Englishwoman did come up from Vallesca in the omnibus, but the hotel staff all say that she left the following day. You see, Laccetti having this conveyance, which he keeps at the foot of the hill, means that we, in the town, witness the arrival of strangers coming to stay at the Albergo del Castello but we do not always see them leave."

"Are there any witnesses besides the hotel staff prepared to swear that the Englishman's amica was Miss Sandoni? That seems a crucial point."

"Ricciardi, the chemist, and two or three others who dine at the hotel say that they saw him every evening during his stay sitting at Miss Sandoni's table on the terrace, and they seem to have assumed that his companion, a woman wearing a white dress, was Miss Sandoni. But they were some distance away, night had fallen. They cannot really be sure. She was not seen with him during the day. That is worth noting, I think. I should have expected her to accompany him and show him where she had made sketches. She talked to me once when she came into my church. She greatly admired a fresco in one of the chapels. Whatever her moral character may have been she was certainly a woman of great intelligence. An artist."

"Another woman, also a foreigner, arrived on the 18th of July, a day before young Smith. That is not disputed, you say."

"No. But according to the hotel people she only stayed one night and was gone before the boy arrived. Laccetti says he took her to the station in his trap."

"And Smith says that she stayed until the 22nd, and that they left together?"

"Yes."

"The hotel register should provide evidence one way or the other if it was properly kept."

"It should. But, most unfortunately, a bottle of ink was spilt over that page," said the priest dryly.

"Then the authorities at Vallesca who made the arrest are depending entirely on the statements made by the hotel people. Obviously they should know if anyone does. They can't all be lying—or can they?"

"The hotel was formerly the Villa Sant Andrina, the country house of the ducal family that is now extinct. It stood empty for many years. At present only a few rooms are habitable. The staff consists of a man named Olivieri, who was formerly a chef at various places on the Riviera, and his wife and her brother. They have all worked in hotels, and they have put all their savings into this enterprise. It is a pity, for I fear it is doomed to failure. Sant Andrina is too remote to attract visitors."

"Would it be permissible to ask your personal opinion of these people, reverendo?"

The priest eyed him thoughtfully. "First I should have to ask you more precisely why you take so much interest in this obscure crime."

"I am investigating on behalf of the young man's family."

"Indeed. He calls himself Mr. Smith, but it is generally supposed that he was passing under a false name. That, of course, has helped to create prejudice. And he has consistently refused to give any information that might lead to his being identified. And yet you tell me that his family have heard of his predicament?"

"They heard of it. It does not matter how."

"They have money—influence?"

"Neither. I have undertaken to do what I can, it may not be very much."

Don Vincenzo sighed. "I have been greatly troubled. I may tell you, signor marchese, that I am convinced of this young man's innocence. I even went over to Vallesca to speak for him, but they would not listen to me. They seem to regard the evidence against him as conclusive. Here, in Sant Andrina, we have less confidence in Mario Laccetti and the Olivieri couple. It was common talk that Laccetti was Miss Shandon's lover and that she lent or gave him considerable sums of money. He is a handsome fellow, and, it seems, not above trading on his good looks. He is engaged to be married to the only daughter of a prosperous tradesman in Orvieto, and it is said that he is urging the parents to allow him to marry her soon. People were wondering what would happen if his fidanzata or her family heard of his other affair."

De Sanctis nodded. "He had got all the money he could from her, and she was becoming an encumbrance, an ageing woman, jealous, possessive. If only he had not yielded to the temptation to make some more money out of the daughter, the mystery of her disappearance might never have been solved."

"You are referring to the young girl who came here and stayed one night at the hotel? Mr. Smith came to me. He sat in that chair where you are sitting now and told me he was trying to trace her movements, and that he had been unsuccessful. Mario Laccetti says they explained to her that Miss Sandoni had left, and they had no idea where she was; and they advised her to go to Rome and apply to the consulate for help and advice. Mario drove her to Vallesca station and put her into the train."

"I expect that is a part of the truth," said de Sanctis. "Actually, I believe, he handed her over to the agents of a powerful criminal organisation, whose heads have built up large fortunes out of the export of women. They have probably been regretting the transaction ever since. They usually handle an inferior article, poor girls who have no friends to rout about after them."

The priest looked at him gravely. "Are you sure of this?"

"I am sure. They have ways of dealing with people who go about asking inconvenient questions. One is to push the questioner down a lift shaft, another is to accuse him of a crime that he has not committed. Their methods are effective, but I am sure they dislike having to take so much trouble. They are used to working a smooth-running machine."

"Then you are in some danger, signor marchese."

"Probably. But I have taken certain precautions. Can you tell me, reverendo, if the hotel is still open to visitors?"

"You are not going there?"

"That was my intention. Only for one night. To-morrow I shall go back to Vallesca and try to obtain a permit to visit the prisoner. After that—we shall see."

"In your place, signor marchese, I would return to Vallesca to-night. You will have time to catch the omnibus if you go at once. You are a friend of Smith, and that may be known. If they have already gone to such lengths to prevent an enquiry into certain matters they will not stop now. You would be alone there in that vast ill-omened building, away from the town, where no cry for help would be heard, with those two men and that woman who are mala gente. I beg of you not to commit such an imprudence."

"I shall be careful. I promise you that. I will come back here for a word with you before I leave in the morning. If I do not reappear I will ask you to inform the police."

"I will do that, but it would be better not to run the risk." He went with his visitor to the door and watched him cross the piazza. The driver of the omnibus had just come out of the wine-shop and was climbing to his seat. His passengers, two old women with laden baskets, were already in their places. There would be time, if de Sanctis changed his mind—but he passed the clumsy vehicle without a glance, and when the horses started forward at the crack of the driver's whip he had stopped to light a cigarette.

The piazza was enclosed on three sides by buildings, by the church and by houses, with narrow lanes and flights of steps radiating from it up the steep hillside. On the fourth side there were plane trees and a low wall, and a sheer drop of several hundred feet to the road that made several hairpin bends on its way down to the plain. The marchese, sitting on the wall, smoking his cigarette and thinking over his next move, presently saw the omnibus, like a child's toy, moving along the road below. He looked to his left where the long stuccoed building that had once been the country villa of the Dukes of Sant Andrina crowned the rocky spur that jutted out beyond the church. The hillside there, from the villa, now an hotel, to the plain below was more or less densely wooded. Guests at the hotel who cared to use a footpath down that hill would save not only five or six kilometres of road but would evade the curious gaze of the idlers in the piazza. There would be idlers on most days, though this evening a cold autumnal wind had driven them all indoors.

The short cut, and Mario Laccetti's trap for hire, would account for the fact that some of those who were seen to come were not seen again.

It was difficult to realise that three days ago he had known none of these people, and that, in a few hours, his life, which had run so long on ordered lines, had suffered a complete upheaval. His wife and children, with their nurse, were on their way to

Scotland. Jeanie had been splendid, cheerful and uncomplaining, accepting the fact that there was no time for explanations. Only as the train began to move, she had leaned out of the window and said wistfully, "You'll be joining us, Luigi, as soon as you can; and whatever this business is that is keeping you and Ronnie, you'll be careful—" There had been something else, but though he ran along the platform he had not been able to hear.

Miss Fordyce and Lily Oram had travelled with them. The older woman had been gruff and monosyllabic, but he had seen tears in her eyes as they shook hands before she got into the compartment.

"I don't know how to thank you. Give my love to my poor Roger if you see him. I feel like a deserter."

Lily had thanked him too. She looked very white and ill, and when the train started she was lying back in her corner seat with her eyes closed.

Ronald had taken his arm as they left the station together.

"Decks cleared for action. A bit drastic, but I expect you are right."

They went back to the flat, deferring any discussion of the next move until they met at breakfast the next morning. It was then that de Sanctis had announced his intention of going directly to Sant Andrina to find out what he could on the spot. Ronald had wanted to come with him, but had been dissuaded. He had been absent a whole day from the consulate, and, though the clerks could carry on for a time, he might be needed, as the vice consul had not yet returned to duty. Finally he agreed to stay on at the flat with Pietro for the time being.

"I brought you into this," he said more than once.

It was true, of course, and the marchese's primary reason had been that he was fond of his young brother-in-law and disposed to help him in any difficulty, but as the case developed his interest had been engaged. He had a natural bent for the unravelling of mysteries, or he would not have been drawn as he had been to the study of the culture of a vanished race, and he had inherited a streak of Quixotism, a tendency to espouse an apparently lost cause, from a grandfather who had fought, in his youth, under

Garibaldi, and whose father before him had spent weary months in an Austrian prison. It was a side of his character unknown to everyone but his wife and his brother-in-law, and well concealed by the bland irony of his habitual manner.

He was reflecting now that the search for Anne Gale had been carried on in the manner of a relay race. First the girl's father, then, when he dropped out, young Fordyce and Lily Oram, then Roger's aunt, and now himself. Of those five one was dead, and one in prison, and the life of a third had been attempted twice.

He had been more impressed than he cared to admit by the old parish priest's evident anxiety as to his safety. He knew that Marucci must have regarded his presence in Frau Haussmann's flat as suspicious. Though they were members of the same club Marucci probably knew very little about him beyond the fact that he was a man of moderate means and with literary interests. If, as was probable, he had since made further enquiries and had learned that he had married a Scottish girl, and that his brother-in-law had a temporary post at the British consulate his suspicion might become a certainty. De Sanctis knew enough of the methods of the Camorra to surmise that the next step might be a more or less obscurely worded warning to him to mind his own business if he valued the continued health and welfare of his wife and children. The mere threat would be enough if the two babies had still been making sand castles on the shore at Anzio, with Jeanie looking on, defenceless and unaware. De Sanctis smiled to himself. Marucci might have a long arm, but it would hardly reach as far as Edinburgh. He had countered that move before it was made, and he was not afraid for himself. The rain had ceased some time before, but the sun had gone down behind a heavy bank of cloud. It was time to make his way to the hotel. He crossed the piazza and went round behind the church and along the narrow lane between high walls that led to the villa. He thought, "In the old days two men could have held back an army here." The castle must have been almost impregnable, but the garrison could be starved out.

There was nobody in the hotel entrance when he entered, but the lamps were lit in the dining-room and dinner was being served to some early arrivals. De Sanctis, who was hungry, was cheered by a very savoury smell. He sat down at an unoccupied table, and presently the woman who was waiting on the other diners came to take his order. She was, he supposed, anything from thirty to thirty-five, heavily built and very dark, with close plaits of blue-black hair framing a face whose ravaged beauty startled him, spoiled as it was by sullenness and by what might have been grief or merely lack of sleep. He thought, "This must be Maddalena Olivieri. She looks like da Vinci's Medusa."

She glanced at him dully and without interest. It was clear that her thoughts were elsewhere. She took his order and came back with a fritto misto of such superlative excellence that de Sanctis complimented her when she brought the next course. She answered indifferently, "Si, signore. My husband is a good cook."

"I missed the last omnibus. Can I have a room here for the night?"

Her heavy face brightened for a moment as she replied that they could give him a very good room. He rose as soon as he had drunk his coffee and she came over to him at once. He told her that he had had a long day and would be going to bed at once.

He followed her up the great marble staircase. The three flames of the cotton wicks floating in oil in the brass lucerna she carried were like marsh lights flickering in the surrounding gloom. Their footsteps echoed along the uncarpeted marble floor of the vast corridor that ran the whole length of the building.

Maddalena said: "It is rather dark. The signore must excuse it. Next year we shall have electricity."

She opened a door on her left and he waited on the threshold while she lit a candle on the dressing-table.

"Will there be anything else, signore?"

"Nothing, la ringrazia."

She wished him good night and left him.

The proportions of the room were magnificent, and the ceiling was panelled with wood elaborately carved with the arms of the Sant Andrina family. The furniture, a cheap bedroom suite, typical of a third-rate commercial hotel, was almost pathetically incongruous. De Sanctis, looking at the rickety chest of drawers and the tiny mat by the bedside, realised something of the scraping and saving, the immense combined effort that had launched the absurd enterprise. He did not doubt that the priest was right and that it was doomed to failure, but it was, in its way, to be admired. He said to himself, "If these people weren't criminals I should be sorry for them."

He opened one of the windows, after blowing out the candle, and went out on to the balcony. The wind had dropped and the night sky was clear, and bright with stars.

CHAPTER XX
THE END OF A DREAM

MARIO Laccetti waited in the station yard while the few passengers who had come by the last train passed the ticket collector's barrier. He was both nervous and impatient, for the person he had been warned to expect had failed to arrive by an earlier train. It had been raining and the sky was overcast. It would be dark long before they reached Sant Andrina. The last person to come out was a big burly man who wore a light grey suit and a Panama hat. Mario, who had an hotel servant's quickness in such matters, summed him up as prosperous, but not quite a gentleman. He glanced about him, and his cold saurian eye rested on the young man.

Mario moved forward with his most ingratiating smile. "Il padrone?"

There was no answering smile. "You are Laccetti? Good. You have a conveyance?"

"My own horse and trap."

Mario's pleasant tenor voice sounded brittle. The padrone's appearance was far from reassuring. He said: "There is a good hotel at Vallesca."

"I am coming to Sant Andrina. I have something to say, not only to you, but to your sister and her husband."

Mario moistened his lips. This was what he had feared. He said: "My sister will do anything for me, but my brother-in-law has been difficult. He needs very careful handling."

"He will do what I say," the other said harshly. "He is too far in to extricate himself."

Mario answered with due humility, "Si, signore."

The springs of the trap creaked protestingly as the big man climbed into the place beside the driver. Mario gathered up the reins and the lean chestnut broke into an awkward canter.

"How far is it?"

"Twelve kilometres by road, but only seven if we leave the horse in his stable at the foot of the hill and go up on foot through the hotel grounds."

The other grunted, "Have you heard from Bertha Haussmann?"

"No, signore. Was she to have written to me?"

"No matter." He clutched the side of the trap as they jolted over a rut. "Attend to your driving. You will have the horse down if you are not more careful, diamine! It is intolerable that I should be exposed to such discomforts." Mario answered submissively, "Si signore." He had been alarmed when he learned that the personage whom he only knew as the padrone intended to pay him a personal visit, and he was realising how right he had been. Marucci, satisfied that his young follower had been sufficiently intimidated for the moment, relapsed into a brooding silence which remained unbroken until Mario pulled up his horse at the foot of the last hill.

"If the signore will get down here it will not take me more than a few minutes to stable the horse and give him a feed—"

"Bene."

Marucci leaned against the gate and lit a cigar while he waited. The wooded hillside loomed up before them, dark against the night sky. He looked up at a few scattered lights glimmering far above. The country was very still and peaceful. He said: "What possessed you to open an hotel here?"

"The views are marvellous. All who have come to us agree about that. And the air is good. In two or three years we shall have a clientèle. Why must they go to Switzerland or the Tyrol when we have mountains here?"

"Too far from the station."

"But when there are more of these horseless carriages, the automobili—" said Mario eagerly, forgetting his awe of the padrone as he embarked on his favourite theme.

"Schiochezze!" said the older man brusquely. "They can't climb hills. And you don't suppose foreigners are coming to a place where their women are murdered, do you? Don't be a fool, Laccetti. You're finished here."

Mario did not answer. His heart sank, but he still hoped that he would be able to persuade the padrone that there was money in his scheme. It had been Mario's experience that very few men or women were impervious to his charm when he chose to exercise it. Of course women were easier game.

The path through the vineyards and the olive orchards wound steeply upwards, and Marucci before long was breathing heavily. He stopped after a while to wipe his face and his neck with a silk handkerchief strongly scented with patchouli.

"Are we nearly there?"

"Si, signore. This is a part of the hotel garden—"

Marucci glanced towards a small building which was just visible among the dense undergrowth a little way from the path.

"Is that where—"

Mario licked his lips which had gone dry and muttered assent.

Marucci did not speak again until they were crossing the terrace. He stopped to stare at the vast formless bulk of the villa. There was only one light, in the kitchen window. He said nothing, but he laughed contemptuously.

Mario winced. At that moment he hated the padrone even more than he had hated Eve Shandon when she ceased to be a source of profit and became an obstacle to his happiness.

In the kitchen Maddalena had just finished washing up the dishes and was putting them back on the shelves. Olivieri had put on his steel rimmed spectacles and was sitting at the table with the oil lamp reading yesterday's *Messagero*. He was in his shirt sleeves, with his arms bare to the elbow, and now and then he killed a mosquito that had come in through the open window and settled on his hands. He was looking pale and tired and he started violently when the door opened and Mario came in, bringing a stranger with him.

"Maddalena, Luciano, this is the signore who advanced us money to pay the last instalment of the price of the villa. He—he has come to see for himself that it is a good investment. I—I have been telling him—scusi—" he brought forward a chair for Marucci, who sat down heavily.

He looked from Olivieri to his wife, and spoke to the woman. "I have found your brother useful and shall again if he can learn his lesson. And this goes for you too, signora Maddalena. You thought you were being clever, I daresay, when you accused the Englishman of having murdered the woman whose body was buried in your garden. But it is one of the rules of our organisation that the police must not be involved in our affairs except in the very last resort. His arrest took him out of our hands. If you had not interfered he would have been effectively silenced before now. As it is, owing to the accounts in the newspapers, his friends have discovered more about our business than they would otherwise have done. We have been put to a great deal of trouble, and have had to take steps that may have unpleasant repercussions. One of our chief depots in Rome, the house in Via della Croce, will have to be closed down, for the present, at any rate. This is a poor reward for the financial assistance you have had from me."

Maddalena answered dully, "It seemed the only way to save Mario. I have not had one moment's peace or one hour of quiet sleep since."

Marucci nodded. "Si capisce. You have been worried. It is very natural. You have not enough to do here. This hotel of yours is an absurdity, a dream that can never come true. You'll cut your losses, and make a fresh start in a place where your talents will not be wasted. I have just taken over an hotel in Naples and I can put you in to staff it. The manager is already chosen, a Neapolitan, who knows the ropes, but if you do well you may take over from him eventually. It isn't a posh place. It's a small hotel of the third, or if you like, the fourth class, frequented by some of the pursers and other officers from the ships that come into port, and may serve as a meeting ground for our agents and a clearing house for our goods. In fact, I am offering you a position of trust. It is more than any of you deserve after the way you have let me down," he added, with a return to his former hectoring manner.

Olivieri spoke unexpectedly. "A drinking den in a Neapolitan slum. That's what your handsome brother has brought us to, Maddalena."

"Be quiet," she said angrily. "It wasn't his fault. He was desperate. He was afraid of losing Laurina."

Mario had been listening, appalled. He could not believe that Marucci really meant to withdraw his support of his beloved scheme. He tried pleading, going over all the arguments he had used before. "We can succeed here if you only allow us a little time—" His eyes shone, his voice shook with emotion as he poured forth a torrent of eloquence. Were all their years of working and planning, all their hard earned savings, to be swept away? If the signore would have patience, only a little patience, every soldo they owed him would be paid back, and they would serve him in any way, he had only to command. He forgot his cheap atheism and appealed to the Madonna and the saints to hear him.

Marucci cut him short. "Basta—" he roared.

Mario's jaw dropped. He shrank back as if from an actual blow. The other two were silent. Marucci waited a moment, glaring at each one of them in turn before he pursued his advantage.

"Don't try your tricks on me," he said brutally. "I'm not a woman. Your pretty face doesn't mean anything to me, my lad. You're starting again from the bottom of the ladder. Make no mistake about that. And whether you rise again depends on yourself. And now, I'm tired and hungry. You can show me to my room and send me up some food. Soup, and an omelette—"

De Sanctis, listening behind the door, realised that it would not be safe to stay any longer. He felt his way back to the foot of the stairs and went up as quickly as he could, holding to the rail. He was only just in time. He could see the three tiny flames of Maddalena's lucerna flickering across the hall below as he tip-toed along the corridor. He was conscious of a certain relief as he reached the comparative security of his own room. There was no key in his lock, as he had already discovered, but he wedged the handle with the back of a chair.

A moment later he heard footsteps passing along the corridor and a door opened and closed.

He sat down on the side of his bed to think over what he had heard. He now had confirmation of what he had assumed to be Marucci's part in the affair. It was Marucci with whom he would have to deal if he was to get anywhere. The prospect was not encouraging. As an influential member of the camorra he would have almost unlimited resources. They would stick at nothing to avoid an open scandal. The death of Francis Gale, the death of the palmist Nefert, could never be attributed to them. That of Gale would always be regarded as an accident. His daughter Anne had vanished for ever. She was past help, and de Sanctis—a realist—doubted if she could be avenged. He knew now what he had previously suspected, that Mario Laccetti had murdered Eve Shandon, and that his sister had been accessory after the fact. But how could it be proved? On the other hand Marucci had made a remark that indicated that Roger Fordyce owed his life to the fact that for the past ten days he had been under arrest.

De Sanctis sighed and stretched himself. He was too tired to be able to think clearly. For two nights he had hardly slept at all, and his bones ached after the journey, after the heat and discomfort of the train, and ten miles jolting over badly made mountain roads in a vehicle without springs. As he frequently and shamelessly confessed to his young brother-in-law he loathed all forms of exercise, and it was due to a natural tendency towards leanness and not to any efforts on his part that he had not grown as fat and flabby as many Romans of his generation.

He would have to try to strike a bargain with Marucci, but in a house where he was outnumbered by four to one common prudence bade him defer any such project until the morning.

He removed his outer clothing and lay down on the bed. When he opened his eyes the sun was pouring into the room through the window he had left open. The air had a delicious freshness and a scent of the aromatic herbs that grew on the hills. It struck him that young Laccetti had been right. It was foolish to go to Switzerland or the Tyrol for what could be found within a few hours' journey of Rome. And then he looked at his watch and was annoyed to find that he had slept much longer than he had intended. Italians are early risers, and he knew that it was only too likely that Marucci had already had his breakfast of coffee and rolls and left the hotel. He dressed as quickly as he could and went downstairs and out on to the terrace.

Maddalena had seen him and she followed him out with his tray. He wished her good morning and she answered with her former lack of interest. He understood her better now. She had nothing left to hope for. Despair acted on her like a narcotic. She was dazed. He said: "Your brother has a trap for hire, I am told. Can he drive me down to Vallesca this morning?"

"He could have done, but he has gone there already with another signore who spent the night here. They left not long before you came down."

"Then I must try to catch the omnibus." He gulped down his coffee and asked for his bill. She had it ready and he counted out the change.

"The Signore will sign the visitors' book?"

"No time for that."

Maddalena did not dispute the point. She neither knew nor cared who he was. It did not matter. Nothing mattered. He had paid for his room and the dinner he had eaten the night before and the breakfast he had not had time to eat, and ready money was very necessary since the butcher and the grocer in the town would no longer give them credit. She glanced up at the façade of the villa, pearly white in the morning light, that had been empty for so many years and falling into ruin and decay, out of which they had planned to create a great hotel, the dream for which they had sold their souls.

A letter had come for Mario by the morning post from the father of Laurina. Her heart had sunk when she saw the Orvieto postmark. The little chemist was shrewd enough in spite of his apparent simplicity, to read between the lines of the sordid story unfolded in the newspapers under glaring headlines. Mystery of

Murdered Englishwoman. Drama of jealousy. Of whom had the young foreigner called Smith been jealous if not of Mario?

The letter, formally worded, had broken off his daughter's engagement.

Privately Maddalena had always thought Laurina a little fool, all frills and giggles, but she knew that Mario cared for her as he had never cared for any woman before. He had given her the letter to read, and had gone off with a shrug of his shoulders, but she had seen that he was seething with rage.

CHAPTER XXI
DEATH IN THE CUP

WHEN de Sanctis came round the back of the church into the piazza there was no omnibus waiting in the shadow of the plane trees. He spoke to one of the women who was drawing water from the fountain, and she told him that he was just too late, the omnibus had left five minutes earlier. There would be another, she said, at noon. He thanked her. She smiled, her teeth very white against the healthy brown of her face, and lifting the heavy copper water jar to her head moved away. The other women whispered together, staring at him and nudging one another. He went over to the priest's house and rang the bell. He would be able to show Don Vincenzo that he was still alive. But the housekeeper who opened the door to him told him that the parrocco had been called away to administer the extreme unction to a dying woman at one of the outlying farms and was not likely to be back for several hours. De Sanctis scribbled a few words on the back of one of his cards and left it with her. He spent the rest of the morning wandering about the steep winding streets of the little hill town. He was anxious and dispirited, feeling that he had begun the day badly and that luck was against him. A delay of three hours in seeking an interview with Roger Fordyce at the prison might not be very important, and he did not really know what he was going to say to the young man if he did obtain permission to see him. Lily Oram had been explicit. She had said, turning to Roger's aunt,

"I hope you won't be too shocked, Miss Fordyce. He told me he was staying at the hotel with a married woman. I think it may have been someone he met on the boat coming home. Mind, that's only a guess. He didn't say so. I gathered that her husband was important and that she was terribly afraid of being found out and not at all the sort who would sacrifice her reputation to get him out of a mess. And so I—I do hope the police won't insist on his producing the other woman before they will believe that she was not Eve Shandon."

Afterwards de Sanctis always remembered that sunny morning of early autumn, spent in drifting about the streets of Sant Andrina, and walking restlessly to and fro under the planes in the piazza, smoking cigarettes and being dogged by small boys who picked up the ends as he threw them away, as one of the unhappiest he had ever known. It came to an end at last, and he was in the omnibus, the only passenger, holding on to his seat as the clumsy vehicle lurched round every bend of the road during the descent to the plain.

The town of Vallesca was two kilometres beyond the station. The omnibus stopped in the Piazza Vittorio Emanuele. De Sanctis got out rather stiffly. He was paying the driver when he happened to look up just in time to see Marucci coming out of a rather dingy little restaurant across the square. The commendatore adjusted his panama at a jaunty angle and walked away. Something about the set of his massive shoulders indicated that he was in excellent spirits and was probably humming a tune.

The eating-house—its name, Ristorante del Sole, was painted on its faded awning—seemed hardly the sort of place he would be likely to patronise, and the hour—it was half-past three—was too late for lunch and too early for dinner.

He did not seem to have noticed de Sanctis, who looked after him thoughtfully, but did not attempt to follow him.

The marchese's goal was the Municipio, a beautiful fifteenth-century building of mellowed red brick, with a soaring campanile. It was the wrong time of day, the hour of the siesta, and he was kept waiting for some time in a frowsty ante-room smelling of drains and stale tobacco before a clerk came to ask his name and his business.

"Permission to have an interview with the Englishman who is being detained in connection with the Sant Andrina murder case? If the signore will wait—"

De Sanctis, waiting, could hear a good deal of coming and going and a murmur of voices in the adjoining office, but when, after a rather lengthy interval, he was shown in, there were only three persons present, the pretore himself, a thin and fussy little man with a notebook, who appeared to be a secretary, and a captain of carabinieri, whose picturesque red and blue uniform was the only note of colour in the dingy, untidy room.

The pretore glanced up over his spectacles. "The Marchese Luigi de Sanctis?"

De Sanctis bowed.

"Why did you wish to see the prisoner Smith, Marchese?"

"As a friend of his family. I represent his relatives."

The captain and the pretore exchanged glances and the latter resumed with a greater show of cordiality. "That is excellent. You can supply us with the necessary particulars."

"Pardon me. I understand that Smith has always declined to give any information about himself?"

"I need not tell you, Marchese, that his silence was ill advised."

"Possibly," said de Sanctis blandly, "but I have not come here to betray a friend's confidence. I may be able to persuade him. I cannot say more than that."

There was a perceptible pause. The pretore patted his head absently where some long strands of grey hair had been combed over a bald spot. He cleared his throat uneasily. He said, "I regret that I have bad news for you. The prisoner has committed suicide."

They were all looking at de Sanctis and saw that he turned very pale. There were three cigarette ends lying on the ground floor just in front of him. He moved them into a line with his foot before he spoke.

"When—and how?"

"An overdose of morphia. We cannot discover how he procured the drug. He must have taken it last night. This morning the jailer was unable to rouse him. He was still breathing, and a doctor was fetched and did what he could, but it was too late. Naturally we have made every effort to ascertain how he came to be in possession of morphia, but without result. I am inclined to believe that he had it on him when he was arrested. He was searched, but not, perhaps, too thoroughly."

"How do you know it was morphia?"

"There has been a post mortem examination. He swallowed it, probably, in his coffee. His meals were sent in from outside. He ordered what he liked. He was treated with every consideration. I can see this has been a shock to you, Signor Marchese, but I think you should consider the affair from his point of view. Personally, at his age, I should have preferred a quick and painless death to fifteen or twenty years of reclusion, and there can be little doubt that would have been the sentence."

"You were convinced of his guilt?"

The pretore spoke weightily. "The evidence was incontrovertible."

De Sanctis did not attempt to argue the matter. It was too late for that. He was sick with disappointment. They had won, he thought bitterly, all along the line.

"The burial must take place within twenty-four hours. That is the law. I doubt if, in the circumstances, a religious ceremony will be possible," said the pretore.

De Sanctis looked up quickly. "I will arrange for that if you will permit it. The parish priest at Sant Andrina will officiate. I will have him fetched here. He is as convinced as I am that the boy was innocent of the crime imputed to him."

"Ah, that one—" The pretore remembered Don Vincenzo's visit. He had been impressed, in spite of his anticlerical bias, by the old priest's unshakable dignity and patience.

"You shall be given every facility," he said.

De Sanctis thanked him and took his leave, after being given a permit to visit the mortuary.

He crossed the piazza and passed out of the cheerful bustle of the streets and the bright sunshine of late afternoon, gilding shop awnings and hucksters' stalls, and sparkling in the glasses of the customers drinking aperitifs at the little tables outside the cafés, into a cold silence broken only by the sound of running water.

The old man who had unlocked the door for him waited on the threshold, while de Sanctis moved forward to stand by the marble slab on which Roger Fordyce lay covered with a sheet, with the clothing he had worn, neatly folded, at his feet.

The marchese turned back the covering from the dead face.

He thought, "How young he looks. Aunt Polly—poverina—will never forgive herself for sending him out here."

He stood there, silently, for several minutes. Miss Fordyce had said more than once that Ronald Guthrie reminded her of her nephew. De Sanctis fancied he, too, could trace a likeness. Was it the modelling of the cheek-bones and the jaw that gave that look of candour, of honest simplicity, that had always made him feel protective where his young brother-in-law was concerned? He thought, "He was as unfit for this business as a sheep dog would be to deal with a nest of snakes."

The custodian, jingling his keys to remind the visitor that time was passing, said, "He doesn't look like a murderer, does he?"

"No."

"He was liked at the prison. He gave no trouble. They're very upset about him going off like that. They didn't expect anything of the sort. They say he always seemed quite cheerful and sure that his innocence would be proved, except now and then when he seemed a bit down, but it soon passed."

De Sanctis was about to cover the face. He said in a hushed voice, "He seems to be smiling now."

"Maybe there's more to smile at where he's gone."

De Sanctis turned away with a sigh. He said, as he slipped a silver coin into the ready palm, "His meals were sent in, weren't they? Do you know where from?"

"Sicuro. The Ristorante del Sole."

It was the answer he had expected, and it brought back to his mind the picture of the commendatore swaggering along the street, setting his hat at a jaunty angle, swinging his cane, ogling every woman he passed, on the top of the world.

Chapter XXII
UNTOUCHABLE

"The Bible was right," said Ronald Guthrie gloomily. "The wicked shall flourish like a green bay tree."

It was late in the evening of the following day. De Sanctis had returned to his flat in the Via Ludovisi an hour previously, tired, dispirited, and cursing the slow and uncertain train service between Vallesca and Rome. He had since had a bath, and was sitting down to a supper prepared by Pietro, more to please that faithful servant than because he felt hungry.

Ronald, walking restlessly about the room, lighting cigarettes and throwing them away half smoked, had listened to his curt and carefully unemotional account of the tragic failure of his mission.

"I suppose it might have been suicide," he said doubtfully. "We can never prove that it wasn't. But from what I overheard at the hotel I knew that Marucci did not want him to stand his trial. I expect he knew that a clever lawyer could pick holes in the case for the prosecution. In Naples I daresay he could fill the court with members of his filthy organisation, but not so far north as Vallesca. The authorities there were very decent. Mind you, I think they are glad to be able to drop the whole thing. They weren't happy about it. It's a racial characteristic, Ronald. It goes against the grain with us to punish a man for being jealous—and that was supposed to be the motive."

"What do we do now, Luigi?"

"Has the vice-consul come back?"

"Yes. He turned up this morning."

"Good. We leave for England to-morrow. There is nothing more we can do here. We've got to break it to Miss Fordyce."

"Oh, my God—"

"I know. I'm not looking forward to it. But she has a right to hear all I can tell her, and I think you may be able to help. She took a fancy to you, and you liked her, didn't you?"

"Yes, oh yes. But is that beast to go unpunished?"

"I'm afraid so," said de Sanctis regretfully. "It's a great pity. Poetic justice is so satisfying; but we live in a world of prose. I wonder if he has gone back to Naples or if he broke his journey here."

"Does it matter," asked Ronald bitterly, "if he's untouchable?"

"Perhaps not, but I would like to see him again if it is only to wipe out that picture left in my mind of him strolling out of that dirty little eating-house, as pleased as a cat that has just caught the canary. Per Dio, I'd like to wipe that smile off his fat face if any words of mine could do it."

"Don't be a fool, Luigi. It would do no good, and you would be making a powerful enemy."

De Sanctis smiled. "He is that already. He will have seen the doctor by now and learned how we rescued Lily Oram. I'll see how I feel in the morning. There would be time. We shall leave by the midday train. And that reminds me, I must tell Pietro to pack."

"You'll take him with us?"

"Sicuro. We'll shut up the flat."

"You know where to find him?"

"Marucci? When in Rome he stays with his mother, the old contessa, who has a villa in the Prati di Castello. Don't you remember that Miss Oram was coming from there when she was taken ill on the bridge? She was giving his little girl English lessons."

"Well, I'd give the chap a wide berth," said Ronald, "unless you can hand him over to the police—and you say you can't. He's dangerous."

"I'll sleep on it," de Sanctis said, but he would make no promises. Ronald looked at him anxiously, but was wise enough to say no more.

"I'll be up bright and early," he thought, "and keep eye on him." He asked Pietro to wake him at six.

Pietro replied indulgently, in the tone he used to Ronald's three-year-old nephew. "What for, signorino? I will do the signorino's packing. Lasci fare. Faccio io."

"So you shall, old bean. But wake me all the same, see?"

When he opened his eyes the next morning Pietro was standing by his bedside with his breakfast tray.

"Splendid." He sat up. "The padrone's still asleep, I hope?"

"No, signorino. He drank his coffee an hour ago, and went out."

"Oh, hell!" Ronald reached for his watch. It was twenty minutes past nine. He groaned. "Why didn't you do what asked you, Pietro? I might have been able to stop him."

"The padrone would not allow it," said Pietro apologetically. "He said you were not to be disturbed. He left a message for the signorino."

"What was it?"

"That if you were in need of occupation you could help me pack his books and papers. I have the case half full already. He is taking all the books on the two lower shelves in his study. We must be going to spend several months away."

"Hard luck on your girl friends here, Pietro."

Pietro grinned. "I have drawn the signorino's bath water. If he will get up now I can pack his pyjamas. We are to meet the padrone at the station with the luggage."

"What about the tickets?"

"The signorino is to take his and mine. If the padrone does not come we are to go without him."

"I'm damned if I do," said Ronald violently. "I can't. Jeanie would have my hide."

They looked at each other. Pietro said slowly, "I am his foster brother. I would die for him. But he is my master. I have to do what he says."

They were waiting on the departure platform of the Centrale five minutes before the train was due to leave. The luggage was in the van, and they had secured three corner seats in an empty first-class carriage. There was no sign of de Sanctis. The manservant's swarthy face was drawn and anxious. Ronald could not keep still. He shifted his weight from one foot to the other, fingered his tie, looked at his watch, strained his eyes to see past the people coming out of the buffet. Their view of the station entrance was often blocked by blue-bloused facchini pushing trucks laden with luggage.

"Only two minutes now. Oh Lord, what are we to do!" Pietro said hoarsely. "Get in, signorino. Take care of the signora and the children. I will stay—"

"No. No. I—oh, thank God—" Ronald's voice cracked. "Here he is." De Sanctis, running towards them down the long platform, waved to them to get in. The guard was blowing his whistle, the facchini were shouting. The train had begun to move as he swung himself on to the footboard. Ronald and Pietro pulled him into the carriage.

No one spoke for a minute. De Sanctis was breathing heavily and his face was white. Ronald produced a pocket flask and poured a little brandy into the cup. His hands were shaking and some of the spirit was spilt.

"Here," he said, "drink this."

"Grazie." He handed back the cup. "Better have some yourself, Ronald."

"I will. I feel like something the cat brought in. Damn you, Luigi, giving us such a fright. My hair will turn white, or fall off, or something. What the blazes have you been doing all the morning?" Some people had gone along the corridor looking for better seats, but they still had the carriage to themselves. The train had left the suburbs and was gathering speed. De Sanctis, glancing out of the window, saw the green undulating pasture land of the Roman campagna, treeless, and marked here and there by crumbling ruins of ancient aqueducts and watch-towers. A wine cart was moving slowly along a rutted track, the driver lying asleep on his barrels under the leather hood, leaving his horse to follow the familiar road. An old man in goatskin breeches was leading a flock of sheep. The sky was blue, the intense blue of lapis lazuli, and the air crystal clear. De Sanctis thought of the raw northern sea mist drifting in from Leith harbour, and sighed.

He said, "I saw Marucci."

"Luigi—"

"He opened the door to me himself. There were no servants and the furniture was covered with dust sheets. He told me he was camping there, fending for himself for a few days before rejoining his mother and his little girl at Sorrento. He asked what he could do for me. I told him that I was in Vallesca the day before yesterday and that I saw him come out of the Ristorante del Sole. He said, 'What of it?' but I think he was disagreeably surprised.

I told him that I knew more than he thought, and that I would advise him to restrict his future activities to his place of origin."

"What did he say to that?"

"He laughed, but I could see that he was angry. He asked me if that was a threat, and I said that I would rather call it a warning. He said, 'You are either a very brave man, signor marchese, or a very foolish one. If you know so much you must be aware that I have a very long arm.' I said, 'Are you never afraid that God may punish you through your daughter?' His face changed. I fancy I had touched the only vulnerable spot in that heart of stone. But he recovered himself quickly. He said, 'Va bene. I have silenced others. Now I shall do the same to you. Look to yourself, de Sanctis. Not that you can prove anything.' I told him not to be too sure of that, and came away."

"And what good have you done?"

"Not much, perhaps. But I think he was shaken. And I feel much better. I haven't told you everything I said to him. I let myself go." He smiled reminiscently as he took a cigarette from his case. "The filthy Neapolitan sewer rat." His smile faded. "These are the canaglia who give us a bad name in other countries; and while our police are too weak or too corrupt to deal with them it must be so. Basta. I am going to sleep." He leaned back and closed his eyes. Ronald watched him with a new-born respect. He had always regarded his brother-in-law as a good-humoured cynic, fond of his comfort, and very unlikely to allow the pleasant and well-ordered routine of his life to be disturbed by any outside influence. He realised that he had been mistaken. He thought, "He's packed his books. That means that he expects to be away for months, or perhaps years. It will be home for Jeanie, and the children are too young to care, but for him it will be exile."

CHAPTER XXIII
THE GREEN BAY TREE

1

COMMENDATORE Marucci closed the door after his departing visitor and went slowly into the dining-room where, ten days earlier, Lily Oram, having lunch with her pupil and her employers, had watched the flashing of the Brazilian diamond on her host's little finger. He took a bottle of vermouth from the sideboard and poured some into a glass and drank it.

He had been conscious lately of a tendency to dizziness and shortness of breath if anything occurred to worry or upset him. He did not look at himself in the mirror, but if he had he would have seen that his eyes were bloodshot, and his coarse good looks marred by a deep purplish flush. He sat down heavily, and after a while he felt more like his normal self.

He thought, "I'll show him. I'll show him."

The Camorra had always found it necessary to make an example of any foolhardy individual who openly defied their organisation. In and round about Naples a more or less spectacular punishment would follow swiftly on the offence. The farmer's stacks would be fired, his cattle disembowelled, the fisherman's nets and his sails slit into rags. In Rome it might not be so easy, but the lesson must be given. The commendatore lit a cigar and smoked it thoughtfully as he considered ways and means for making the Marchese Luigi de Sanctis wish he had never been born.

He was quite alone in the villa, for the contessa had taken the servants with her to the furnished house he had taken for her at Sorrento. That suited him well enough, for he could make his own coffee in the morning, and lunch and dine at a restaurant. His spirits were not affected by the darkened rooms and furniture swathed in dusting sheets. In another day or two, when his business in Rome was concluded, he would go south and join the old lady and Carmela. He was fond of his mother, but he thought chiefly of his little girl. Delicate, perhaps, but she would outgrow that. She would be a beauty one day. She was shy, he thought fondly, easily hurt, but she trusted her babbo and he would protect her. He frowned, remembering that she had become attached to her English teacher. English. It wasn't safe to undertake any business in which they were involved. In future he would steer clear of them. Hadn't he heard that de Sanctis had married an English woman? He sipped a second glass of vermouth before he went out and strolled along the embankment under the planes to the nearest cab rank.

He climbed the dark stairs of the house in Via della Croce to the second floor. Doctor Donati came to the door. He was wearing a dirty dressing-gown and bedroom slippers, though it was getting on for noon, and his scanty dark hair was dishevelled. Marucci looked him up and down with angry contempt, noting the leaden tinge under his sallow skin.

Drug peddling was very profitable, but the agents who became addicts were soon worn out, though for a time, of course, their warped and atrophied moral sense made them useful tools. Marucci thought the doctor might last long enough for his present purpose.

He said brusquely, "I'm coming in. I want to talk to you."

Donati raised a shaking hand to hide the uncontrollable twitching of his facial muscles.

"You—you're very welcome. La—Laccetti is here."

"Laccetti—"

Mario stood up as the commendatore entered the surgery. He was wearing his best suit. Marucci was struck by his amazing good looks. In his opinion they were too remarkable to be an asset. Women would always be running after him and getting him into trouble, and their adulation had already made him so vain and so self-willed that he was almost unmanageable. But the commendatore did not allow his adverse opinion to appear in his manner. He greeted Mario indulgently, with a clap on the shoulder and a smile that seemed to make ample allowances for youthful impulse.

"I did not expect to see you again so soon, caro. What are you doing in Rome?"

"I came hoping to find you, signore."

Marucci's smile faded. "You should know perfectly well that people in my employment await their orders, and do not come to me unless they are summoned."

"Padrone—" Mario fumbled nervously with the brim of his hat. "You have heard that the Englishman committed suicide in prison?"

"I heard it. You should be thankful. The Sandoni affair is now finished. The trial might not have gone so well. You and your sister might have lied your way out of the mess, but I fancy your brother-in-law would have broken down under cross-examination."

Mario answered submissively. "Si, signore. We are very glad. Maddalena and I thought that as there would be no more scandal about that you might be willing to give the hotel another chance—"

"You thought. Do you think that I should have a villa here, a flat in the best quarter of Naples, horses and carriages and servants and clothes and jewellery, if I was in the habit of throwing my money down a well? When I said no I meant no. I shall not change my mind. You'll close down when you receive my instructions, and your sister and her husband will go to the house I told you of in Naples. I may have other uses for you. In fact, I can use you now, and if you do well you will rise from the ranks so quickly that soon you will be able to laugh to think that once your greatest ambition was to make a success of the Albergo del Castello. Draw your chairs up to the table, you, too, doctor."

Mario looked downcast. Donati shuffled forward, slavishly obedient. Marucci lit a cigarette and embarked on an explanation of what he wanted done. The other two listened silently though once or twice they exchanged furtive glances.

"This affair has gone badly from the beginning," said Marucci. "The frau bungled it. I had to go to Naples on business and when I came back she had to confess that she had let the girl slip through her fingers. We had been dangling the bait, but the fish wouldn't bite. I warned Bertha to be careful, but I daresay she lost her temper. The little fool took fright, and—" he shrugged his shoulders.

Mario stared. "Do you mean that she escaped? Then how is it they have not found her?"

"No. No. Bertha was clumsy, but not so clumsy as that. And she knows the ropes. Something of the sort happened two years ago. A Polish lady's maid. Her mistress died in Rome, and the frau found a new place for her with a lady who was going to the Argentine. The night before they were to leave to join the boat she became hysterical, screaming fits, shrieks for help, Heaven knows what. It had to be stopped. They thought she went out and drowned herself, but her body was never recovered from the river. These things happen in our business. The only way is to cut one's losses. Basta." He stopped to light another cigarette. "A certain person came to see me this morning. He was here yesterday—no, the day before. You know whom I mean, Donati. The Marchese de Sanctis. He is a member of my club, and I got his address from the porter on my way here. 118, Via Ludovisi. He knows too much, and he threatens to make use of his knowledge. That must not happen. I leave the method to you, Laccetti. It is a chance for you to show what you can do. Here is a hundred lire for any incidental expenses. But I expect quick results. I give you up to twelve o'clock tonight. You can report to me at my house in Prati di Castello. It will be quite safe, as the servants are away."

"Give me a little more time," urged Mario.

"No. I want the matter settled before I go for my holiday to Sorrento. It is up to you. The lift accident was neat, the attempt on the Oram woman less so. Poison is always a doubtful weapon. Use your hands. Did Nefert tell your fortune, by the way, before—"

Mario moved uneasily. "It—it was all rubbish," he muttered. "I didn't listen. For God's sake don't remind me of it."

"Surely you aren't squeamish?" said Marucci, with his cold smile. "To-morrow, if I am satisfied, I will send you to South America. You will travel first-class and enjoy yourself. But there must be no failure, no botched work. I shall want a detailed account. The marchese has annoyed me."

He flicked the ash of his cigarette off his sleeve and got up. "To-night, between twelve and one. As for you, Donati, you'll have to clear out if I find another tenant. I shan't use this house again for our business. Damn the frau and her son. If they've gone back to Germany he'll be dead before Christmas, and serve the fool right. Moral sentiments won't mend his lungs."

Donati went with him to the door, and came shuffling wearily back to where Mario sat with his head in his hands.

Mario looked up at him curiously. "What did he mean about the German woman and her boy? Aren't they still in the flat above? I went there before I came to you, but I could not make anyone hear."

"The Frau has been very worried lately. Her son was beginning to take too much interest in her business, and to ask awkward questions. What she has done she did for his sake, but that wouldn't help her if there was a show-down. She thought he was so wrapt up in his music that he wouldn't notice how she earned the money to pay his teaching fees, to say nothing of the butcher and the baker, but I warned her she would have trouble with him presently. They slipped away a few nights ago. God help them, if the padrone finds out where they've gone. He doesn't forgive a thing like that."

"Is he really going to turn you out?"

"Why not? I'm finished. Thirty years ago, my boy, my professors foretold a brilliant future for me. Brilliant. Never mind. I'm fifty-five. Finished. You thought I was older, perhaps. How long have you been working for him?"

"Only since the spring. I answered an advertisement. Someone with capital to invest. But it wasn't what I thought. He lent money, and in return I was to act as his agent when required in collecting girls to be trained for the chorus of an opera company that was going to tour in South America.

"Of course, I knew what that meant, but I picked up two or three for him in Vallesca—and then the one that has caused all this bother. Diamine. He's made me do things I didn't want to do and wouldn't have done if he had not promised to help us carry on the hotel. That's all I care about. And I've lost Laurina."

"But you'll go on doing his dirty work, I daresay, until you're like me, with nothing but the hope of another shot of morphia between you and hell."

"No, I shan't. If I'm in his power he's in mine. If I was arrested I should tell them I only carried out his orders."

"Your word against his, and who would believe you? He endowed an orphanage in Naples. That's why he's a commendatore. A wealthy philanthropist. I've noticed you argue with him. You haven't realised yet how powerful he is. If you had lived in Naples as I have you would know what it means to get in the way of someone high up in the Camorra. A flick of his fingers as he walks through the Galleria, and before you reached the end of the Toledo someone would have fallen against you and knocked you down in front of an oncoming tram, or you would be lying in a gutter with a knife in your back. And you'll have to go to Naples to embark on that fine sea voyage he promised you."

Mario's eyes narrowed. "You think that's a trap?"

Donati shrugged his shoulders. "There's no way of telling. He promised me a lot, but I never got more than a bare living. There is always something really handsome in the way of a reward in store when you have done the next job."

"I see."

2

The commendatore passed the rest of the day pleasantly enough. After a leisurely lunch he spent the afternoon in the gardens of the Pincio watching the children, in charge of stout, beribboned nurses, playing in the shade of the trees. Then he went for a drive in a vettura along the Appian Way and dined at a roadside osteria. He was not alone. He had picked up an acquaintance, an elderly Austrian professor, in the Piazza di Spagna, and had taken him along as his guest, and he prevailed on the old gentleman to come with him afterwards to a performance of *Rigoletto* at the Teatro Nazionale. The professor was an old bore, but if Laccetti bungled his job it might be useful to be able to prove an alibi. After the show they walked back together to the Hotel de Russie where the Austrian was staying, and Marucci went on alone, on foot, across the Ponte Margherita.

Rigoletto was one of his favourite operas and there had been a new tenor with a fine voice. Marucci was humming "La Donna e mobile" as he lingered on the bridge to look down at the Tiber. There was a moon, and the dark water was streaked with silver. Beyond the trees of the modern embankment loomed the sombre mass of Hadrian's fortress tomb, with its bronze angel, sheathing his sword. Marucci, who thought religion a good thing for women, to keep them quiet, was not interested in angels. He moved on, still humming the duke's aria. He had quite recovered his spirits. If Laccetti had done his work efficiently the tiresome and unsatisfactory affair in which these English had intervened, in their absurd search for a young compatriot to whom they were not even related, could be written off.

The villa stood alone, in a small garden enclosed by a low white wall, with a gate of wrought iron, heavily gilded. Everything of the best, Marucci had told the contractor when the house was being built. He was genuinely fond of his mother, and the house in the Prati de Castello had been a birthday present to her. If she had been at home there would still have been a light in her room, and she would have called to him when she heard his key turn in the lock.

"Sei tu, figliuolo?"

But she was at Sorrento with Carmela, and the house was dark and silent. He found the light switch, but no light went on. Another fuse, he thought irritably. He felt his way into the dining-room. He had used his last match, but there would be a box on his writing-table near the silver casket in which he kept cigarettes. As his fingers felt about among the odds and ends on the table something sharp-edged caught on his cuff and slid away. He grasped it as it was falling with a shattering of thin glass. He knew it must be the large framed photograph of Carmela in her white first communion frock and veil which stood in the place of honour. He had saved it, but the glass was evidently badly broken. As he laid the picture down he felt something warm running down from his wrist.

He must have cut himself somehow when he was trying to save the frame. He hoped the picture had not been stained. At first he was merely annoyed by his own clumsiness. And then, as the handkerchief he had hastily wound round his hand turned into a gluey, sodden lump that filled like a sponge with every throb of his pulses, he realised that the razor-edged sliver of broken glass had severed an artery. With that knowledge came fear.

After a horrible moment of blind panic he made an effort to pull himself together. He was alone there, in the dark, but Laccetti would be coming soon, and he could make a tourniquet and fetch a doctor. Laccetti. He had always been more trouble than he was worth, but he could be really useful at last. The front door must be opened for him so that no time would be wasted.

But the familiar dining-room had become a strange unfriendly place. He stumbled once over a stool, and again over a chair, and each time he fell heavily and had difficulty in struggling to his feet. When, at last, he reached the front door and opened it, after a good deal of fumbling, he had to lean against the wall to rest.

Some time had passed since he met with his accident. He did not know how long, it might have been five minutes or an hour. All the while he had been losing blood and using up his strength.

That picture in its silver frame had been a birthday present from his little girl to her babbo. His Carmela, his precious one, with ugly red smears on her pretty white silk frock.

There was a ringing in his ears, and a voice, small and clear, as if it came through a long-distance telephone.

"Are you never afraid that God may punish you through your daughter?"

He felt sick and faint. His knees were giving way under him; he was falling, falling for ever, through illimitable space, through eternal cold, and everlasting night.

Doctor Donati was spending the night on the dingy sofa in his surgery. Lately he had seldom troubled to undress more than once a week, when, as a concession to civilisation, he still changed his shirt. He was awakened, towards five o'clock, by the ringing of his bell. He got up, yawning and shivering, and lit a candle before he went to the door.

"Who is it?"

"Me. Open, for God's sake."

Donati pulled doubtfully at his lower lip. He recognised the voice of Mario Laccetti, loud and uncontrolled, obviously on the verge of a nervous breakdown. If he was not admitted he could not be trusted not to make a scene in the street below. He opened the door and followed his unwelcome visitor into the surgery.

"Why have you come back here? I've had enough—"

He looked more closely at the young man, and as he looked his jaw dropped and he shrank back.

"Your hands. And you've been treading in it—"

"You don't have to tell me," said Mario savagely. "That's why I'm here. It's getting light. I can't go to the station like this. Listen. It wasn't me. I didn't do it. I haven't done anything. I went to the place he told me of in the Via Ludovisi, and the porter of the flats said the Marchese de Sanctis went away with his family this morning. They took a lot of luggage with them, and he thinks they may be gone for some time. I was afraid to tell the padrone because I knew he would be furious, though it wasn't my fault. I picked up a girl in the Trastevere, and we sat drinking in an osteria, and we each had a plate of pasta con pomodori, and she wanted me to go home with her, but I knew I'd have to have it out with that animal sooner or later, so I got rid of her and went off by the river bank to the Prati quarter. A fine night, with a moon, and I didn't hurry. I knew he expected me round about midnight, but I thought, let him wait. I found the house easily. The name was on the gate. There were no lights showing, but the front door was open a few inches. I called out, 'Is anybody here?' No answer, not a sound, and the place was as black as the mouth of the pit. I went in and nearly fell over something lying on the floor. I struck a match and saw him. There was a lot of blood—it was on the door-handle and underfoot. That's how I got it on me. I swear I never touched him. I came away."

"Was he—dead?"

"Per Bacco—"

"Stabbed?"

"I don't know. I saw no weapon and no wound. I tell you I came away at once. I want to wash."

"You can rinse your hands under the tap."

"You must give me a pair of your shoes."

"I have only one pair, and they would be too small for you."

"It can't be helped," said Mario feverishly. He kicked off his shoes and sat down to force his feet into the doctor's. "I've never seen you wear anything but those old slippers." Donati shrugged his shoulders resignedly, and sat on his sofa looking on as Mario washed his hands under the tap, scrubbing his nails hard with an old brush. He examined his neat blue suit carefully, found two blood spots on the turn up of the trousers, and washed them off. Then he produced a pocket comb and combed his hair.

"I need a shave, but my hand isn't steady enough." He glanced at Donati. "You'll keep your mouth shut?" Donati nodded.

"Make a parcel of my shoes with something heavy, and throw it in the river."

"I can't go about the streets in my slippers," Donati said listlessly.

Mario eyed the older man for a moment uncertainly and then took a handful of money from his trouser pocket and counted out some silver on the table. "This will pay for another pair."

The doctor had seen the flash of a diamond. He thought, "He's taken the commendatore's ring. He must have killed him."

But he said nothing. He had been in the power of Marucci for a long time, and hatred for his task master had crawled in his drugged mind like a torpid snake.

Mario nodded to him. "I'm off now. You won't see me again. Addio."

When he had gone the doctor blew out the candle before he shuffled over to the window and threw open the shutters. It was a perfect September morning and the air was deliciously fresh. Sparrows were twittering in the eaves. He watched Mario hobbling painfully down the street in the shoes that were too small for him, until he turned the corner. Then slowly and deliberately, indulging the luxury of anticipation, he turned back the frayed cuff of his shirt and bared a lean forearm before he opened the drawer where he kept his hypodermic needle.

CHAPTER XXIV
THE SEARCH IS ENDED

RONALD Guthrie and Penny Fordyce sat on the river wall of Stratford churchyard watching the leaves from the trees drop into the water and float away. Penny had been crying. She had cried a good deal in the last three days since Ronald and his Italian brother-in-law had broken the news of Roger's death to her and to her aunt. The marchese had gone on to join his wife in Edinburgh, but Ronald was staying on for a few days at the White Swan. He spent a good deal of his time with Penny. He had decided that she was his sort of girl, not exactly pretty, but sensible and easy to talk to; and Penny was glad of his company.

"I ought to be looking after the shop really, but we aren't awfully busy as the season is over, and Lily can manage."

"Is she staying on with you?"

"I think so. Miss Briggs is going to be married to a farmer at Alcester. He's been coming to our place for a cup of tea on market days for a long time now. We'd have to have somebody, and we like Lily and she likes us, I think. I say, Ronald—"

"Yes, what?"

"Do you think she was in love with Roger?"

"I don't know."

Penny blew her nose. "Let's not talk about it. Do you like Shakespeare?"

"Pretty well." Ronald's tone was luke-warm, and Penny looked at him reproachfully. "You'd have to if you lived here, though he dies down a bit in the winter. I've got a pash for him really, in spite of his beard. Beards aren't so bad if they're well trimmed. I think your brother-in-law looks sort of romantic with his, like Drake or Raleigh or somebody."

"Shall I start one?"

"Certainly not. I should hate you with one."

"All right. Then I won't. Where's Aunt Polly off to?" He had met Penny coming away from the station after seeing Miss Fordyce into the train.

"She's going to Brighton, to St. Ursula's, to see the head-mistress."

"What for?"

"Well, for one thing, I'm not going back—I simply can't face it—I should never stop thinking of Anne—and she's going to try to wangle it that Miss Blane doesn't insist on the term's fees instead of notice. But that isn't the real reason. She's got to break it to Miss Blane that Anne—that Anne is gone. She was going to write a letter. She was trying last night. She made several starts and tore them all up. It's difficult when we really know so little for certain. So she decided to go down for the week-end and see her before the term begins."

"How old are you, Penny?"

"Sixteen. I know it's young, but I haven't any brains so it's really just a waste of time," said Penny rapidly, "and I'm quite good at making cakes so Lily and I can carry on when Aunt Polly is in the sere and yellow, though that won't be for ages yet, thank goodness, because she's a lamb even when she seems to be biting your head off."

"Oh, quite." Ronald cleared his throat. "I say, Penny, would you care to come and stay with my people in Edinburgh? My mother and my sister Jeanie—you know—the marchesa. They'd love to have you—"

Penny looked pleased. "I'd love to come. Oh—could we go to Cawdor? Just for a trip, I mean—"

"I daresay," he said vaguely. "I don't know where it is exactly. What about it?"

She gazed at him reprovingly. "Ronnie! You can't have forgotten. 'Glamis thou art, and Cawdor: and shalt be what thou art promised'."

"Oh, that. Well, anyway, we could have some tennis. We've got a hard court."

"Does the marchese play?"

Ronald grinned. "No fear. He loathes any form of exercise."

"Talking of exercise, we'd better be getting back to Sheep Street. You'll have lunch with us?"

"I've been hoping to be asked."

*

Miss Fordyce, meanwhile, was on her way to London, safely entrenched in a corner seat of a third class compartment labelled Ladies Only. She had brought a book, but she did not read. She sat with her eyes closed: they ached and the lids were reddened, for she, too, had shed tears, not so freely as Penny, but hers were the more difficult and bitter. The marchese had been very kind, but he had not been able to rid her of the feeling that she was to some extent responsible for Roger's death. And yet, if she had had to live through the last three weeks over again she knew that she would not have acted differently. The test had come when they knew of Francis Gale's death. A certain man went down from Jerusalem to Jericho, and fell among thieves. Were they to follow the priest and the Levite and pass by on the other side because this time the victim was a child?

She opened her eyes and looked out of the window over the stubble fields where the last of the harvest was being carried. Roger had failed, but she would always be proud of him.

That woman—Aunt Polly found it hard to be charitable when she thought of her—that woman who had inveigled him on the ship, coming home—what would she feel when she saw the notice which had been sent to the *Telegraph* and *The Times*.

On the 3rd of September, Roger Fordyce, aged twenty-four.

Nothing much, perhaps. Roger himself had said that it was all over, and that it had been a mistake. If he had lived would he have asked Lily Oram to go back to Malaya with him when his leave ended? Miss Fordyce sighed, and began to collect her belongings.

The train had reached the outer suburbs.

It was a little after four when she got out of a cab at the gate of St. Ursula's. She was dreading the coming interview. She asked for Miss Blane, explaining that she had no appointment, but that her business was urgent. She was kept waiting for a few minutes in the hall and then shown into the headmistress's study.

Miss Blane shook hands with her. "You are Penny Fordyce's aunt, of course. Do sit down. You are just in time for tea. Parsons is bringing another cup. I am afraid I am very busy. The children will be arriving on Monday. Did you wish to see me about Penny? She's a good child, but not, I fear, very brainy—"

"About her, in a way. I meant her to leave at Christmas, but she's been a good deal upset about Anne Gale—they were great friends, you see, and she does not feel she could bear it—"

"Really? Do you take sugar? One lump?"

"Yes, please," said Miss Fordyce distractedly, looking at the scone she held as if she did not know what to do with it. "You see, about Anne, I'm afraid I'm going to give you a great shock—"

"I know about the poor child's father, Miss Fordyce, that he died last month in Rome as the result of an accident."

"Oh—you know that. He came to see you, didn't he, when he came back from his honeymoon, to find Anne had run away from the house of the elderly relative with whom she had been staying?"

"Yes."

"He came to us afterwards. I believe it was your suggestion. We talked it over with him and agreed that she might try to join her mother who had been staying in Italy. After his death we—we carried on. The child was so young, and there seemed to be no other relations to look after her. We—I won't go into details, Miss Blane, but we had evidence that she had fallen into bad hands. I—I am so sorry to have to say this—it is terrible to think of—but I am afraid there is no doubt that she is lost to us for ever."

Miss Blane showed no emotion. She gazed at Miss Fordyce for a minute before she said. "Are you sure of this?"

"My nephew and I both went to Italy to make enquiries on the spot. I think I could convince you, if you can't take my word for it, but it is a long and complicated story. We had not, and I haven't now any proof that would satisfy the police."

"My dear Miss Fordyce, I don't doubt your word for a moment. But you have taken me by surprise. I had no idea that you had taken any action or I would have communicated with you before. You actually went to Italy? Fancy that. I think you had better hear Anne's account of her adventures from her own lips."

"I—I beg your pardon?"

Miss Blane smiled. "She is staying with me for the present. Quite safe and sound."

Miss Fordyce said nothing. She had turned very pale. Miss Blane rang the bell and asked the maid who answered it to tell Miss Anne that she was wanted in the study.

The young girl who came in and stood shyly by Miss Blane's chair, waiting to be spoken to, had a breath-taking charm. Her photographs showed her to be a very pretty girl, but no camera could do justice to her flower-like grace. Miss Fordyce, staring at her, understood her niece's infatuation. To good-natured, blundering, clumsy Penny this exquisite creature must have seemed a miracle.

Miss Blane said: "Anne, dear, this is Miss Fordyce, Penny Fordyce's aunt. You have not written to Penny, it seems."

"I'm sorry. I meant to, but there was such a lot to say, I didn't know where to begin. And I'm not much good at letter writing. Penny always did write two to my one. Will you give her my love, please, Miss Fordyce?"

Miss Fordyce opened her mouth and shut it again without saying anything. She did not feel that she could trust herself to speak just yet.

Miss Blane said: "Sit down, my dear. I have just learnt that your friends have been very worried about you. I have not asked you many questions as Mr. and Mrs. Bland didn't wish you to be reminded of what happened to you in Rome, but I think Miss Fordyce has a right to hear all about it, so suppose we have it all from the beginning."

Anne sat down obediently, and folded her hands on her lap.

"Well, Daddy couldn't have me, and I went to Cousin Agatha, but I couldn't stay there because she was so queer, and the house was full of cats. I thought I could stay in Daddy's flat in London, even if he was away, but there were people there, and they told me he had married again and was on his honeymoon. I—it was a shock, and I felt pretty awful, because Daddy and I had always had such fun together and I felt sure a step would spoil everything. I thought I'd go to mother if I could manage the fare. I knew she was in Italy, staying at a perfectly gorgeous place up in the mountains. She sent me some sketches when she wrote. I gave one to Penny. So I pawned my watch and Grandma's ruby

ring that Daddy gave me when I was fifteen and took a single
ticket to Rome. The journey wasn't bad, people were nice to me,
and when I got to Rome I didn't have to leave the station. An
old gentleman who spoke a little English took a ticket for me to
a place called Vallesca and put me in the train and spoke to the
guard about me, and when I got there the guard saw me into a
funny sort of omnibus full of women with coloured handkerchiefs
tied over their heads, who were carrying live chickens and even
a sucking pig, who stared as if I was some sort of freak. I was
tired after so much travelling and I slept most of the way, and
when we got to the place the bus driver took me to the hotel and
carried my suit case and he seemed to be asking questions, but,
of course, I couldn't understand a word, so I just kept on saying
Albergo del Castello."

Anne looked enquiringly from her headmistress to Miss Fordyce.

"Do you want to hear all this?"

"Yes, dear. Go on."

"The hotel was queer. It was on the edge of the hill, with a
perfectly marvellous view, an enormous building, and it seemed
to be almost empty. I asked for mother. I was very excited and
a bit nervous because I was taking her by surprise, you see, and
I did hope she would be pleased. I hadn't seen her since I was
quite small but I remembered how lovely she was. Dark. I was
terribly disappointed when the waiter said she had gone away.
He was very nice. Young and good looking, and he spoke English
quite well. He said that anyhow I must stay the night there, and
in the morning they would see what could be done. And in the
morning he said he had consulted his brother-in-law, who was
the manager or something, and he was being allowed a day off
to take me back to Rome, because they weren't sure but they
rather thought mother was there, staying in a pension they had
recommended. He took me down the hill by a short cut through
the hotel grounds to a stable where he kept a horse and trap, and
he drove me to the station and left the horse at a sort of inn just
down the road. When we got to Rome he seemed suddenly in a
great hurry to get me into a cab, and angry because people stared.
That's what he said, but I fancied he was frightened, and I still can't

think why. And when we got to the pension it was a flat at the top of a house, and the woman who kept it was a German, very fat, with a red face and gingery hair scraped back and fastened into a tight little bun, with lots of pins, rather like that fräulein who only stayed one term, Miss Blane, but much worse, and she stared too, and said: 'Ach, where did you find this?' And they both talked away in Italian so that I couldn't understand, which I thought was a rotten thing to do as they could both speak English, so at last I said, 'Where's my mother, please?' And the woman said: 'You are very tired. I will show you to your room. Your mother is not here, but I can tell you where she is. It is not very good, but you must be brave, is it not so?' I said: 'Has anything happened to her?' And then she said that mother had married again and was on her way to India. I said: 'I don't believe it. She wouldn't without telling me.' And then I remembered that Daddy had, and mother—well, she's always been like that. I mean, when she was in Kashmir I didn't have a letter from her for nearly a year. The landlady was quite decent, and put her arm round me and called me Liebchen. I told her I would have to get back to England somehow, and she said she would take care of me and we'd talk it over in the morning when I had had a good rest, and she unpacked my suitcase for me and helped me undress, and she brought me a cup of hot soup, and I think now there must have been something in it because I felt awfully sleepy afterwards and I didn't wake until quite late the next morning. She brought me my breakfast in bed and said everything would be all right, but I must not go out because in Italy young girls weren't supposed to without a chaperone, and she was too busy to take me. She asked me if I'd ever done any dressmaking, and I told her I had always wanted to but had never had a chance, so she brought me a dress length of flowered silk—awfully pretty it was, very pale blue with pink roses and leaves—and a paper pattern and a sewing machine, and told me to do the best I could with it. It was for me, and she promised not to be cross if I spoilt it. I was quite excited, because it really was lovely stuff, and the pattern had full instructions in English. You'd think the time would have seemed long, staying in one room, but it didn't. And after a time she brought me a novel by Mrs. Hungerford, a Tauchnitz edition."

"I wonder how she knew you would like that," said Miss Fordyce.

"She told me that before she married she was fräulein in a school at Eastbourne for a year. I asked her if she liked the English, and she said she did, but I don't think that was true. I believe she hated us."

"I thought you said she was kind to you?"

"Yes. It was the way she looked at me with her little piggy eyes."

"Didn't you see anyone else?"

"I heard a man's voice at meal times, and in the evening some-one practised the violin. It was the next day that the frau told me that a friend of hers had called and would like to see me, so she took me into the dining-room, and there was a big dark man there. She didn't introduce him properly, she just said, 'This is Anne—' And he smiled and shook hands. I thought from the way he talked that he might be a South American. He stared at me very hard, and he said: 'I hear that you are at a loose end, Miss Anne. Your father has married again, eh? I know. That is never very pleas-ant for the children of the first marriage. You do not wish to be at the beck and call of a stepmother? That is very natural. Well, it is a bit of luck for you that the frau told me about you, and I will tell you why. I am a theatrical manager. I have many touring companies travelling all over the world, and, as it happens, I can offer you a small part in one that is leaving Naples next week for the Argentine. I pay good salaries even to beginners, and the work is not hard. It is an amusing life, you will meet people, have fun.' I said, 'Thank you very much, but I couldn't possibly. I couldn't act even in the school plays.'"

"True enough," said Miss Blane drily.

"The frau said it wouldn't be a speaking part, just a little sing-ing and dancing which I could easily pick up. I should be given a few lessons. She said: 'My dear child, you're too young and inexperienced to realise that it is an extraordinary privilege to meet a famous manager like this, informally. It happens that you are just the type he is looking for, or he would not be making you this very generous offer. I can assure you that there are young actresses of proved talent who would give their eyes to be in your shoes standing at this moment.' I wanted to laugh because it always sounded funny when she misplaced her verbs, but I was beginning to be worried, too, because I was afraid I might seem rude and ungrateful if I kept on saying no. I said it was most awfully kind of them but I didn't want to go on the stage. I just wanted to get back to England, and I'd rather earn my living as a mother's help or something, or perhaps go into a shop. The man said, 'Is this your last word?' And the frau answered for me, 'Give her a day or two to think it over.' He told me to go back to my room, and I heard them talking together for some time before he left the flat. Afterwards she came and scolded me, and said I couldn't expect people to help me if I wouldn't take the chances that presented themselves, and that the English were a thankless race, and I was upset and cried. I was awfully lonely and homesick that evening, and after supper I began to feel really ill. I was ill in bed after that for I don't know how long. I was sort of muzzy—"

"My dear Anne," said Miss Blane.

"Well, I mean, dazed. Then, one day when I was feeling better, the frau had another talk with me. She was quite kind again and she said she was very sorry she had bad news for me and that Daddy had been killed in a lift accident. She showed me an obituary notice, cut out of an English paper, so I knew it must be true. Then she said, 'You must realise that I am a working woman. I can't afford to keep you here indefinitely.' I said if she would lend me the money for my fare back to England I would promise faithfully to pay it back, and she said that was impossible. She said, 'My friend's offer is still open, but not for much longer. You must decide and let me know to-morrow.' I said, 'I'm sorry, but I won't go on the stage whatever happens. I should hate it.' She said, 'You little fool—' and she went out, slamming the door. I got up and dressed. I thought I must go away. But when I tried the door it was locked. I sat down and tried to think what I ought to do. I was crying because—because of Daddy, and I was frightened."

Anne's voice shook slightly and as she looked past her hearers, staring unseeingly at a picture on the wall, the pupils of her eyes dilated until they looked quite dark. Miss Fordyce, whose heart had been hardened against her, relaxed a little. It was not the child's fault that lives had been thrown away.

"I had been crying for a long time when someone knocked at my door. I knew it couldn't be the frau because I had heard her go out, and she never knocked anyway, so I said, 'Who is it?' A man's voice answered, ' Never mind that. Come out and be quick, because there isn't much time.' I told him I was locked in and he said he would let me out because the keys of the other doors fitted. I said all right, and when he had opened the door I went into the passage. He was quite young, not much more than a boy, and he looked very ill. He said, 'Herr Gott!' so I knew he was German, though he spoke English quite well. I told him I had heard him playing. He said, 'Yes. She's my mother. You've got to get out of here before she comes home.' I said, 'Where shall I go?' He said, 'The British Consulate. But don't put the police on to us.' I said, 'Why should I? You haven't done anything.' He said, 'Quite right. Forget about us as if we were a bad dream. Get your hat quickly.' I wanted to look for my suitcase, but he said there wasn't time. My knees were so wonky after being in bed so long that I nearly fell down the stairs, but he held my arm. It was dark by that time and we walked for miles through streets, most of them narrow and smelly, and at last, when I was simply dead beat, he stopped and said he had brought me to the English quarter, and I must manage for myself, and he left me."

"Good Heavens," said Miss Fordyce involuntarily.

"It was all he could do," explained Anne. "He had asked me why I had come to his mother's pension, and I told him, and I said she was angry because I wouldn't accept her friend's offer of a theatrical engagement, and he said, 'So that's it,' and after that he hardly spoke at all."

"What happened after he left you?"

"I was simply dithering with fright. I felt sick and my heart was thumping as if I'd been running a race. There was an hotel just opposite, with lights in most of the windows, and two cabs drove up full of English people who had come back from a theatre, and they were all talking and laughing, and I went over and tried to speak to one of the older women, but she just brushed past me as if she hadn't heard, and then another party arrived, and I wanted to speak to a man who looked like the father of the two girls, but he pushed me away and said something about it being disgraceful and having had trouble enough with the beggars at church doors. And they all went in, and there I was. I—I just burst out crying. I couldn't help it. I simply howled. And then a middle-aged couple came up, and the man asked me what was the matter and where my folks were, and I couldn't tell them because it was such a long story, and she said, 'You poor child.' They were so kind that I felt worse than ever, and everything went black, and when I came round I was in bed, with a nun taking care of me. I learnt afterwards that I had hit my head on the kerb when I fell and had slight concussion. I didn't have to bother about anything because Mr. and Mrs. Staunton Bland said they would see about everything, and we came back to England by easy stages. They are Americans. They had a daughter who died when she was three, and she would be about my age now. They want to adopt me and take me back with them to the States."

"And you want to go?"

"Yes. Yes, I do. I love Aunt Hattie, and Uncle Elmer is a lamb."

Miss Fordyce glanced at the head-mistress. Miss Blane answered her unspoken questions. "The Staunton Blands brought Anne to me while they visit friends in Scotland. I think she is fortunate. They are charming people and have been most kind to her, and their references are unimpeachable. Run along now, my dear."

"Yes, Miss Blane. Good-bye, Miss Fordyce. Will you give my love to Penny and say I'll be writing to her?"

Miss Fordyce cleared her throat and said rather gruffly, "I will. Good-bye, Anne. My very best wishes."

When Anne had gone and the door had closed behind her she said, "You are sure they are to be trusted?"

"Quite sure. They really are charming, rather old-fashioned, but kindly and sensible, and, I could see, devoted to Anne. He's chivalrous, as so many American men are, and I think he finds her child-like directness and simplicity very appealing. We had a long conversation, when Anne was not present, and I told them all I knew about her unfortunate parentage. I warned them that the mother might claim her, though I did not think it was very likely. They are trying to get in touch with her, but the lawyers told them they often did not know where she was for months together—"

"I can help you there," said Miss Fordyce. "Mrs. Gale, who had resumed her maiden name and was known as Miss Shandon, was murdered in Italy towards the end of July. The case was reported in the Italian Press, but the victim's name was given as Eva Sandoni which, I suppose, accounts for the fact that it was not referred to in the English papers. You might tell the Staunton Blands, and leave it to them to enlighten Anne or not, as they think best."

Miss Blane looked shocked. "Murdered. What a dreadful thing. Could it have been those people who so nearly got hold of the child?"

"I am afraid so."

"Was the murderer arrested?"

"No." Miss Fordyce rose slowly and rather stiffly from her chair. She felt that she could not bear to answer any more questions.

Miss Blane said, "You look very tired. You've had a long tiresome journey. It was good of you to exert yourself on Anne's behalf. I really should have told her about that so that she could have thanked you for your kind efforts."

Miss Fordyce winced. "Oh no. Please."

Miss Blane went with her to the door. "All's well that ends well," she said brightly.

"Yes."

Miss Fordyce walked back to the boarding-house where she had booked a room for the night, along the sea front, through the cheerful noisy crowds of holiday makers. She knew that she ought to be glad. The horror they had hardly dared to think of had not come to pass. The clear stream had not been fouled, the flower had not been trodden into the mire. But she would have been more than human if she had not felt that Roger's life had been thrown away. She stood for a while by the railings, looking out to sea, and going over it all again in her mind, and again she realised that in spite of the loss that would darken the rest of her life there was nothing that she wished undone. And that knowledge brought peace. It was still early. Yielding to an impulse she turned inland and climbed the long hill to the old church of St. Nicholas. The church was open, but there was no service going on. She knelt for a while in a pew in the nave. Presently the old verger, who had been pottering about in the chancel, came to her.

"I have to lock up for the night now, ma'am."

She got up at once, not wearily, but with her usual briskness. "I'm ready."

EPILOGUE
1940

"THIS is the place," said the young airman. "They give you scrumptious teas, and they have a very tasty sort of gingerbread, a speciality of the house. It's run by a Mrs. Guthrie and a Miss Oram. They must be getting on. They've been here donkey's years."

As they passed in his friend glanced up at the painted sign of the Poor Player swaying gently in the breeze that blew up Sheep Street from the river.

It was the middle of the morning and the shop was crowded, but they were fortunate enough to secure a table for two. The prettier of the two girls who were running about serving coffee and cakes and ices came over to them.

"Hallo, John, are you home on leave?"

"Yes, Polly. How's Mrs. Guthrie and Aunt Lily?"

"Mother and Auntie are well, but run off their feet, poor dears. Still, we're lucky to be doing so well."

"This is my friend, Fatty Harrison. Miss Mary Guthrie." Harrison bowed and Polly smiled at him. "What are you having? Coffee and biscuits?"

"Some of your gingerbread, please."

She shook her bright head regretfully. "Sorry. It's off the menu. We can't get the materials. It's an Italian recipe, you know. Aunt Lily learnt how to make it in Italy. They call it panforte."

"Did she? Gosh. I didn't know she'd ever been out of Stratford."

"It was a long time ago," said Polly vaguely. "Before I was born. I don't think she liked it much. She doesn't often refer to it. It must have been very different. No passports and no cars. Practically the Middle Ages."

The two young men laughed and John said, "That reminds me. I picked up rather a decent little sketch just now for five bob. It was at that auction room round the corner. They're selling a lot of old junk turned out of people's lumber rooms."

He removed a brown paper wrapping, and laid a small water-colour drawing on the table between them. It had been pasted for framing on a bit of cardboard and was rather ragged and dirty at the edges. It represented a statue of Pan, with one arm missing, his grinning head and muscular shoulders gleaming white against a background of purple wistaria.

"It's rather good, I think," said its new owner, "though I suppose it isn't by anybody well known. It is signed E.S. and the date is 1905. Does that convey anything to you?"

"Not a thing," said Roger's niece cheerfully, and sublimely unaware that her mother, sitting in the desk across the shop counting out change, might have given a different answer. "But it's rather nice. Cover it up or you'll be spilling coffee over it. You did say two coffees, didn't you?"

She hurried away.

Harrison, who was shy with young women and had not uttered a word while Polly was within hearing, was suddenly moved to speak.

"Thirty-five years. Isn't it queer to think that bit of paper that a baby could tear into fragments, that you could burn up with this match"—he lit his cigarette—"in less than a minute, has outlived millions of men. The last war, and now this one—and Pan still grinning—"

"That will do, Fatty," said his friend repressively. "I'm going to ask Polly if she'll come with us to-night to the pictures."

Harrison opened his mouth to protest, but he was too late. Polly was coming back with the coffee. Harrison looking at her— she had no eyes for him—had to admit that she was a pretty girl, not glamorous, but undoubtedly pleasing. That crooked smile—

he was not to know how that smile, so like poor Roger's, had still the power to wring Lily Oram's heart.

The invitation was given and accepted. They drank their coffee, and paid for it. Penny Guthrie, at the desk, said, "Hallo, John," absently, for she was just wrestling with a bill that would not come right and counting surreptitiously on her fingers. They walked away down Sheep Street towards the Clopton bridge. There they paused to watch the river running under the arches, and John chose this moment to look again at his sketch.

"They might have given me a better bit of brown paper," he grumbled. "Oh hell, here's an officer coming. I'll have to salute."

He sprang to attention, and the sketch slipped from under his arm over the parapet and floated away gently down stream.

"Shall we get a boat and go after it?" asked Harrison.

"No use. Look, it's sinking. And, if it doesn't, it would be over the weir before we could catch up with it."

"I suppose so. And, if he sticks in the reeds, that's the right place for Pan."

They walked on over the bridge as a swan, crossing the river on his lawful occasions, thrust the sodden scrap of paper under the surface with his strong yellow beak.

THE END

AFTERWORD

A BRIEF NOTE ON THE CAMORRA AND WHITE SLAVERY

THE criminal events which Moray Dalton depicts in *The Murder of Eve*, which is set primarily in 1905, could have been drawn straight from newspaper headlines from the first decade of the twentieth century. The loosely-knit Italian criminal organization known as the Camorra—whose origins are vague but is known to have operated illicit gaming houses in the city of Naples as early as the eighteenth century—was much in the news in the early years of the 1900s, having been the subject of investigation in 1901-02 by the Saredo Inquiry into corruption and bad governance in Naples and prosecution in 1911-12 at the Cuocolo trial, which concerned the murder of a couple of reputed Camorrista police spies and resulted in the conviction of twenty-seven Camorra bosses and their sentencing to lengthy prison terms.

The Cuocolo trial received attention around the world, including in the United States, where many Camorristi had emigrated on account of the poverty of southern Italy and in the New Country were blamed, like their criminal brethren the Mafiosi, for multitudes of crimes, including the coercion of young women into lives of forced sexual servitude, or "white slavery," as it was popularly termed—even though most of the true victims of this abhorrent practice were not white. In the United States popular panic over the supposed epidemic of white slavery led to the passage into law in 1910 of the Mann Act, which criminalized the interstate or foreign transport of "any woman or girl for the purpose of prostitution or debauchery, or for any other immoral purpose." White slavery panics continued to recur periodically over the next few decades, with blood chilling exposés claiming that naïve young white women were being preyed upon by slave gangs all across the country at such seemingly innocuous locales as ice cream parlors, fruit stands, movie theaters and amusement parks.

In New York City in 1917, when pretty eighteen-year-old Ruth Cruger disappeared after paying a call on an Italian man's motorcycle shop to have her ice skates sharpened and was never seen alive again, crusading celebrity attorney and crime investigator Grace Hunniston accused the Italian, Alfredo Cocchi, of being a white slaver and agent of the Camorra. However, in actuality the man, who indeed murdered the poor girl, seems to have been a garden-variety sex criminal. Rather than having coerced Ruth Cruger into a lowly life of prostitution, Cocchi simply had assaulted her, beaten her to death and buried her in his cellar.

In 1926 after years of investigation, the League of Nations held a slavery convention which produced an agreement obliging signing nations to eliminate slavery and the slave trade, while two years later an internationally bestselling book by French investigative journalist Albert Londres, *The Road to Buenos Ayres*, highlighted the intersection between so-called white slavery and the prostitution business in South America. Throughout the 1920s and 1930s crime thrillers as well as more respectable detective novels employed white slavery as a plot device, while true crime magazines ran lurid stories about it, complete with titillating covers portraying attractive captive white women in bondage. Although today the white slavery panic of the early decades of the twentieth century is deemed by experts to have been highly exaggerated (and to have greatly overlooked the mistreatment of African and Asian women), that it was a widely held concern is unquestionable.

Curtis Evans

KINDRED SPIRITS . . .

Why not join the

DEAN STREET PRESS
FACEBOOK GROUP

for lively bookish chat
and more

Scan the QR code below

Or follow this link
**www.facebook.com/groups/
deanstreetpress**